THE PARALLEL LIVES IN COAL

LINDSAY WILSON

ISBN : 978-1545406113

Cover design by John Norton and Spencer Williams.

Futureproof Publications.
Contact: futureproof@aol.com

For my family.

Dedicated to a world in which better things happen and
Tim Henman won Wimbledon.

LINDSAY WILSON

CHAPTER ONE:
"How strange…"

I'm standing in front of a ticket booth, presumably waiting for a ticket, which is quite odd given that a second ago I was driving along the M1 heading towards an intriguing engagement off Junction 39; looks as though I might struggle to keep that appointment.

Nothing else seems out of the ordinary, although the ticket booth is a bit over fancy with mahogany edging and bits of swirling marble – but I'm being distracted and it's a very bad time for this – because clearly there are matters much more pressing and I really need to stop ignoring them. What I should really be focusing on is why I'm standing here, where's my car and more importantly what if it isn't too late to get to that appointment?

Usually I'm stressed at the thought of being late, or, heavens forbid, missing something. 'Reliability is my reputation!' is my motto-boastfully embossed on a dust – gathering pile of business cards. Or at least it was – because resting above the impressive wooden cabin housing the ticket seller is a clock which, as well as telling me I am several hours late for my meeting, also obligingly provides the date. I think missing my meeting is going to be the least of my worries. I expect they've already given up on my attendance because it would appear that the meeting ended over five years ago.

*

Someone nudges me rather pointedly in the back, alerting me to that fact that the queue has moved forward. I turn round to glare but am unexpectedly disarmed by a grinning, curly topped face, so I settle for a meek apology.

I take a step forward and instead puzzle over where I am and why and how I got here.

At least I know *when* I am; but so far, that has offered little comfort. A second prod lets me know it's now my turn to offer up some request to the ticket seller. I begin to panic as I realise that I don't have a destination and even worse I don't have my bag so I am just on the verge of another apology when I see that I'm already holding a ticket.

"How can I help you today madam?"

I look up at the ticket seller and am surprised to see a round, doll-like face smiling patiently down at me. Why does everyone around here appear to be so cheerful?

"Oh – hello madam – are you keeping that or does it need changing?"

I've no idea but I don't think I can cope with any more dilemmas.

The doll-faced ticket seller is pointing at my ticket. I glance at the date which appears to collude with the information on the ornate clock.

I hold it up and two large emerald eyes gaze at it and then look expectantly at me.

"Is this for today?" I ask her.

She inspects the ticket more closely.

"It is indeed."

I hear a muted titter behind me.

"Do you want it changed?" she asks again.

Do I? I look at the ticket seller's beautifully round and serene face and consider testing her tolerance by explaining my predicament but I don't know where to start. Instead I make a general apology to anyone within earshot and slink pink faced away. But at least I have something that may offer a flicker of a purpose; a valid ticket.

So far I haven't had the opportunity to assess my surroundings. Obviously I'm in a station; a particularly grand one with high ceilings, decorated with complicated swirling marble motifs and impressively spotless floors – but there are no signs indicating where I am or information boards offering a choice of departures.

I look again at the ticket: 'Gate 8 at 15.30.' I glance back at the clock and realise it's now almost twenty past three and I'm consumed by fresh anxiety.

Perhaps this new panic is another misguided distraction from more pressing worries but nevertheless I'm compelled to rush forward and find platform 8.

There are surprisingly few people about, none of whom look like guards, and they're all moving far too quickly for me to stop them and ask for help. I can, however, see they're all heading in the same direction and that to fall in step with them ought to give me better odds of catching my train. So I do just that.

For a few moments I'm confident I've made the correct choice as I pass a series of corridors indicating the escalating number of platforms but after number 7 I come to a dead end. Alarm surges through me again as I sense time is running out – and the only clue to my present predicament may be lost forever.

It's then I notice that just below the sign for Platform 7 is a small, tattered piece of cardboard bearing an arrow and a number 8. The arrow seems to be pointing towards a wall but on closer inspection I can see a narrow staircase, heading downwards, which nobody appears to be using. I think I can hear the rumbling sound of a train approaching from below so, uncharacteristically, I sprint down towards it.

As I reach the bottom, I see that a single-carriage train has already arrived at the platform. The doors slide open and I await an eruption of passengers but nowhere along the platform are there people either getting on or off. I'm all alone. A bell rings and I only have a couple of seconds to decide whether to board or not. I'm tempted to stay put and find help but I can't allow the closing doors to make this choice for me so I leap on.

The carriage is almost empty but I look at my ticket anyway to see if I have a seat number. I do and feel immediately cheerier that I now have a particular place in this unfamiliar world.

I look at the seat number nearest the door and realise my seat is towards the front of the carriage, where almost all of the other passengers are sitting. I walk up the aisle smiling awkwardly at a couple of girls who are the only occupants of the lower end of the carriage. They are both very pretty and are dressed almost identically in brightly coloured sixties style shift dresses and striped tights; reminding me of the type of girl found on the pages of Doctor Seuss stories. The smaller of the two looks up at me and smiles with the same patient expression as the ticket seller.

As I approach my allocated seat, I realise that, embarrassingly, this would place me next to some stranger. I don't like sitting near unfamiliar people for any length of time, in case they turn out to have some bad smell or make an annoying sniffing noise. Although I feel uncomfortable not following the correct procedure, I decide to risk taking the empty seat in the row behind.

I sit down and finally have a moment to think about my situation.

I already know I'm not carrying a bag, so I check my pockets. A phone would be useful but I don't have one. I do however find a key. It's not mine. I think I'd remember a key that was attached to a small toy microphone. Curious. There's also a small bit of dirty bent metal and a scrap of paper with an address – some place called Field View Cottage. Never heard of it. In my other pocket there's a glove that appears to be covered in soil and finally a folded piece of A4 paper, stained with what looks like a nicotine thumbprint in its corner-what have I been up to? When I unfold the paper, the only writing I can see, written in capitals, is:

"PLEASE PLACE EVERYTHING IN THE FOLDER."

Even curiouser.

What folder? What everything? I can't believe someone would go to all this trouble for a key, a scrap of old metal and a soiled glove.

I study my ticket a little more closely. I didn't have time to find out my place of departure so I'm keen to at least discover my destination.

The ticket doesn't appear to have a golden glow suggesting it possesses magical powers. In fact, it appears to be a single ticket to Peterborough. Now why would I have a ticket to Peterborough? I can't even remember ever having been there -I would have been less surprised if it had been a day return to Mars.

Although I support the custom of ignoring all people on public transport I think, given the unusual circumstances, I should attempt to make contact with someone from this future in the hope of gleaning some useful information. I glance in the window to get a rough idea from the reflection of who's sitting in front of me. It appears to be a reassuringly normal looking man; probably in his thirties. I summon up a bit more courage and shuffle stealthily along my seat to get a better look through the space between the seats. The gap is almost entirely filled by a mass of irregular curls, a ruinous collapse of ancient ionic columns that rest precariously on what looks like a rather expensively suited shoulder. Not scary, alien-like, or sounding to have a cold, so I pop my head round and ask:

"Do you know if this train stops at Peterborough?"

I'm quite prepared to be told that we are indeed going to Mars but his reply is even more unexpected.

"It might do," he says. "Are you Sarah?" he adds.

I nearly bang my head on the side of the arm rest.

"Do I know you?"

He does look vaguely familiar but instead of answering or before I can take a better look, his face disappears and is replaced by an orange folder.

My name, which incidentally *is* Sarah, Sarah Norton actually, is written neatly on the front of the folder.

Now it's interesting, because when I was on my way to the meeting near Leeds this morning – or maybe five years ago – I had in my possession a very similar document. Okay, not just similar…

"Where did you get this?" I ask him.

"It was in the seat pocket attached to a reserved sign. This is your seat isn't it?"

"Oh yes, sorry."

Why do I feel the need to apologise to every stranger I meet? If indeed he is a stranger.

"I didn't realise you could have things delivered to trains," I mumble. "I think I may have lost that a long time ago."

"Yeah sure you did. Here then."

He shoves the folder into my hands and turns back to his reading.

"Thanks then."

When I had the folder in the car this morning I'm sure there wasn't much in it; maybe some blank pages of A4 lined paper and a letter of invitation from a client. But now I'm hoping the contents are a little more revealing.

Inside are a quite heavy sealed envelope and a loose letter, addressed, of course, to me:

Hello Sarah! I expect you're feeling confused right now, but it's quite normal to suffer memory loss.

Normal?

The note you're reading was written by yourself. It's just to reassure you it was your decision to be here and do this. I hope you're not suffering too much – a bit dizzy maybe? You agreed to take this very unusual and exciting job. No point in trying to explain it all now because, as you probably realise, one of the side effects is memory loss, but rest assured your reliability is intact.'

Yeah right, no point to whom? I think a bit of explanation would be most welcome right now – and what about my reliability being intact – could that mean I actually got to the meeting near Leeds? I carry on reading with interest.

Which means that, knowing you, the first thing you'll feel is relief that you didn't miss your meeting!

Maybe it really is me. No one else would suggest that getting to a meeting on time would be more important than solving the problem of five missing years.

You need to take out the envelope and then put everything in your pockets into the folder and re-attach it to the reserved sign. The train will stop soon and you need to get off. Wait until you get outside the station before you open the envelope. You'll find another ticket to Peterborough to use later. Don't worry about how well you're doing, the fact that you're reading this means you're doing a good job. Reliable as ever! Just trust me when I tell you that this is worth all the confusion. Good luck and until you read this again, goodbye. P. S. You should keep the glove.

Right then, so that clears that up – as long as it's worth it.

What could be worth all this though? Certainly not half a pair of gloves.

Perhaps there is one thing.

Unless this is some kind of joke. Am I about to be swooped on by cameras and self-satisfied presenters while I pretend to look shocked and delighted? But I'm not the kind of person that something like that would happen to. For a start I would need prank-loving friends or at the very least *have* friends. So what am I to think, that I'm telling myself the truth?

I look around me. Could all these passengers be working for mysterious clients?

And what exactly is the job I'm doing so successfully? There must be more to it than walking around aimlessly in train stations and putting keys in envelopes.

And looking at the key now I'm not sure I'm even capable of that. As far as I can tell, it's the only tangible thing I have in the world. I can't just immediately give it up just because this 'so called me' said to. If 'so called me' really knew me, she'd know that 'this me' would rather just hang on to it for now. I check that no one is looking and rather guiltily slip it back into my pocket. I put the address back too – no point having a key without somewhere to unlock.

I suppose I could give up the piece of paper. What possible use could it have? I don't even have a pen. But before I have chance to talk myself out of it, I refold the paper and add it to the rest of my booty.

That leaves the letter and the bit of damaged metal which looks like it could be the broken-off end of a memory stick. I'm too conscientious, or cowardly, to return the folder completely empty and because the instructions are in capitals I feel obliged to put at least something in it. I reluctantly put in the letter and, as I can't imagine ever having the need for a bit of broken metal, add this too.

I tap the hairy man's shoulder and a pleasant brown eye looks questioningly back at me.

"Did you say this train is heading for Peterborough?"

He twists around a little further but I can still only see the one twinkly brown eye.

"I said it might. I don't honestly know." His eye quickly scans me, and I guess I must have passed his assessment of my trustworthiness, for he moves in a little closer and adds clarification.

"It may sound a little odd but I've just been to an interview and I'm not sure whether this is some kind of test but I was told to get on this train and told to get off at the final terminus, so you see I really don't know."

I'm keen to discover what kind of job might require someone to go on some mystery tour when I'm distracted by a long, thin arm which reaches out towards me from across the aisle.

"You want me to put that back for you?"

"What?"

I turn to locate the source of this long arm and find it to be attached to a woman, probably in her early fifties and wearing thick expensive clothes in varying shades of green. She has a long thin face bordered by a severe brown hair cut which seems rather out of keeping with a large, oddly shaped crystal pendant around her neck. She has the look of a woman who has suffered multiple disappointments and yet still feels it her duty to keep a stiff upper lip; like the type of governess who tends to fare badly at the hands of their spoilt young charges.

"How do you know it needs to go back?" I ask, hoping she won't realise it doesn't hold all it ought.

"Because they always have to go back," she replies, in a tone that sounds like rolling eyes.

Do I know this woman? I don't think so – could we be work colleagues? Or maybe she's my boss?

I turn towards the man in front but his eye has gone.

There's a loud, giggling sound which the green lady ignores as she takes the folder from me, and before I have a chance to consider returning the contraband from my pocket, I watch as it disappears back into the seat in front.

"I know you'll be fine."

Be fine at what? I consider making further enquiries but my attempt to formulate a probing question is interrupted by more giggling. I get the impression I'm already the subject of much mirth and I'm reluctant to attract further ridicule.

The giggling gets louder, but I can't work out where it's coming from.

"Just relax dear. Sometimes it's for the best not to know everything."

"Do you know what's going on here?" I ask her but she has already turned her back towards me.

"Or where we're heading?"

The giggling erupts into laughter.

The green woman retakes her seat and I now locate the source of the laughter.

Frankie?

CHAPTER TWO:
"...and miraculous..."

A small head grins back at me from further down the aisle.

"We're not going anywhere you idiot."

How could I have mistaken this horrid child for my beautiful son?

He looks about the right age but that's where the similarity ends. He has short dark hair and a face of sharp features like it has been hurriedly chiselled out of cheap wood.

"Are you talking to me?" I ask, hoping this direct approach will embarrass him into turning away.

More giggling.

"The train isn't really going anywhere. It just appears to be. Less chance of frazzling your brain I suppose. It's really going round in a circle, a bit like a very fast roundabout, in order to give a higher gravitational potential which of course creates a gravitational time dilation. Basically it makes the clocks run faster inside than out so you get there quicker. Simple, huh?"

The annoying little boy stares expectantly at me – waiting to be rewarded with a reply.

"Get where quicker?"

I've clearly given him the response he wants as his thin mouth spreads into a self-satisfied grin.

"The future, of course."

Who is this little Smart Alec and why is he trying to wind me up? I won't even have laser eye treatment in case my eyeballs explode and even kiddie theme park rides make me dizzy, so it's very unlikely that I would volunteer to be spun at ridiculous speeds into the future.

"Really?"

"Here we go," a fourth passenger a little further ahead grumbles.

The new speaker also seems rather odd. Not so much that he'd stand out in a crowd but maybe just a touch too colourful and bouffant. He looks to be someone self-important like a professor and wouldn't be out of place holding a cane or quoting Oscar Wilde.

"I wouldn't listen to him – he's just trying to wind up you 'memory losers'.

"Memory Loser? What's that?"

How could he know? He tuts. I try again.

"So we're not moving into the future?"

"What do you think?"

The boy giggles again but I stare at the man hoping he'll reveal something more.

"And then always the same annoying questions. I expect you're wondering how we all got to be here, right?"

"Is that such a ridiculous question?"

"Not ridiculous, but very predictable. I certainly can't be bothered."

"Sorry."

Why do I keep apologising? Rude man.

Now that I'm the centre of everyone's attention I feel I might as well go the whole hog of having a proper look at the carriage. I hold onto the edge of my seat and look nervously around me as I mentally count seven passengers. There are three females: the older one in green and the two young girls sitting further down the carriage and then two men; the grouchy Oscar Wildish guy and the hairy guy – and then there's a sixth person who I can't make out at all who is sitting right at the front. Finally, there's the child. Although he only looks about eleven, there's something menacing about his appearance that suggests he's much older. Perhaps it's because, although he is the only one to be wearing modern clothing of jeans and t shirt, he seems so out of place.

The train jolts a little, causing me to slip and look even more ridiculous.

"Just as well we're not going fast," I joke lamely in the direction of the boy.

"Only about one-hundred-and-eighty-five thousand miles per second, at the moment."

The train jolts again and the Oscar wildish guy turns to look at me.

"I believe you're getting out here?"

"Do I always?"

Even I'm getting the impression I'm predictable, though my actions are not obvious to me. Am I the only one clueless? I stand up, tightly holding my pocket which contains my envelope – my only hope of answers – and walk back towards the exit.

I look out of the window. It looks very much like the platform I boarded from but I can't see any place names or any people. Surely this isn't Peterborough.

Am I sure this is my stop? My letter said to get off soon but my ticket says Peterborough.

"Do you know if this is Peterborough?" I ask the girl who'd smiled at me. She doesn't answer but continues to look at me look at me benignly.

Maybe there's a connection.

Having committed myself to the decision to leave I try to stand confidently by the doors hoping someone else would validate this as a good choice by joining me. I glance back up the carriage but no one else is getting up.

The doors open and I hardly have time to step onto the platform before they shut again. The place is deserted. I look for an exit and see only one small set of stairs next to a cardboard sign with a number eight on it. It all looks very familiar.

I head up the staircase and once again enter a marbled hallway. Can this really be the same station I was rushing through only a few minutes ago? Surely not.

But as I walk back towards the entrance I can see the outline of the ornate ticket booth. Could the little boy be right – that I have just moved forward in time? If only I'd had the time to find out where I was before I boarded.

Although it's more probable that the stations just look alike rather than me being transported into the future on a train, I head towards the booth to see if there's anything there that could confirm or disprove the idea. But when I reach the booth, it is closed and the area where I imagine the clock and date to be is obscured by shutters.

It doesn't feel late and yet the place is deserted; clearly the opportunity to buy tickets has passed so with no other option I follow my own instructions and leave the station.

I hesitate at the large glass doors with their 'Exit' sign surrounded by intricate golden spirals. So far my whole new life has been spent either on the train or in this station. I haven't been outside at all. What if it's not safe?

I step out and don't go 'poof' but neither am I anywhere I recognise. I'm in a rural lane which seems at odds with the rather ostentatious station but explains the lack of commuters.

I walk to a seat next to a normal looking bus stop sign and sit down to read my letter. I tear open the envelope and a key drops onto the pavement. Inside the envelope are a five pound note, a train ticket and another letter from myself.

"Hello Sarah!

How's it going? You may not know who our clients are, but be assured they have our best interests at heart. We are also being generously recompensed. In fact you're headed to our own country retreat right now. True!

Also in the envelope is some money for your bus fare, your train ticket and the key – which you had better pick up before you forget it.

Am I usually this annoying?

You've got about two hours before the train leaves so you need to be back here by 3.15. If something happens, stay put. Someone might help – eventually. Ha, just kidding, just pray it's not little Pete! But don't worry, one of the reasons we were chosen was for our dependability. Remember our motto, 'Reliability is our Reputation!'

The Number Eight bus should be coming, so pick up the key and get on. Ask for Field View. Field View Cottage is ours.

That's it. Be back for 3.15? Wasn't it already 3.30 when I got on the train? I glance at my wrist and am alarmed to discover no watch. I never go anywhere without a watch.

And what's all this about being chosen?

The number eight bus does indeed approach. I hurriedly pick up the key, which looks just like the other one except instead of a toy microphone a plastic double-decker bus is attached to it. I put it in my pocket. There's no more money in the envelope. Will I have enough?

The bus pulls up. I tell the driver I want to go to Field View and to my relief he seems to know it. I hand over the five pound note and he smiles as he punches out the ticket and gives me change. Phew.

"I expect you'll be wanting to know where to get off?" he asks.

How come everybody knows more about me than me?

I take a longer look at the driver. The amused eyes looking back at me look familiar – or at least one of them does. And then there's the hair – a mop of disorganised brown curls. But he can't be the same guy from the train who's still surely heading off to some job interview. For a second I wonder if this was the job he was going for, but clearly there's no way he could have got off, been successfully hired and still had time to change into a bus driver's uniform.

I can feel the eyes of impatient travellers showing disapproval for what can only be a couple of seconds' delay.

"Yes please," I say. "I expect you get a lot of lost people coming off the train?" He doesn't look like he's been rumbled. I guess the planet is bursting with curly haired, brown eyed men.

"Some I suppose, but it's only you who seems to be lost *every* time you get on."

"Every time? So I've caught this bus before?"

"Yes – a few times – not that you seem to remember."

"Sorry!"

"There you go. Every time I mention it you apologise and look all confused as though you've never been here before. I always make sure I'm on time, just in case. I was running late once, coming back, and it was like you were going to be late for your own funeral."

I'm on the verge of another apology when he pushes the bus into gear and sets off.

"Better not keep you waiting," he says, "but then I always say that don't I? Don't worry I'll stop when we get there."

I find a seat, glancing around to see if I know anyone, but if I do, they're all successfully disguised as middle aged shoppers.

The bus trundles down a country lane with open fields on both sides. I start to relax and consider the option of just staying on the bus. Surely it would eventually arrive some place from where I could negotiate a way home. If you can call a half empty flat a home? Maybe that's why I only gave myself the fiver, to stop me from going elsewhere?

"Can I sit down a moment?"

A young woman stands just behind me, struggling with a couple of shopping bags. I pointedly look around at the expanse of empty seats but she doesn't take the hint and sits down anyway. Where did she come from? There wasn't anyone standing up when I glanced around a moment ago and she would certainly have stood out.

"Do you remember me?" she asks.

I can't even remember what I was doing an hour ago but then I realise who she is. She was one of the pretty girls sitting on the train. I remember she looked old fashioned – like someone out of sixties cartoon book.

"You were on the train," I say. "I didn't realise anyone else got off."

I'm pretty certain they didn't and she definitely wasn't at the bus stop.

"Sometimes I do," she adds as though this explains anything.

My letter didn't say anything about meeting someone on the bus. If she's one of the travellers who will help me when I get stuck, why's she here now? I haven't even got to the cottage yet. Is she coming with me? I don't know if that would be reassuring or not.

"My name's Sarah," I tell her.

"I know," she replies. "Just listen, because it will be your stop soon and you'll be getting off. We haven't got much time, less than we thought, that's why we think it'll have to be today. I'll sort out the bus and get him back to you but you need to get the Alternator from the cottage and sort out the rest. Just think – this could be your day to get him back at last."

"Field View," the driver calls out. It's only taken a few minutes.

Am I supposed to know what this girl's going on about? I don't want to appear stupid, but what on earth is an Alternator and who's coming back? Why would it make it my day? I haven't a chance to ask these questions as the bus stops and the driver looks back at me expectantly.

"Hurry up then," the girl says. "You'll know what to do when you get it. I'll see you back on the train."

Not knowing what else to do I get off.

The driver smiles down at me looking lost on the pavement.

"Aren't you going to ask when the bus heads back to the station?" he asks.

"Oh, sorry."

"I'll be back in fifty minutes."

Where's my watch?

"Thanks."

"You usually head in that direction," he says.

The bus has dropped me next to a fancy stone built bus shelter – a little extravagant I feel, given the isolation of the area. Apart from perhaps the occupants of the small row of cottages up ahead there would, I feel, be a very low demand by bus passengers.

I head towards the cottages in the direction the driver indicated. At the end of a stone track is a reassuring sign declaring it to be Field View. The numbers go up in twos although there is no sign of where any odd numbered buildings might be. There is no suggestion of any of the cottages being inhabited either – no vehicles or twitching curtains or indeed any traces of human activity.

The fourth cottage along, number eight, has an oval plaque hanging from a bare trellis helpfully labelled Field View Cottage and surrounded by a border of white daisies. Quaint. Just how I'd imagined my ideal country cottage would look. Did I choose it myself? Did I choose the daisy plaque? It was certainly chosen by someone with my taste. I can't wait to see what I've done with the inside.

I take out the two keys and place one above the other – apart from the novelty key rings attached to them they're identical. Why would I need to return a key just to have it replaced with the same one, only with a different key ring? I suppose it's always handy to have a spare though – especially if you're me. I look at the bus and microphone and momentarily wonder who made these choices before I put the newer key with the plastic double decker bus back in my pocket and the microphone one in the keyhole. As I twist it I hear the satisfying sound of the door unlocking.

I feel suddenly excited, as though the cottage is some large, unexpected Christmas present.

CHAPTER THREE:
"…is life…"

And as with most large, unexpected presents, I'm disappointed. The pretty floral wallpaper, the oak dressers, the lacy tablecloths, the vases brimming with sunflowers and daisies and the soft but comfortable sofa and armchairs are all missing. In their place is something more like a student bedsit. It is a lot smaller than it looked from the outside with just a moderately furnished room consisting of a blue leather sofa, which I would never buy, and a couple of red chairs, not even matching.

Immediately off the so called lounge – and it smells literally off – is a small bathroom housing a grimy bath and toilet. And above the light switch, in keeping with the grim student theme is a poster of an old *Star Wars* film peeling down a brownish wall. I've never liked *Star Wars* much apart from the small woolly creatures in the third one or is it sixth if you count the later films as earlier ones? If we're talking space adventures I always preferred Star Trek, except for the episodes when the crew stayed on the ship; especially, and ironically, the one with the small woolly creatures in it.

I leave the toilet before I gag and head back past a door leading to a small, yellowish Formica covered kitchenette. I can't believe I would have been so excited to tell myself about this windfall. Maybe I couldn't be trusted after all. Unless it wasn't me who had written those notes – I certainly don't remember doing it. But why bother? If someone really wanted to go to the enormous trouble of making me believe I was the owner of this cottage then they should have at least attempted to be more convincing by replacing the plain dark walls with a few flowery prints.

I am nevertheless starving; I hope there's some delicious food here. This would be a good test because if it really is me who chose the food then there will be tasty jalapeno-strewn vegetarian pizza and a nice bottle of white waiting for me.

I make my way through the ugly yellow kitchen towards what I assume is a fridge and am once again underwhelmed. Despite the anticipation of delicious bounty, the inside illuminates nothing, apart from what looks like a small lunch box. I grab it and switch off the fridge at the socket; no point in wasting electricity for a solitary plastic tub.

I give the tub a tentative shake. Maybe I'm on some secret mission and this container will self -detonate after I've read its contents. Or not. And although this all feels a bit 007-ish I'm disappointed to see the tub is marked with J.J. not J.B. I sigh and open it.

Inside are a small brightly-coloured package and a small carton of milk. I didn't know you could get them anymore. Do they still give them out free in schools? I open it and the smell nearly makes me gag. I pour the putrid lumpy substance down the sink and instead take a few gulps of tap water. Was this supposed to be my reward for a job well done? Well I'm not impressed – or not doing such a good job.

I take a cautious look at the package and am surprised to see that it is a napkin decorated with tiny festive scenes mainly involving cute reindeers and the heads of irritated looking Santas. I know how they feel. Could it be Christmas? It certainly didn't feel particularly cold outside and judging by what I saw from the bus I would guess it was more like late summer or early autumn.

Anyway, here's hoping it's something better than rancid milk.

Not much better. Inside is a sad looking sandwich curling up at the edges like the dry gills of a stranded fish. It doesn't look green and I really am quite hungry so I give it a tentative nibble.

Yuk!

I spit out the contents of the sandwich into the napkin and see that it is covered in black dust. Disgusting. Why would anyone sabotage a sandwich like this? Is it April Fool's day? But again, why bother? – I'm nobody – nobody special anyway; certainly not the kind of person who would be worthwhile hoaxing. And whose idea of fun would involve making someone retch? I spit again and stare at the filthy black granules in the wrinkled face of an irritated Santa.

It looks like coal dust. I stare at it for a few seconds hoping for a revelation but my brain remains unresponsive.

I turn the dry bread around to look for clues and inspect the contents more closely – but although it is apparent that at one time the sandwich might have contained a more delicious combination of cheddar cheese and onion – the inexplicable addition of the coal dust remains a mystery.

Except I've seen something resembling this dust quite recently. I poke around in my pocket to locate the singular stained glove. Could this be why I needed it – to examine a sandwich?

I sprinkle the contents of the napkin onto the side of the sink and turn it this way and that and hold it up to the window – but if there is any cryptic meaning secreted within the folds of paper then it remains hidden to me.

I look back at the cheesy remains. Is this what I was supposed to return to the train station – the thing the girl on the bus talked about? Or is there something I've missed – what was it she said -something about an Alternator? Is there an alternative sandwich? The girl said I would know what to do. Clearly she doesn't know me very well.

I suddenly feel exhausted and just want to lie down for a bit. I know I only have so much time. Time! What time is it? I have to be back at the station by 3.15 and I have no idea what I'm supposed to do, how to get back or what will happen if I don't. I look around for a clock but I can't see one. How do people manage without watches and phones? I guess I'm about to find out.

I'm torn between my nauseating fear of being late and the rising desire to just give up this stupid game and look for more food. I drink some more tap water and gather up all my new things. I am just about to toss the napkin into the bin when I change my mind. Instead I carefully fold it and put it neatly at the side of the sink; I've never been very good at throwing things away.

Thump!

Someone or something is moving noisily around above my head. I stand very still while I decide what to do. This could be the opportunity to find out what is going on or. I don't like the 'or.'

Before I can make any decision, a door I hadn't notice near the entrance to the lounge opens.

"What are you doing here?" a woman screeches at me.

She's probably in her thirties, quite small and would look rather pretty if it wasn't for the angry distortion of her petite features. She also looks vaguely familiar. Am I imagining it or did I know this woman before I lost my memory?

She remains staring at me expectantly but I am clueless as to what to say.

Her eyes look as though they should be capable of firing lasers but this aggression cannot prompt any better answer than: "I don't know."

The woman sighs, but more with resentment than sympathy.

"You're not supposed to be here."

I'm not sure if I'm relieved or not so I resort to my usual response in times of uncertainty.

"Sorry," I reply.

"How did you get in?"

At last – something I know the answer to.

"I have a key."

"Clearly not the right key."

"Well it seemed to fit okay."

"Well it would," she answers cryptically.

"I'm sorry," here I go again, "if I'm not supposed to be here, but I got a note."

"Saying what?"

"That I was to come to this address."

And that there would be nice food – but I tactfully keep that bit to myself as the woman in front of me doesn't look like the type to open up her cupboards to weary travellers.

"And who wrote this note?"

Now this is a bit awkward.

"Well I believe it was written by me."

Silence, just a steely gaze. She is clearly waiting for an explanation and I immediately get a tight feeling in my stomach that I haven't experienced since school. School! I have a vague feeling that it's there that I know this woman from – but she must be a few years younger than me and I rarely mixed with kids from lower years. Nevertheless I am still feeling intimidated.

"Well it said it was from me."

"But you don't remember writing it?"

I don't really feel like explaining my circumstances to this unpleasant woman.

"So anyone could have written it?" she adds.

"Maybe I should just go."

If I don't get a move on I might miss the bus and although I'm pretty sure I can't have done what I was supposed to do here, I feel an obligation to get back to the train. Hopefully it will take me home. I edge towards the door.

"In a hurry – a train to catch perhaps?" she laughs maliciously and for a second I think I can hear a child's giggle. "Fine. Perhaps this time you'll bring back the right key."

Is she talking about the key with the little double-decker bus on it? How could she know about that? Perhaps if she'd been a little friendlier I would have revealed the contents of my pocket.

She stares at my pocket. Can she read my mind?

"You sure you don't have anything else you shouldn't have?"

What can she mean? The nasty sandwich perhaps? I glance towards the kitchen and she immediately brushes past me. She strides towards the sink and picks up the Christmas napkin.

"Was there anything in this?" she barks.

"Just a rotten sandwich," I tell her and indicate the blackened slices of bread.

The woman scoops up the sandwich in the napkin and leaves.

Why is she so interested in my pocket? Is there anything else I shouldn't have? Apart from the key, surely there is only that blank piece of folded paper I resisted putting into the folder? I put my hand in my pocket and take it out. The PLACE IN FOLDER instruction stares up at me. But as I unfold the paper I see something more. I gaze open mouthed.

There's some comment about an alteration being complete and an address for a Simon I've never heard of, but that's not what's making me tremble. I feel sick. What is this? What it says here can't be right. It can't be.

Just then the door reopens.

The woman stares at me and looks at what I am holding.

"What are you still doing with that?"

"You know about this? Is it true?"

Instead of answering, she sighs and for a second I think I see pity in her eyes.

"Is this true about Frankie?" I repeat.

"I'm sorry. I didn't want to do this."

Do what?

"I promise you it's for your own good but it's hard to know what the effects will be – doing this again – so soon."

"Doing what?"

She strides over. I see a glint of metal in her hand and feel a sharp pain on my wrist. Has she stabbed me? I look down at my hand but there is no wound – no mark at all.

Before I can work out what's happening she reaches for the paper that I'm still holding. I lift it up but she manages to grab it. I refuse to let it go. I think she sees the determination in my eyes for instead of trying harder to pull the paper away she brings up her other hand and rips off the bottom part.

"I'll take this with me. And to think you like to describe yourself as reliable! You'd better borrow this too in case you get into more bother."

She hands me another key, turns and disappears.

I feel a bit woozy and all I can think is that I need to go. I take a final look around and leave.

As soon as I get outside I look at the torn paper but there is nothing written on it. How is that possible? Why did the woman take it away? How could it be for my own good? All I need to know is what happened to my son. The light-headedness is getting worse and it's making it hard to think clearly. The paper is in my hands but it's blank. Did I just imagine that I saw something? A wave of nausea rolls through me leaving a sense of relief, as though I've been cleansed. Of course there was nothing written there.

With a renewed sense of purpose I pull the door towards me and see that the key with the microphone is still dangling from the lock. No wonder that weird woman was able to get in. I consider locking her in and ringing the police but I don't have my mobile and what exactly could I tell them? I don't have any proof that this place is even my own; it could end up with me being the one carted off to the station.

I hurriedly take out the key and stupidly realise that I am already holding a key. If the woman came in this way she must have seen that I still had a key; except didn't she say it was somehow wrong? I look at the one she handed me – it is attached to some kind of spiral fossil – an ammonite I think. I hold it against my key and see that they are identical – so how could mine be wrong?

What is this thing about keys? I now have three of them. Even for someone as inept as me this is too many. Back when I had a normal life and home, I always kept a spare key hidden on a hook behind the little number plate outside my flat.

I look at the little daisy plaque that seems so out of keeping with the rest of the cottage and gently lift it up. Immediately I hear a jangling sound resembling the clanking of a full key chain. There behind the plaque are several hooks with half a dozen or so keys, all attached to novelty key rings. I think I may have had this idea before.

I add the microphone and little bus to a hook with only two key rings on it – a plastic yellow balloon and a small hairy gorilla. It's just like one of the monkey-type toys that Frankie could never get enough of – his room was littered with hundreds of various-sized apes and chimps. I'm tempted to release the little gorilla from its metal chain but what would be the point? Instead I take one last look at the strange cottage and turn back towards the main road.

"Ow."

I'm pretty sure there wasn't a big wooden pole blocking the path on the way in. I look up and see a sign in the shape of a yellow balloon. I take a couple of steps back to see what is written on it. It's a 'For Sale' sign. How did that get here? I know I've messed up my so called task but whoever is orchestrating this charade can't have arranged for me to lose my cottage this quickly.

It seems very unjust. I give the pole a wriggle and it becomes loose. I need to give myself some time to work out what is going on and who's going to notice if the sign mysteriously disappears around the side of the cottage? Kids eh? I drag the sign out of sight and head back towards the main road.

I look for the bus stop but there doesn't appear to be one. Hadn't the bus driver dropped me off by a small bus shelter? I may have imagined it – though you would think I would take greater care over noticing what is going on around me given my recent experiences. Instead there is just a sign that indicates that should you so desire, a bus will stop if you put your arm out. I estimate I have over half an hour to catch the train and that the bus wouldn't take more than ten minutes to travel the three miles or thereabouts to the train station.

I look up the lane and can see it winds for some distance before disappearing beyond a row of cottages similar to the ones I've just left. Where is my watch? I find it very hard to function without one. Even though I am excellent at predicting the time and always wake up before the alarm goes off, I need its reassurance and it gives me something to look at in between tapping my fingers and glancing anxiously in the direction of whatever it is I am anxious about.

I am now doing a lot of tapping and my glances, unbroken and unsteadied by being unable to look at a watch, are turning into nervous glares. *Where* is the bus?

How much time do I have left? Should I start running? Yeah right. Not likely. Hitch a lift maybe but with what? There's no traffic, not even the mandatory tractor.

The fact that I have a good view of the road is not helping, for even if it did come over the hill I would still be tortured by the ensuing wait. I have to start walking and at least attempt to put less distance between me and the station. Surely the bus would still pick me up if I put out my hand.

The tension of missing my train is making my head pound and the wooziness I felt as I left the house is back. My arm feels like it is being bitten by an army of red ants. My head feels like it will burst. I turn round once more to see if I'm being caught up by the bus; but nothing. I look forwards to see if I can see or reach the next bus stop; but nothing. Just pounding and more pounding and an overwhelming fear that the consequences of missing the train will not be good.

Then…

CHAPTER FOUR:
"...offering..."

I'm standing at a bus stop, presumably waiting for a bus, which is quite odd given that a second ago I was driving along the M1 heading towards an intriguing engagement off Junction 39. I might struggle to keep that appointment.

I glance down at my hands for inspiration or at least a bag containing a clue as to what I'm doing here and see that I am holding a ticket. Relief swiftly turns to dismay as I read that the ticket is for a 3.30 rail journey to Peterborough. Why would I be going to Peterborough? I don't think I've been there except for passing through on my way to London. And why 3.30, when my meeting was for 9am? I check my watch. It's not there. I never go anywhere without one, my reputation is built on my reliability, and despite my ability to accurately predict the time I still need the reassurance it provides.

My panic increases as I realise that as well as missing the meeting I am now also going to miss this train. I don't even know where the train station is. I don't even know where I am. The only thing I do know is that the meeting isn't in Peterborough, but maybe that doesn't matter, for unless British Rail have started to issue their tickets several years in advance, I believe my colleagues gave up on me long ago for according to the date on the ticket, the meeting ended over five years ago!

I try to take the edge off my panic by scanning my surroundings more closely. The bus stop is on a country lane I have no recollection of seeing before. As well as there being no bus, there doesn't appear to be any kind of traffic. Where is everybody? Am I the last survivor in a post-apocalyptic world or are there others waiting in Peterborough.

I just have to get there. By finding a fully functioning train and transport staff?

There must be some reason why I'm here or at least an explanation as to how I got here. Perhaps I've had a bump to my head and five years have just evaporated. Maybe I had a car crash on the motorway. I've been in a coma and I've just woken up and walked out of hospital. I look at my hands and see they are slightly blackened by something like coal dust. Maybe I was trapped down a mine for five years.

I check through my pockets for clues. A key attached to a toy bus, about three pounds in loose change and some scraps of paper, one bearing an address I've never heard of. Perhaps I live there now, but because of the terrible accident I get blackouts and have to write messages to myself for when I walk down country lanes and forget who I am and where I need to go?

The next piece of paper is torn and blank except for the instruction 'PLEASE PLACE EVERYTHING IN FOLDER.' What folder? And why is it ripped? I put it in my pocket and focus on the last bit of paper which is a letter, addressed to myself, which backs up my blackout theory. I read it but it doesn't make sense. If I was trying to help myself out why would the letter be so cryptic? It hardly seems appropriate to take advantage of my condition and write silly and misleading notes to myself – which clearly I don't remember – about keys on floors and references to mysterious clients and child travellers. I like the idea of being given random property and I do have a key but I'm afraid the most likely explanation is that I am completely bonkers and have escaped from some nice rural mental institute where there is probably a lovely inmate or warden called Peter. They are without doubt, looking for me right now. As if on cue, a car stutters into view and slows down as it approaches.

The car, which is red and has visible signs of rust and DIY tape attached to a dent above one of the wheels, draws up alongside me. The window opens and a red faced man, clearly distressed, looks up at me.

"Thank heavens I've found you," he gasps. "I knew you'd be along here somewhere. I looked for you at your usual bus stop but I might have guessed you would have eventually kept going. Are you okay?"

"Do you know what time is it?" He looks puzzled. Surely it's not the hardest of questions. "Are you Peter? Sorry, you're probably not him. I just read about him a moment ago. Some note I wrote to help me remember I think. Didn't do a very good job did I? I can't remember a thing."

At last he grins.

"Well at least that hasn't changed – and you're still apologising. I just wasn't expecting you to be quite so calm. Your head nearly exploded last time I was late and that was when you actually caught the bus. I was half expecting to see bits of you dispersed all over the hedge rows. It's just turned four."

"What?"

"You asked the time. Were you supposed to be somewhere?"

I show him my ticket. Maybe train fares have become so expensive that you need to book years in advance to afford one.

"Sorry. It looks like you've missed this."

"Thought as much, not that I knew why I was going. Maybe that's where I live, though between you and me I think it is just as well you caught me as I haven't the foggiest where home is. Oh, unless it's called…"

"Field View?"

"Yes. Are you a doctor there?"

Finally I feel I'm getting some grip on my reality.

"I'm a bus driver."

Well, I suppose you can't expect them to send busy doctors after every patient that decides to wander off.

"Sorry, of course not. I mean of course you could be a doctor. I mean if you'd wanted to be."

I need to shut up.

"I think Field View is a bit small to warrant its own doctor."

So maybe I'm already better. Excellent.

"Oh right, so it's a like a convalescent home. I thought it might be some place for mad people."

"I've no idea. I only ever drive past it but I've never seen anything like a home on this stretch of road. I guess it might be some half way house for one of the hospitals like Barton. It would certainly explain a few things. I should have guessed you were from some kind of institute."

He looks a little upset, as though I'm not the right escapee or perhaps he's disappointed that I don't recognise him. However, now that he's calmed down I can see he has a friendly face, slightly weathered with swirls of laughter lines and a head of chestnut curls. He's very trustworthy looking.

"I only came because I thought you might be in trouble. When the bus broke down in town I was worried that you would be panicking."

"What bus?"

"The one you're waiting for. I don't normally go after my passengers." He looks harmless enough but why would a bus driver be coming after me in a car? I don't know what to say to him but he seems happy to keep talking and he thinks he knows me. "There is something unusual about you," he tells me. "Not just because you turn up every now and then and never remember where you're supposed to be going but because you're always so polite and surprised that I recognise you."

Well he's got that right. I am polite but I try to remove my look of surprise.

"I think I must look forward to you arriving out of the blue and on the return journey you're always waiting to get on. I felt responsible that I wasn't there to pick you up so I borrowed this car and came to find you. Don't you remember me dropping you off earlier?"

"Sorry."

"Blimey, you've lost your memory again? You are in a pickle."

"So you're not from any home?"

"No."

"And you've not been sent here to take me back to one?"

"No, but I could still give you a lift to the train station."

"Is that where I normally go?"

"Yes."

"I don't suppose you have a timetable?"

As he looks in his jacket pocket I notice that he is wearing an outfit commonly favoured by bus drivers and he also has a paunch, the size of which suggests he may have been a bus driver for some time.

He passes me a small booklet.

"Here you go but I'm afraid I know for a fact that there won't be one for quite a while."

How does he know that? Why has he given me a bus timetable?

He suddenly snatches it back.

"How stupid of me, of course you wanted to know about trains. Look, maybe I should just drop you off somewhere?"

But was there really any point in going to the station? Even if I did get another ticket, how would I end up in the right place or time? If I was being met, would they wait? Who would be waiting? Would it be a good thing? I'm not sure going to the station is such a good idea after all. I look closely at this man. Can I trust him? The alternative, apparently, is hanging around for a broken bus which I am reliably informed won't arrive for quite a while.

"Maybe we could call the station. I don't know where my phone is but if I could use yours?"

I am eager to see where five years of technology have taken the mobile which is now probably solar charged and integrated into watches or coat sleeves.

"Of course."

Well that's a promising response.

He dips his hand into the inside pocket of his jacket and produces a small phone.

As he taps his finger against the screen I try to think who I could call to help me find out what has happened to me. It is a dishearteningly small list.

"I'm sorry," he says. "I don't seem to be able to get a signal. I suppose we are in the middle of nowhere."

Fair point, or convenient excuse? So much for future technology.

I throw caution to the wind. Things could surely only improve.

"Can you give me a lift to Field View?"

"You remember where you get dropped off?"

"I have this." I pull out the scrap of paper with the unimaginative address and show it to him.

"Right," he gestures to the passenger seat and I get in. "I'm Andy."

"Hi Andy the bus driver. I'm Sarah. Or at least I used to be."

"Sarah the bus rider. Hi."

Funny.

I'm surprised by how quickly we reach Field View. I don't even have time to imagine all the potentially gruesome outcomes of getting in a car with a strange bus driver called Andy.

He pulls up outside a very pretty cottage.

"Will you come in? I might need some help explaining where I've been to the warden or whoever is in charge."

I try the door. It's locked. I try knocking. Nobody answers. I get out the key with the ammonite attached and am relieved that it seems to fit. Voila. It works.

I lead the way. Inside opens into a space that is exactly how you would imagine a cottage in the countryside to be decorated. Or at least the way I imagine it would be.

The walls are covered with bright flowery wallpaper and in the corner of the room is a beautiful pine dresser. In the centre of the room, covered with a delicate, lacy tablecloth, is a large table upon which is a vase full of white daisies.

"How lovely!"

"A bit twee."

I give Andy a stern look. Typical bus driver.

There is a soft floral sofa in the corner and I fall onto it gratefully.

"Any luck with the phone?"

Andy tries it again.

"The signal strength seems to be fine but there's no ring tone. I don't know what's going on with it."

He holds the phone out to me and I take it and press a few buttons and although the screen lights up which suggests the battery is fine there is nothing else going on.

"It's not my fault," Andy says, "the network must be down or something."

Something?

"While you're up would you mind having a look and see if there's a kitchen and maybe a fridge with food in it. I'm starving."

Andy disappears mumbling something about manners.

He comes back with a plastic tub.

"There's only this – what does JJ stand for?"

"No idea."

"Is this it? What about the cupboards – maybe there's a pizza or a bottle of wine lurking in one?"

"No idea," he replies pointedly.

I give him a pleading smile and he turns and heads back to the kitchen.

I'm pretty sure I don't know anyone with the initials 'JJ'. Maybe it belongs to the genuine owner. I hesitate briefly to prove to myself that I have some integrity and then prise open the plastic lid.

Inside is a crumpled winter themed serviette.

Judging from the mild weather outside I don't think that it's winter – but that doesn't mean much – I tend to shove unused festive napkins into drawers ready to be discovered the following January.

I tentatively unwrap the small package. The bread looks ok and a quick peek inside suggests some kind of cheese, so because I'm particularly hungry I give it a little bite.

Ouch.

I pull the cheese away before it rips out my teeth. The cheese is not just cheese. Lodged inside is a roundish object wrapped in a torn off bit of the paper napkin I try to unwrap it as I reattempt the cheese. Yuk – moulding red Leicester.

It seems to be a lump of coal. I look at my hands which still look a little dusty. Did I put this here myself? I turn the lump of coal in my hand something sharp snags at my thumb. I look closer and see something metallic poking out from it. Interesting. It's small and oblong with a couple of holes in it, a bit like the clasp of a bracelet. It reminds me of a child's toy, intended to teach kids about archaeology in a fun way – you'd crack through sandstone to reveal skulls and bones which had to be put back together. I gave my son one once. Maybe I'm supposed to chip away at the coal to reveal a prize or a clue.

Bang.

What was that?

Andy comes running in and I instinctively cover up the sandwich.

"What was that?"

"Will you have a look?"

He makes for the stairs and I stay seated. I want to have another look at my coal while he's preoccupied.

I unfold the napkin and look at the coal again. What am I supposed to think?

It is impossible for a bit of metal to be inside coal unless it was around millions of years ago in some prehistoric swamp, or someone has gone to a lot of trouble to make a very realistic fake piece of coal. And how did it end up in the fridge of what may or may not be my property?

A few moments later Andy returns.

"Have you any idea what is upstairs?" he asks.

Is he still testing me? The soft sofa is zapping my will to think, never mind move.

"Do you want me to guess? How about a bed – ooh a lovely comfy bed."

"Not even close and I think we can rule out this being a half-way house…"

I turn around but I'm too late. What the...?

CHAPTER FIVE:
"…infinite…"

Andy suddenly lunges at me. I jump up just in time to allow him to hit the cushions.

I hope he's not dead. I was just getting used to not being isolated from the rest of the universe and he was proving to be quite handy.

I don't think he's dead. There's no knife sticking out from his back, in fact no blood at all and he looks to be breathing. I think I can hear giggling from the direction of the staircase. The noise stirs a memory. A child. My child perhaps? I look back at Andy. Surely nothing is going to be gained by going up there. It won't help Andy unless he was poisoned and the antidote is waiting at the top of the stairs.

Andy starts groaning so I can ignore the stairs for the moment.

"What the? Ow. What the?"

The blackout seems to be affecting his ability to form sentences.

"Are you ok? Do you know what happened?"

"What the…? Did you just hit me on the back of my head?"

"While sitting on the sofa in front of you? And I only have the standard length of arm."

Andy ignores my attempt at humour and as he pulls himself back up he snarls at me.

"Fine," he says, "so perhaps you saw who did?"

"There was nobody behind you. You were just about to tell me the secret of Upstairs when you fell onto the sofa almost crushing me."

"Well excuse me for disturbing you but I had little to do with the decision."

"Sorry."

His face softens.

"I just can't understand what just happened."

"Could it have anything to do with what you found upstairs? What was it?"

"Guess."

"We did that already. Just tell me."

"Ouch."

Andy disappears behind the sofa again. He can't have been hit again – I was looking right at him and there was definitely no attacker. Maybe he's had a relapse.

Just as suddenly his head pops back up and he looks at me strangely. Surely he can't *still* think it was me. He looks down at his hands and then appears to come to a decision:

"I think it will be better if I just show you. Come on."

Andy jumps up with more energy than I thought him capable of and I follow reluctantly. The sofa seems a more preferable option. I glance at it longingly before being tugged towards the stairs.

"You'll never guess." He's right there. I won't. "What it's doing upstairs is the mystery. I mean how did it all get there? You don't look the palaeontology type."

The what now? As it happens he's not exactly fitting my idea of the typical bus driver.

At the top of the stairs there's an open door. Andy beams at me as though he's discovered a hoard of treasure. Here's hoping.

The room is dark and I feel along the side of the room for a light switch.

"There's a switch on the wall," Andy offers. Cheers Andy. I finally locate it and it turns on several spotlights. They still don't offer a lot of light and it takes a few seconds for my brain to begin to make any sense of what they are illuminating. The whole effect of the room reminds me of an old fashioned museum. Andy is jumping about behind me. "So, do you recognise it?"

"I can safely say that this is the last thing I expected to see, so no, I don't think I recognise it."

"Isn't it amazing?"

Now it's been a while since I've been in a museum – probably only once since I left school, when I took my son to a local museum one miserable morning during an autumn half term break. I remember thinking what a shame it was that one of the most interesting places in the city was so poorly attended. It didn't even cost anything. They provided sheets full of pictures of objects in the museum that you could tick off when you found them. There were items from the Iron Age that had somehow survived for thousands of years. I can hardly keep a mug for a week without it breaking.

Now that my eyes are getting used to the dim lighting I begin to look more closely at the contents of the room. In the corner is a large lump of stone shaped like a claw. "That's a dinosaur's footprint! Isn't it great?" Right. But surely the most pertinent question is …what is it doing here? I try it out. "What do you think it's doing here?"

Andy furrows his brow and puffs out his cheeks – a reasonable answer.

"But look closer," he insists.

"Okay."

Being unfamiliar with dinosaur parts I'm really not sure what I'm looking for. I turn and shrug.

"In the middle, where the pad is – can you see it?"

We seem to be returning into game territory -I bet he's great to have around come Christmas Day afternoon. Not. I humour him and look closer.

"You mean that indentation in the middle, like a baby footprint?"

"It's not a baby footprint. It's an adult footprint -a human adult footprint."

He says it like a da da daah! but I'm none the wiser. So there's two footprints in one, is that so amazing?

"So?"

"So, forget those seventies films with scantily clad cavemen doing battle with Tyrannosaurus Rex. It never happened. Man came along about 200 million years after the dinosaurs."

"Those movies weren't authentic? They looked realistic enough to me."

"Ha ha."

"So?" I'm still a bit confused. I can't really see why it's a big deal.

"So, this footprint shouldn't be here."

"You're not wrong."

How come Andy the bus driver is an expert in archaeology?

He scowls. His easy going demeanour is slipping again. "There was something just like this found in a riverbed in Texas."

"So they're practically commonplace then."

Another scowl.

"Except the footprint in the Texan dinosaur print was about twice the length of a normal adult."

"So not only demolishing the theory of evolution it also proves the existence of giants."

I don't wait for a response. I leave Andy staring intently at the dinosaur anomaly while I look at some of the other items.

There is a selection of fossils. I recognise an ammonite. I can remember quite clearly being shown some at school by an over keen student teacher who had spent her summer searching the cliffs of the East Coast for fossils. She'd managed to avoid the usual pupil offensive by being oblivious to all attempts made to wind her up and instead of sending her crying off to the staffroom she actually engaged us all with her enthusiasm.

I even remember her telling us that the name ammonite, meaning Horn of Ammon, came from some Italian guy called Pliny the Elder (how could I ever forget) who used it to describe them because they looked like the ram's horn headgear worn by the Greek god Ammon.

I'm not sure what she would have made of this specimen though, for lodged into the rim of the outer spiral is a bit of metal. I can't see it properly but I do recognise it as having no business being there.

I move to the next item on display. This one is a larger stone with some markings of a fossilized fish or it could have been a reptile. This one also has an addition. It is the size of a postage stamp and looks like a microchip. The theme continues along the display with a variety of ancient stones all with half hidden anachronistic extras.

I put check the bit of coal in my pocket. It doesn't seem so peculiar anymore. This must be where it came from, but for what reason? If only I could remember something more useful than the origins of fossil names. Miss Clyde – that was the teacher's name! Equally unhelpful.

There are two pieces left. One is dark and heavy looking and looks like a lump of iron. I pick it up and twist it round carefully to prevent my thumb from being caught on the now familiar piece of jarring metal protruding from it. I don't waste too much time inspecting it as my eye is drawn to one final piece and it is lovely. It shines under its lamp like a dollop of solidified sunshine. It's a necklace. This time the chain is in an appropriate position attached to a loop which in turn is fixed to the biggest piece of amber I have ever (I think) seen. I can't help but pick it up and admire it. More intriguing though is to see what it contains.

There have been plenty of pieces with examples of prehistoric foliage and insects but I anticipate this will be more interesting. I hold it up to the lamp and yes I can make out an unusual shape.

I turn the amber around to try and get a better look but I don't recognise it. It's unlike any of the other bits of metal, including my coal. It is more elongated with an oval tip and has some indentations or slots at the end of it; a bit like a key but not like any I've ever seen.

Before I have time to think about it, I slip the necklace around my neck and tuck it under my shirt.

All this time Andy has been fully absorbed by the dinosaur and muttering excitedly about rewriting history.

"Do you think cavemen used computers? Come and look at these." I steer him towards the other exhibits.

"What is all this? It's not genuine is it?"

He stares at the ammonite with the microchip attached.

"I don't think cephalopods were around in the late twentieth century," I say.

"A cephalowhat?"

That Miss Clyde must have been one hell of a teacher.

"Cephalopods fossilized into ammonites. They're the swirly ones."

"Right, or maybe there were just computers in the Jurassic Age."

"Actually cephalopods were around from the Carboniferous Age."

"Pardon me," he says. "So you were just pretending not to know anything about ancient history"

"Sorry. I didn't mean to be rude. Honestly, I only know about ammonites from school."

"Must have been a very memorable lesson."

It was.

"This is amazing. Who would do such a thing? I mean how on earth did they manage it and why?" He pauses, looks at me. "...what's it doing in the attic of a quaint little cottage in the middle of nowhere that supposedly belongs to you?"

My recent memory loss is now proving to be a bit of an asset. I'm sure, even if I knew the answers it would be too complicated to explain.

"I wonder why this one is empty."

Andy is staring at the vacant stand which recently housed the piece of amber. I am about to show him the necklace but pause for a second. Maybe I'll keep it to myself for the moment. Instead I take out the coal that I have been carrying.

"It isn't. I mean it wasn't. I was just looking at this a little more closely." I show him the piece of coal.

"That's a bit odd."

I expect him to be looking at the bit of metal, which frankly in the land of the odd seems rather tame compared to the other oddities surrounding us. But he's actually looking at the napkin.

"Why is there a tissue around it?"

He's looking at a piece of coal with some impossible piece of metal sticking out of it and he's more puzzled by the fact that it's been wrapped in a napkin?

"To keep it clean?"

He takes the coal from me and lifts it up to his face.

"Smells of cheese," he adds cryptically and places the coal on the stand.

"Better keep it all together for now."

I wonder why, but I don't disagree.

It is at this moment that we hear another inexplicable noise. This time it is coming from downstairs. While Andy is distracted I reach onto the stand and pocket my coal. I just get it out of sight before Andy turns towards me and puts a finger to his lips as if I'm going to alert a mad axe man to our whereabouts.

"You wait here," he whispers.

As he turns towards the stairs, his hand briefly reaches into his pocket and I watch as he pulls out something unexpected.

"Andy," I call quietly and he turns. "You're not a bus driver are you?"

CHAPTER SIX:
"...possibilities..."

Andy grins.

"Sure I am."

He holds up the metallic object. Why don't I keep my mouth shut? I take a step backwards keeping my eyes fixed on the glinting metal while working out the best place to hide. He grins again.

"Don't be so jumpy. It's just a standard issue Tommy Swift. It's a type of taser." That's all right then. I take a step back but he just smiles. "All drivers have them. You never know when the locals are going to get violent. A few too many beers on a sunny afternoon can turn any passenger nasty. Remember the Manchester City bus Killings? Wait here."

He turns and heads down the stairs. I don't remember any Manchester bus killings, obviously, but he could tell me any old rubbish and make it sound fairly plausible. And as for dangerous locals, well I haven't seen any. And since when did the public allow bus drivers to carry weapons? Maybe I really have woken up in an apocalyptic world.

Andy's reached the bottom of the stairs and I peer down to see what's going on. It's quiet and I don't fancy waiting around. I'm sure I never used to be the type of person who blindly obeyed the instructions of dodgy strangers. Or at least I'm sure I'm not the kind of person who likes to think she's missing something. I go down quietly. I still think there's a good chance of someone dangerous being around and I doubt it's one of Andy's disgruntled passengers.

When I reach the bottom I look carefully around. I should have brought one of those rocks down with me; at least I would have some defence against a mystery assailant.

It seems very peaceful and the flowery furnishings seem out of place with the imagined terror I expect to occur any second.

Where's Andy?

I'm in the kitchen when I hear a giggling sound coming from the lounge. I think it is the same giggle I heard earlier.

I head cautiously back towards the lounge and the giggling gets louder. Again the room is empty. The giggling is coming from the sofa but no one is sitting on it. I move quickly to the end of the sofa in order to catch out the person making the noise and who is surely hiding behind it. But no one is there. The giggling continues. Where has Andy vanished to? Exactly how long did he expect me to wait upstairs? Is it possible that I missed him and he's looking in the attic for me?

As I'm heading towards the stairs I notice that the front door is slightly open. I open the door a little wider. Nothing. The light is starting to dim but even in the approaching evening gloom I can tell there is nobody there.

I decide to take a look round the side of the cottage but the moment I step away from the door it slams shut. I rush for the handle to catch whoever is on the other side but it is locked. I pull on the handle harder but the result is the same.

"Andy!" I shout and start hammering on the door. "Andy!"

Nothing, just that giggling again, faintly. Andy's red car is still parked up so he hasn't left, or at least not by car. Possibly his optimistic prediction of not being knocked out twice in one day was wrong.

I need to get back in. What did I do with the key? It's not in my pocket so I might as well take a trip round the side of the cottage after all and see if there's any alternative means of entry. There is a small patch of grass that looks like it has been recently mown – by whom I wonder?

The edges also look neat with borders of small flowers I don't know the name of. I'm doubt it is my own handy work. I turn the corner and almost walk head first into a thick wooden post.

I step back and realise someone has dumped an estate agent's 'For Sale' sign and left it leaning against the side of the cottage. 'Brightstone and Nephews' reads the sign, which for some reason is written inside a large yellow balloon. I presume this was dumped here after the cottage was taken off the market, but there is Sold sign. I push past it and head towards the only window on the wall. I peer inside and realise it houses the toilet – useful to know – but doesn't reveal anything except that there is a poster of Darth Vader on the wall. Why would there be such a tacky poster in there? I'm pretty sure I've never been a particular fan of *Star Wars* and it seems very out of keeping with the rest of the decor. There are no unconscious bodies lying on the floor as far as I can tell, and as there is no obvious way to open the window without a brick. I move to the back of the cottage where there is another locked door.

This must be where the kitchen is. I look through the window a little further on and vaguely make out a sink and a couple of cupboards which seem to be painted in a ghastly shade of yellow. There seems to be something on one of the work surfaces. I rub some of the dust from the glass to get a better look. On the work surface is the messy remains of someone's attempt at sandwich making. A loaf of bread is spewing its last remaining slices from a paper wrapper and an open jam pot is nestling against an upturned margarine container. A knife, its red tip dripping, hopefully with jam, is lying abandoned by the sink. How come Andy didn't come back with one of these instead of that weird coal sandwich?

I come to a final window. It's getting darker so it's difficult to make anything out apart from the fact that this one looks into the lounge, though the sofa appears oddly bigger and shinier and I don't remember there being any armchairs.

I scan the room and see a movement near the now shiny sofa. It must be Andy.

I'm just about to tap when I realise that the body is much too short and skinny to belong to him. I strain for a better look. It appears to be a young child and for an idiotic second I imagine it to be my own.

Without warning the child looks directly at me. A face I don't recognise comes close to the window and stares out at me. It belongs to a boy of about eleven. What is he doing in there and how did he get in? The boy's eyes twinkle with malice and he pulls a face and giggles. He's been in the house all along. Surely he can't be responsible for Andy's attack. The boy suddenly smacks the window and I back away, nearly tripping over a hedge. By the time I recover, he's gone.

"Sarah!"

I turn round and see a familiar face – Andy. I'm so relieved to see him, dodgy or not, I dash towards him.

"Where have you been?" he asks anxiously. "I looked all over for you. I went back upstairs and you'd gone. How did you get out here?"

I'm tempted to state the obvious but just shake my head.

"Where's the boy? Did you see him?"

His puzzled expression reappears.

"I couldn't find anyone," he tells me. "The place is empty. When I saw the door was open I thought whoever it was that hit me must have left. You're lucky I didn't try and stun you."

Yes, that would have topped off the day nicely.

"The door was locked," I explain, "that's why I was round here, trying to find a way in. I was just looking to see if I could get in through a window when a young boy appeared and banged on it. You must have at least heard him. And he was giggling, exactly like before. Don't you remember? It was just after you were knocked out?"

Okay, so maybe he couldn't hear too well when he was unconscious but he must have heard the banging.

"Honestly, I didn't hear anything."

Honestly? It is almost dark now and there is still the possibility some mad kid is lurking around ready to bash me on the head so I think it wise to invite Andy back in.

The front door is now wide open. Could it have been Andy who slammed and locked the door when I went out? But then why would he come and find me and lie about not seeing the boy?

"Where did you find the key?"

"I thought you had it."

"But the door was locked. How did you get out?"

"I just walked out. Honestly, it was open."

Maybe the door just got stuck." Honestly again. The man protests too much. I suppose it could have stuck. Where *is* the key?

We go in and head into the lounge bit. I take a good look but the place really isn't big enough for hiding places.

"Were there some armchairs in here before?"

"Before?"

Keep up.

"Yes, before we went upstairs and before I went outside."

"Why would there be armchairs here then? Are you beginning to remember this place? Did you used to have armchairs here?"

"No. I mean maybe, no…I mean no, I don't remember but when I was looking in from outside I'm sure there were two armchairs and the sofa …it was bigger and it sort of reflected in the light like it was plastic or something. And…do you know where the loo is?"

Andy looks relieved for a second. It's clearly a question he can answer.

He points to a door to the left of the entrance.

"Yeah, it's just there, I went in it when I was looking for you."

Ok no need to justify yourself. Why do people always feel like they need permission to go to the loo? Like at school. The toilet is small and there is no *Star Wars* poster. As I take advantage of the facilities, I scan the entire room. Empty bath, empty sink with just a bar of suspect dried green soap, and that's it. No cupboards to hide or secrete a poster behind, not even a flowery shower curtain or toilet brush holder. So unless it was stuffed and flushed down the toilet it has to have been removed, but why and when? I was only looking at it a couple of minutes ago. Andy confessed to being here earlier but as I leave the bathroom and begin to ask, I already know his answer.

"A what poster? No I'm pretty sure I would have remembered that. I love *Star Wars*. Which film was it?"

He's missing the point.

"Andy, when I was outside looking in, the whole place was different. I thought it was just because it was getting dark but now I'm sure it wasn't the same."

"Like a different building?"

"No, just the stuff in it, like the furniture and the poster. It was like this except it was furnished differently as though it was someone else's cottage."

"And the boy was in it?"

"Yes."

Andy is looking doubtful and who wouldn't be.

"Are you sure you weren't just looking in at next door. Maybe they've got a kid who's a science fiction fan."

"Personally I'd class it as fantasy." It's probably the wrong time for this conversation. "And no, I wasn't looking in the wrong house."

I sit down. I'd forgotten how comfortable this lovely sofa is and I feel exhausted. I realise I haven't seen a bedroom. Andy has done the full tour so I ask him where it is. I could really do with some sleep.

"I was wondering that. There isn't one. Not that I could find and I've looked everywhere. Twice. There's just this area here and that weird exhibition up the stairs – unless you saw differently from outside."

No need for sarcasm Andy. I give him a glare.

He ignores this and instead.

"I could do with a drink," he says. "Shall I see if there's anything else in the kitchen, tea or something?"

I wouldn't mind a glass of wine.

"Please."

He wanders off to the kitchen.

"Are there any jam sandwiches in there by any chance?"

"Not that I can see. Why?"

"No reason."

"Okay." He doesn't sound convinced.

"Just be careful. A mad axeman could still be around. "

I sit up and look over at him. He really doesn't seem bothered. Why? Why isn't he bothered? He's only still here because I don't want to be alone. But what if it's him I should be worried about? After all I didn't see anyone hit him and there wasn't any mark. Could he have just pretended to be hit so I would feel sorry for him or so that I would feel scared and need him to protect me? Well it worked. He looks so honest with his little paunch and curly brown hair.

"I can only find some cereal bars and funny little cartons of orange, or there's tap water," he tells me from the kitchen. "Hang on I'd better just check the juice, they weren't even in the fridge. It seems okay."

"Orange then."

If this was my home there would at least be one bottle of wine lurking in a cupboard.

He smiles as he sits down next to me and passes me a couple of breakfast bars. I'm just being paranoid, I decide. All he's been is nice.

"So, how's your orange?"

"Fine."

"So, has anything come back to you? I must say it's been a bit of a funny day."

I'd like to think it's not typical for me either but I don't know.

"Me too, I think. So when do you think I was last here?"

"I picked you up from your usual bus stop near the station a couple of weeks ago. Do you even remember getting on today?"

"No."

"So what do you remember about today?"

"Nothing, until finding myself at the bus stop in the middle of nowhere."

"Okay, well you must have left the cottage and gone to the bus stop across the road and when it didn't arrive you set off walking towards the train station. So at that point you must have known what you were doing. You got about a half mile before I discovered you at about ten to four. Remember – you asked me what time it was?"

"Yes I was checking if my train would have left."

A momentary realisation that the train might have been delayed induces feelings of guilt. Even if I really did think I'd gone mad and escaped from a home, I know my natural instinct should have been to at least check it out.

"So you do remember that you were going to catch a train?"

"No, but I found a train ticket in the envelope with the letter and stuff."

"Envelope?"

He looks expectantly at me.

This is the moment I decide if he is to be sent packing or become involved in all of this. I don't even know if he wants to help. Why would he? Surely he has buses to drive at some point?

But I guess at the moment he's all I have to help me figure out what is going on and it's not like I forced him to bring me here.

"Sorry, you don't have to show me it."

Reverse psychology; always a winner. I pull out the envelope and pass it to him.

I watch him closely as he reads the letter, looking for signs that he too will conclude I'm not quite the full picnic and I'm ready to move aside should he make a dash for the car.

"Ah."

"What is it?" I ask hopefully.

"I wondered why you thought I was called Peter. I don't think I'm particularly small though."

How on earth did he manage to read that letter and take it as a personal insult?

"What's with the dear you/me. What's that all about?"

I need answers not more questions.

"Don't know."

"So you got off a train."

"Maybe."

"Yes. So *maybe* you get off a train and you have this letter, but, according to the end of this, it says my bus is approaching. So you probably don't read this until you are at the bus stop. Which means..."

"What?"

"I don't know, but if you only read this just before the bus came, then you can't have had the letter for long."

"Unless I get these blackouts regularly and they are like memory prompts."

I take the letter from him and read it again.

"It's not the most helpful note I could have written. Surely a few useful names and contact numbers would be better than silly comments about dropping keys."

"And how is it connected to the mysterious travellers and the weird room upstairs? Very odd."

You're telling me.

"I just can't imagine how I could be involved in anything like this. I'm not really the kind of person to be mixed up with mysterious events and characters."

"Well looks like you are now. It's not like the letter was written for someone else. And I know you've been coming here on and off for some time."

"For how long?"

"I've been doing this route for a couple of years so at least that long. It could have been longer."

"So why can't I remember anything?"

"You never do. Each time you got on the bus you acted as though it was the first time you'd ever made the journey. That's why I remember you. I used to look out for you and make sure I was on time. I was hoping to see you again before I leave..."

"You're not going to be a bus driver? How will I manage?"

I laugh.

"That's why I can't believe the bus had to be towed back to the depot today. I was really worried."

How sweet. At least someone was looking out for me. But shouldn't there be someone else? Someone I know, for example.

"I didn't know you owned this place though. What on earth is it that you do that pays out in country cottages? What did you do before you lost your memory, are you a rich businesswoman or maybe some kind of international spy?"

"I used to run a small agency and as far as I know I still do."

"Doing what?"

"Mostly being hired by people to investigate insurance fraud."

"Oh."

Clearly being a spy would have been more acceptable to Andy. It's not like he has some high powered job that allows him to look down on other professions.

I take out the business card that proudly boasts my reputation as being reliable – I can't even rely on myself anymore – and hand it to him.

"Maybe you got a new job."

"Perhaps. The last day I can remember, I was on my way to visit a new company to discuss a job. The invitation indicated 'favourable' terms, which is unusual, but if they were typical of most insurance companies, it would have resulted in being paid as little as possible and a tedious morning spent with some rather dull executives. But it doesn't look like I ever got there."

Andy turns over my card as though expecting a more interesting job to be revealed on the other side.

"What's wrong with being an insurance fraud investigator?" I ask.

"Nothing. Well it is kind of up there with traffic wardens isn't it? Sneaking around, checking if people really do have leaky roofs or watching to see if they really do need crutches."

How rude. But he has summed it up quite well, only you rarely needed to leave the office to find evidence of some apparently physically challenged person whooping it up on some public network site. Even though it was a small business I always made enough for us to get by and I was never out of work.

"Reliability is my Reputation!" Andy laughs.

"I was really good at it."

"Yes, you even own your own business cards."

"Thank you."

I hold out my hand for the card but instead he pockets it.

"Good, but it doesn't help to explain what's happening to you now. I suppose we'll just have to wait and see if this Peter or someone turns up and fills us in."

I ignore the 'we' bit for a second because I realise that the turning up bit has more than likely already happened.

CHAPTER SEVEN:
"…to follow…"

It's getting late and I'm tired.

"Did you notice any blankets while you were looking around?" I ask Andy.

"There're some cupboards that I haven't looked in." Oh good, maybe the wine will still show up. "I'll check if you like. Then I guess I should be on my way…unless."

I really want him to offer to stay but I don't like to ask in case it's awkward but I don't feel safe by myself. I put on an innocent smile and hope he gets it.

"Unless, if you're a bit anxious?"

Yes.

"Yes."

"I guess I could stay, if you think you'll feel safer."

I will, though he's the one that got whacked on the head.

"That would be good. Thanks. I'm sorry there are no beds though. Someone decided to convert the bedroom into a wacky exhibition."

"That still might be you," Andy says, banging cupboard doors.

"Any sign of a bottle of wine?"

"Not yet – just some bits of paper and – I'll just see if this torch works."

The banging stops.

"Andy?"

Nothing. One more bang. Then the lights go out.

"Andy!"

Surely he hasn't been knocked out again.

The lights come back on.

"Over here," Andy calls. "Come and look."

What now? Perhaps he's found a hidden stash of *Star Wars* memorabilia and some armchairs stuffed into a cupboard.

I find him crouching in front of a chest of drawers.

"Oh, that's odd."

There's a change! Andy is holding a pile of A4 paper.

"What's odd?"

"When you turned off the lights I shone the torch over the contents of the drawer and I swear one of these pieces of paper was covered in writing. There were lists of names and addresses. I was trying to have a better look because I recognised one of the names. When the lights came back on there was just this pile of blank paper. I wasn't imagining it."

"What, like phantom furniture and children?"

"I thought you said there was just the one child."

Ouch.

"Anyway, whose name do you think you saw?"

Andy picks up one of the blank pieces of paper and turns it back and forth a couple of times.

"There was a few but the one that jumped out was none other than Simon Greaves."

"Right. Who exactly is Simon Greaves?"

"Only one of the most famous people in the world."

"Did he by any chance get famous in the last five years?"

"Maybe. He was in a reality talent show a few years ago."

"You don't look the type to watch talent competitions."

"Well, no one watches them now, but anyway that's not what he became famous for."

"Intriguing. Go on."

"I can't believe there is someone who hasn't heard of him."

"Yes, well there are a few things I haven't heard of. Does he have something to do with the Manchester massacre?"

I feel like I'm showing off.

"No, he's famous for being dead."

"Right, well that's hardly unique. I believe there are billions of dead people, so what's so special about him? Was he such a bad singer he was mobbed to death? Mind you, that could have happened if he was good. Or was he killed by one of those music snobs who think only kids who start in garages have any validity in the music business."

I'm on a roll and think I'm quite funny until I notice Andy's frown.

"Sorry. Did he win?"

"No. He should have done though."

"Ha! You voted for him. I never used to pick the winner either, all that money wasted on phone calls. For nothing. They hook you at the beginning and then you feel responsible for them and you have to keep voting."

He frowns again.

"Sorry. Go on."

"Sure you're finished?"

"Yes, go on."

"Well, it was the live final and millions of people were watching the last two performances of the finalists, one being Simon of course. Are you listening?"

He's like a teacher.

"Yes."

"Well, the first finalist, Alison, sang the so called winner's song."

"So Alison won?"

"No."

Now I'm confused.

"But Simon didn't either?"

"No. Are you okay?"

"I feel fine."

Great, actually.

"The show had to be abandoned. Simon was singing his money note when part of the stage collapsed on him. They took him off in a helicopter, and all of this was watched by millions of people, billions probably when the footage was replayed on the internet. By the time they got him to hospital he was already dead. You can imagine all the media hysteria, especially with so many people seeing him killed live on TV. There were loads of theories about terrorists and publicity stunts that went wrong but the upshot was that the family sued the company and everyone involved for billions of pounds."

"Did they reveal who would have won?"

"I don't think you grasped the main point here."

I thought that was the only point of these contests – to see who wins.

"Anyway, everyone went bankrupt, so there was little point in winning. Alison wasn't that good anyway."

Now who's missing the point?

"Well if he's that famous it's not surprising his name is written a lot – even on invisible paper."

"I can see the paper all right. It's the ink that's disappeared. Maybe if I hold it up to the light I might be able to make out something."

Andy gets up and heads towards the brighter lights of the kitchen.

I am feeling really dizzy. Possibly due to lack of food.

"Are there any more cereal bars?"

"Oh yes, get us a couple will you. They're next to the sink."

Fine.

Andy goes through each piece of paper, holding it up to the light.

"Anything?"

"There's nothing, but at the corner of each sheet there's a small yellow smudge. I wonder what that's all about."

"A yellow smudge?"

"Yes, look."

Andy walks over and passes me one of the sheets.

"I've seen this mark before. Hang on."

I tip everything out onto the kitchen worktop.

"I have no idea how long this stuff has been here."

There's the envelope and letter, a scrap of paper with this address on, the ticket to Peterborough, some coins and a piece of torn plain A4 paper.

Andy picks up the torn scrap of paper.

"This sheet has a smudge in exactly the same place," he exclaims, I don't suppose…"

"Still no memory," I tell him.

"Hey, you don't know what I was going to say."

"Sorry. But did it have anything to do with me remembering if I'd ever seen writing on it before?"

"Maybe."

"Are you sure it is just a smudge? We should look for a magnifying glass. Maybe it's a hidden code."

"In very tiny writing?" he scoffs.

"Hence the need for a magnifying glass."

"Why didn't I think of that? I'll just get mine from the car."

"You've got one in the car? You're kidding."

"I am. I left it at home next to my directory of yellow smudges."

"A no would have been enough."

"But that reminds me. There's a rug in the car – I'll go get it. Will you be okay for a couple of minutes?"

"Longer than that I hope."

"I meant…oh right, yes. Well I'll be as quick as I can."

He puts the torn sheet of paper in his pocket and heads for the front door. Then he pauses.

"I didn't realise you'd found the key," he says.

"Neither did I. I mean I didn't. Where did you find it?"

"In the keyhole. I'm sure it wasn't there earlier or we'd have seen it."

"It must have been there all the time."

I wonder if I sound more convinced than I feel. I definitely did not put the key in the lock. Andy goes out and I'm struck by a childish urge to get up and lock the door. I resist of course but go to look at the key. It puzzles why it is even in the lock. It would only be there if someone had used it to lock the door from the inside. I reach out for it and instinctively turn it for a second. The lights go out again.

I try to open the door to get out but it seems to be stuck. I compose myself and hear a noise from behind me. That giggling.

"Who is that? Who's there?"

More giggling.

"Stop that. Tell me who you are."

Still nothing. It's that kid. I can't see him but I can tell he's there. He has to be there. Why would I be hallucinating a child? I don't feel mad. But it's still a possibility. I don't know for certain that I haven't been institutionalised for the last five years. It can hardly be eliminated from the list.

Giggling. Is he laughing at me? I'm suddenly aware of someone tugging at the door handle.

Andy.

"Andy, the door's locked," I call to him.

"Did you lock it?"

I suppose I did.

"I didn't mean to. Hang on I'll try the key again, it got…."

The key turns easily but the lights don't come back on.

Andy comes in carrying the rug.

"What's with the lights?"

I flick the switch in vain.

"They don't work."

"It'll be a fuse, I expect that's why they went off earlier – we can try and find one tomorrow if you like; lucky we've got a torch."

Very.

Suddenly I'm blinded by a powerful beam.

"Oh you found some bedding stuff."

Huh?

I look round and there, illuminated by the torch, are a couple of camp beds and duvets behind me.

What do I say? Luckily Andy isn't expecting a reply.

"Excellent," he says and grabs one of the beds and begins unfolding it. "This certainly is a house of surprises Am I to put it up here?"

He starts to unfold it then stops and picks up a scrap of paper from the carpet.

"Is this your paper? Look at it at now."

"This can't be it. You must have got it from the cupboard."

"No. This one is ripped. It must be yours."

Yeah right. You'd hardly need membership of the Magic Circle to pull that one off.

Anyway, I let that slip in favour of being more interested in the apparently newly visible words. It is just an address and a sentence. As per usual neither looks familiar. The address is for somewhere I have never heard of and the sentence seems devoid of sense. "Alteration Complete." I turn the paper over again. PLEASE PUT CONTENTS IN FOLDER is still written on the back.

"Let's have a look."

Andy studies the paper for longer than should be necessary for so few words but eventually looks up.

"Interesting."

"And?"

"I don't suppose."

"Well. Don't you want to know what is going on? This might be the lead you're looking for."

I was looking for a lead? I'd still prefer a glass of wine actually.

"Lead?"

"A clue to why you keep turning up and forgetting why. Don't you want to know what's happening to you?"

"Hang on Sherlock. Maybe."

"You'd rather just keep wandering around with mysterious bits of coal and strange notes."

"Maybe. The note said someone would collect me." Hopefully someone other than the creepy kid. "Perhaps I should wait. It might turn out that I am a missing patient after all."

"But that wouldn't explain the weird stuff like the wacky museum upstairs."

"It might. Maybe it's some kind of art therapy."

"Fine. How about you sleep on it, see if anyone comes for you? But there's one more thing, the address on your bit of paper."

"What about it?"

"Well I was only able to look at the information about Simon Greaves for a moment but I could have sworn that it's the same address as the one you have here – it's definitely the same village."

"Weird."

Andy sounds hurt but I'm too tired to think.

I grab a duvet. I'm shattered and it doesn't take a moment before I mercifully blank out.

CHAPTER EIGHT:
"...any path..."

It is quiet and light. I am relieved and surprised that I got some sleep. Normally I wouldn't be able to nod off until I was confident of not being disturbed; particularly by unknown quantities like potential snorers. So either I was too exhausted or Andy was a considerate sleeper. I open my eyes. Andy isn't even here. No camp bed, no Andy.

"Morning, mum, thought you were never going to wake up."

I sit up quickly and look in the direction of the chipper voice coming from the toilet. I can't believe it. He's here? I feel a surge of excitement. When was the last time I saw him?

"Isn't it about time we got rid of these posters mum? I haven't watched a *Star Wars* film in years. It's embarrassing. I am nearly twelve."

The boy who walks out of the bathroom is not my son.

"And another thing, why are you sleeping down here again fully clothed? Too much wine? What if one of my friends came round?"

I glance down and realise I've been lying on a blue leather sofa. Horrible.

"How did you get in?"

"I live here of course, not that I wanted to mum."

"Stop calling me mum. You're not my son. Are you Peter?"

I am almost certain this is the same boy I saw at the window last night.

"Still am mum. What a stupid question. And of course I'm your son, exactly how much *did* you have to drink yesterday? And remember I want to be called Pete now. Peter is so lame. Why couldn't you have called your son something cooler like Frankie."

I did, after his granddad Frank.

The boy giggles.

"Sorry, just joking. Frankie is way worse. Don't you think?"

What does he know about Frankie? Where is he?

The boy glares menacingly, then grins.

"Only messing mum. Do you want a sandwich? Though there's not much to go in it. You really ought to do a proper shop."

He suddenly leaps onto the edge of the sofa and leans against my arm. He smirks as I pull away from him.

"Sorry. Maybe you could do with some water or there's some milk. Where on earth did you get those little cartons from? I thought they were just for school kids. Not wandering into the local primary, stealing are we?"

Without waiting for a reply he springs off into the kitchen and I take the opportunity to go to the loo. On the inside wall facing the outside window is a tatty poster of Darth Vader. I rip it down and re-enter the lounge. The flowery décor and comfy sofa have gone and been replaced by the disgusting blue leather sofa and a couple of large red chairs.

"Here, this should make you feel better," Peter says returning. "Though you ought to get some of those long life cartons – these milks don't last very long."

He holds out some bread and a little carton decorated with blue cartoon cows. I don't move, so he just drops it onto the sofa.

"Say thank you then. You're always telling me to do it. What's the matter, cat got your tongue?"

He giggles again and makes a strange lapping sound.

I pick up the sandwich and sniff it.

"I couldn't find the arsenic, so you'll have to make do with raspberry jam."

I look up at his little round face that wouldn't be out of place in a Beano comic.

"Where's Andy?"

"Who?"

"The man who was sleeping on the camp bed last night."

"Oh mum. You've got to stop bringing strange men home. It could be dangerous. And think how it might affect me, all these different uncles coming round. I could be psychologically damaged."

Another giggle.

"Just tell me where he is."

"There's just you mum. If you did bring someone back they've obviously gone. Is he why you didn't come to Peterborough? You were supposed to be meeting my uncle. Remember?"

Here we go again. Will people stop asking if me if I can remember things?

I take a bite of the sandwich and pick up my jacket which is lying over the back of an armchair. I feel about in my pocket for the train ticket that I *do* remember and pull it out.

"There you go, see? You were supposed to get the 3.30 and meet us at the station. We tried ringing you but it just went to voicemail. Have you turned your phone off or have you lost it again. Poor mum, always losing things."

I look at the ticket. It does say to Peterborough. But I'm sure I don't know anyone from there; certainly not a brother. Do I have a brother? I don't think so. Even if my parents were still alive I don't think it would have been likely for them to have produced a son in the last five years.

"And I was supposed to catch this when?"

I hold up the ticket hoping that he would at least accept that the date was absurd.

"Yesterday. The eighth – that was yesterday."

"And it's the right year?"

Even I realise that this sounds a bit of a stupid question.

"You've had one of your fits again haven't you mum? I told Uncle George it was too soon for you to try and do stuff by yourself. But no, he said you would be fine if we moved to the middle of nowhere – that you would be less likely to get run over or mugged after one of your turns. But it hasn't stopped you running around clueless with any Tom, Dick or Harry." What a horrid little boy. He surely isn't anything to do with me. "And you didn't think about me did you? I hate it. There's nothing to do, no one to play with." Just for a second he really does seem like a little boy. But there's something about his dramatics that is not at all convincing. "And I hate you. You've spoilt everything and it's all your fault!"

"Now then Peter, that's enough," a man's voice booms from the door. "If it's anyone's fault it's yours, actually."

The voice belongs to a very imposing man, aged about fifty and wearing rather formal clothes that look like they've come straight from the stage of some early twentieth century period play.

Peter also jumps and I notice the tension between the two of them. Peter's confidence seems to evaporate.

"Yes, sorry uncle."

So this is supposed to be my brother. Really? A bit old I think.

"Hello Sarah,"

I shrink back.

"So you're not remembering us today are you?"

He doesn't sound threatening but neither do I feel reassured. I stay quiet, expecting him to explain.

"Have you got your photos and your notes? You should have a picture of me and Peter in your pocket, along with the rest of the family and pictures of important things like the cottage."

I've been through my pockets enough times to know they don't contain any photos.

"And the notes? Did you black out here? Where?"

How does he know I blacked out?

He isn't playing the part of the concerned relative very well. He just seems really irritated, as if I've messed up his plans.

"I don't know," I say. "Not far away, just down the road. I think I was trying to catch a bus."

What happened to my bus driver, Andy?

"So how did you get back here?" the man says. "Have you got your notes? Anything else?"

"She says there was a man here called Andy but there's no sign of anyone," Peter says.

I want to look out of the window and see if the red Ford Escort is still there but I have the feeling that I've already said too much about Andy and not because it might upset Peter's fragile psyche.

Instead I pick up my jacket and pretend to look for photos I know aren't there. However, I do feel some unexpected stiff pieces of paper. I pull them out and see beaming faces looking at me and I see myself smiling too, all conveniently standing in front of the same backdrop – this cottage.

"See," giggles Peter, "a whole host of family and friends!"

There is a small assortment of characters, usually no more than two at a time, standing either side of me and grinning, but I can't remember anyone. Surely I should have knowledge of my own relatives before the last five years?

The faces are a little fuzzy. There are a couple of youngish girls and a couple of older ones but the only person I recognise is myself – and in each one I am wearing the same outfit, the one I am still wearing. I turn one of the photos over to see if there is any information written on the back but there is nothing. The photos are in remarkably good condition to say they have supposedly occupied my pocket for the last few years. Suddenly Peter snatches them from me.

"That's me and Uncle George. Do you remember now?"

Idiot boy. I ignore him and turn towards his so called uncle.

"How come all the photos have been taken here? Why aren't there any from other places or from different times? And more importantly how come I don't know any of them?"

'Uncle George' sighs heavily. He rubs his forehead with the air of someone who has performed a role too many times and whose words are delivered without thought.

"Always the same questions," he says.

"Not to me they're not."

"Trust me they are."

"Well I don't mean to be boring."

"No, I realise you can't help being repetitious, but it gets so draining. The photos in your pocket are supposed to help you, along with your notes with your info and numbers. Maybe they are just confusing you. Perhaps we should think of something else."

I pat the outside of my pocket again; they are the only belongings I have and I don't want to lose them. I remember the letter, key and a bit of money, probably bus fare, and that strange lump of coal. Where's that gone? I check the other pocket; it's definitely gone. I feel a sense of panic and I look behind the sofa. I glance at my 'relatives' expecting some bewilderment on their faces, but there is just resignation from the man and a smirk from Peter. I won't give up and pour out the contents onto the floor.

"There see."

I look towards what 'Uncle George' is pointing at. It's the ripped, A4 paper, now resting on the tasteless carpet. How does he know about the strange sometimes blank but always smudged paper, cryptically destined to be replaced in some mythical folder? I reach to hide it from this intruder but he is surprisingly swift and swoops down and lifts it up.

"Here we go."

He reads off the paper:

"Hello Sarah! Hello again. Hello me."

The letter! But that wasn't written on the torn paper.

"I expect that you/we are feeling confused right now, it's quite normal to suffer some memory loss."

That's not my letter.

"You have epileptic amnesia. If you are reading this, it probably means you have suffered another attack. Try and get back to the address that you should also have on you."

Epileptic amnesia? Never heard of it.

"Don't panic. Someone will help you."

'Uncle George' stops reading.

That's it? That's supposed to reassure me?

Uncle George looks over again with a smug expression that suggests I should now clearly be cured of my irrational behaviour.

"Where's my lump of coal?" I ask.

Peter giggles again. I know that I sound stupid and that this is just backing up their theory I have certain health issues but I also know what I know, which is that I definitely had a lump of coal, and no ordinary lump of coal at that. I decide to keep back the detail about it being embedded with a bit of metal.

"I had a lump of coal. Have you seen it?"

I take another, more determined look behind the sofa, partly so I don't have to continue looking at Peter who can now barely contain his giggling and is now clutching at his stomach. However, it's impossible for me to remain bent over for long and as I return upright I find he is still squealing and writhing like some victim in an amateur production of an Agatha Christie play.

"Do you remember what your doctor told you? That because of the repeated attacks, the damage to your brain tissue is getting worse? And because it is mainly on the right side of your brain, it is affecting your visual memory? You don't always accurately remember what you've seen and it's hard for you to process directions and objects. That's why it's easy to get lost and think you've seen something that isn't really there."

It all sounds plausible and does explain the waking up clueless at the country bus stop. And maybe the coal with the strange bit of metal in it could be written off – but what about Andy and the exhibits upstairs? This reminds me of the fossilised amber necklace that I snuck round my neck. If that's still there then I can't have false memories of everything that I think I remember. I brush my fingers against my neck. I'm certainly wearing a necklace. I want to tug it out of my shirt triumphantly but part of me believes what George is saying. What if I pull out something else? I need to check it alone – and I need to see what's upstairs.

"I feel confused and tired. I think I'd better lie down for a while," I say.

Peter has stopped convulsing and moves towards me.

"Good idea mum. Have a little kip on the sofa."

"I think I need a bit of quiet. I'll just pop upstairs for a bit."

"Ok but remember we're supposed to be somewhere."

"Peterborough?"

"Not exactly," he giggles, "don't worry about it. Have a rest mum, then we'll get off."

Stop calling me mum.

I head up the stairs, but I know before I get to the top that there will no longer be any weird lights shining on even weirder exhibits. I flick on the switch, fully expecting an ordinary tasteless bedroom containing an equally tasteless Darth Vader strewn bed. I'm half right.

CHAPTER NINE:
"…or profession..."

Not the half I was expecting. The exhibition stuff has gone but in its place is a single light shining on a box-like object in the middle of the room. Do George and Peter know about this? It looks a like a safe.

It seems to have two sections, the top half with a hole, presumably for a key, and a lower section that looks like a combination lock. Am I supposed to be able to open it? I know that as far as I can remember, which I realise isn't very long, that I have not been given a code for a safe unless it was on the apparently blank, then not so blank paper with smudgy marks on it. I did sometimes have a key, but if I looked for it, that would mean going back downstairs and dodging past the dodgy relatives.

I crouch down and take a closer look. Perhaps it isn't even locked. I reach for the handle and give it a hopeful tug. Nothing. I notice something glinting in the back of the room. As I strain to look at it my eyes adjust to the darkness and I make out something that my brain interprets as a camera. It's one of those security types that are fitted into the top corners of rooms to monitor what's going on. I wish it would tell me. I can't tell if it's switched on but it's aimed directly at the safe and me. The camera might have been justified in guarding the weird museum stuff but why is it here now? Could *I* be the one who's being monitored and if so, by whom? Are George and Peter watching me right now or maybe even Andy or someone I don't know?

Or I could be being super paranoid. Actually I feel surprisingly calm. That's an interesting point, why am I so calm? I have no idea what has happened to me in five whole years, which is three hundred and fifty times five days. Could I possibly have gone through over seventeen hundred days like this one?

It's exhausting just thinking about it and I already needed a lie down. Why couldn't there have just been a simple comfy flowery bed to lie on?

I want to give the safe a good kick but I have enough disadvantages without adding a broken foot. I sit down in front of it.

If this is my home then surely I should be able to get into my own safe. Have there been any clues about numbers? I haven't come across anything yet that suggested it might be a code. The only number I've come across is that of this cottage. I try entering an eight. I mean who would try just entering one number; genius! Or not. The door remains shut. I try it again, though even I realise I am unlikely to mess up with just one number. Nothing. Except it's not just one number. To the right of the numbers is a button marked C. How many numbers would I be idiotic enough to enter without cancelling previous entries? If I have been trying to get into this safe for five years would this be the first time it has occurred to me to cancel the previous seventeen hundred attempts. Surely not, but I'm still here aren't I? I push the C button and re-enter 8. Stupid idea.

Or if I had a hairpin I could insert it into the keyhole and wiggle it about until it broke and scuppered all future attempts of entry. It isn't a regularly-shaped keyhole. It has zigzags up and down the sides that look somehow familiar. Where have I seen that shape before? Not on the door key I'm sure of that and it was recently – not in my former life. So that leaves the last few hours. Of course, I'd almost forgotten why I'd come up here in the first place – the amber necklace. I pull at the chain and there it is. Ha 'Uncle George' you missed this one – I'm not imagining this.

I hold it up to the light and look closely at the amber –there's a small metallic bar with similar indentations. But if this is this is the key to the safe, how do I get it out of the amber?

I sit and stare at it for a while. I don't know how to get into it and yet there has to be a way. Maybe I could put it in a hot oven. Do I even have an oven?

Judging by the rather limited fare of sandwiches I would guess not, but surely the most basic of kitchens would have a microwave. That would be an interesting experiment. Frankie would have liked the idea, especially if it worked and we were left with a piece of metal – which even I know shouldn't be put in microwaves. Once again though, that would require returning downstairs and I don't think I would get away with quietly blowing up a necklace.

So back to option A; the combination code. If I set the combination myself it must be a series of numbers that I would know off by heart, like my birthday for instance. I push the C first, of course, and then try it with a reasonable amount of confidence but a realistic amount of doubt and succumb to the latter. I guess it would be too obvious and easily found out by anyone. So what other numbers do I know? Dates obviously – of birthdays and anniversaries and maybe some telephone numbers. I try various dates without success. Finally I am left with the date I am most confident I would have chosen. The best day of my life – despite the twenty three hours of crippling stomach cramps before he finally arrived.

The handle doesn't budge. I'm about to give up when I realise that there is one more significant date that I have not yet tried, probably the worst day of my life, he day Frankie disappeared. I put in the numbers with trembling fingers but I need to stay focused. I need to get myself out of this confusing mess and surely getting this dammed safe open is going to help. I pull the handle and at last it gives way.

I hardly dare look – what if it's empty? It isn't. I look up at the camera as though I should be able to detect if it approves of my success or if it is laughing at me but it remains inactive. No matter, either way I'm going in.

The first thing I see is a small mound of tissue. I pull it out and feel something powdery on my fingers. Soot. I place the tissue in my hand and carefully unwrap it to find two more lumps of coal. What is it with coal round here?

These pieces are smaller than my lump and less interesting – no danger of snagging my fingers on sharp metal here. I carefully place the pieces down on the tissue and realise it's no ordinary piece of tissue – beneath its blackened exterior there are traces of a feint outline of Santas. This is the same type of paper that was used to protect *my* coal.

I pick up one of the pieces and study it carefully. It has small indentations along its centre, a bit like the scales of a small fish. This isn't a different piece of coal, it's *my* piece of coal. I turn over the other piece and see a corresponding string of small dents. Where's the metal thingy gone? I look into the safe in the hope of finding it there pull out some crumpled papers.

As I straighten one of them out I read the words 'Break the coal'. Well thanks a bundle. Why didn't I get this information when my lump of coal was intact? Was it me who left this pointless suggestion? Did I think it would amuse me? How little I know myself.

I wrap the pieces of coal in the crumpled paper for added protection – again forgetting to use my glove. I don't want to leave the coal but I don't want a pocket full of soot either. I put the bits in my pocket, but with little confidence they will remain there. I feel about the safe for anything else. Less surprisingly there is a letter and even though it seems likely that this really is my safe, I am still astonished to see that it is addressed to me.

Dear you/me etc.

What are you playing at? Remember our motto: 'Reliability is our reputation!'? Clearly you don't. This isn't a game you know, this is deadly serious.

I can't believe I'm being told off by myself. Don't I know what I'm going through? And it's not like me to be so confrontational or dramatic; what's with the 'deadly serious'? I actually feel quite annoyed. I would have hoped that if I'd bothered to go to so much trouble, and actually succeeded in solving the riddle of the safe, I'd be rewarded with something more useful than an admonishment. Why not tell me why I've accumulated new relatives or why the cottage keeps self-refurbishing? I'm tempted not to carry on reading if I'm taking such an uppity tone with myself but it would be ridiculous, after all the effort I've gone to, not to read what I've got to say for myself. So I sulkily continue.

I know you don't enjoy hearing this but we promised to do a job. You were supposed to break the coal and catch the train, remember?

It's like talking to Andy again. No, actually I don't remember and if this was me writing I should know that. How does this me that's writing even know about the coal or that I didn't do anything special to it? And actually it is broken now – so what's the problem? I sneak a look at the camera. Maybe it's me up there and I'm watching myself through some kind of wormhole video link.

I guess you are wondering how I know all this. It's just sufficient for you to know that our clients have prepared for every eventuality and permutation. Something was bound to go wrong at some point. You need to get back on track.

Hilarious, even when I'm cross I can't resist an opportunity to pun.

Some of the other travellers will come for you. Do exactly as they say.

If I'm referring to those two downstairs, how can they be part of this mysterious coal business if they're trying to convince me I'm mad? I know that the other note mentioned a Little Peter and hope he's not the one to find me, but why would he pretend to be my son? He's not even using the right name.

My gut definitely says to not trust my so-called relatives, which would mean I don't trust myself. I wish Andy was here and I really hope he's okay.

There is nothing else on the paper and I'm on the verge of tearing it up into little pieces when I'm struck by an idea. Since when did I start telling people off and being over dramatic? I'm usually the one to be relied upon to be inappropriately flippant in a crisis. I hold the letter up to the light and yes, there's a yellow smudge in the top corner. I just need to magically make it turn into something else, hopefully something a little less hurtful.

Simple.

Actually it could be.

CHAPTER TEN:
"…the potential..."

I might not be a rocket scientist but I have not failed to notice that odd things occur in the dark. I get up and reach for the light switch. Could it be this simple? I flick it on and off. No it couldn't. The letter is exactly the same and still scolding me. I should have taken the rocket science course. Okay, what else?

Things changed after I'd been asleep and when I went outside looking for Andy and shortly after he found the sheets of paper in the cupboard. All combined with the lights going off. Yes, I already know that, so what else?

I locked the door while Andy was getting the rugs for the magic camp beds. The door was also locked when I was outside and that's when I saw the cottage with its posters and awful sofas for the first time. But nobody went out when Andy was looking at those sheets…. unless someone else came in? It's worth a shot. I have to go back downstairs eventually and it's probably a sensible idea going out and locking that dodgy pair behind me – I just hope the key is still in the lock.

I tiptoe downstairs feeling like a character from an American graphic novel about to be apprehended by some evil nemesis.

As I reach the bottom I take a sneaky look towards the living room. I can't see anyone and neither can I hear anything. I would feel safer it I could hear the two of them chatting; at least they would be distracted and perhaps I could pick up some hint as to what they really wanted from me. They have gone to too much trouble with photos and diagnosis to just let me wander off.

"That was quick. Are you feeling better?"

I nearly jump out of my skin as I turn towards the kitchen. Peter is standing to my right holding, what is proving to be a very popular snack around here – a jam sandwich.

"I'm fine. Where's your Uncle George?"

"Who? Only joking."

Again he seems a lot more confident when he's on his own.

"So where is he?"

"Ooh a bit tetchy aren't we, clearly the nap didn't help after all."

"So?"

I'm wondering if he's just being awkward or trying to stall me.

"He'll be back in a minute, just checking the car before we leave."

"He's outside? I'll go help."

This is my chance to get to the door without raising suspicion.

Peter leaps in front of me as I reach for the door. His face contorts into an ugly smile before erupting into those familiar giggles.

"Now then mum, no need to get over excited."

He puts his puny little arm across my torso and to say he's only supposedly twelve, he has surprising strength. For the first time though, I am beginning to feel angry. It seems one step too far in this weird world to be bullied by an annoying little boy, so I push back – but he gives way and I slip embarrassingly down onto the linoleum floor. As I hit the ground there is a loud crashing sound, which I don't think is coming from me. Then darkness.

For a moment everything is very quiet. The giggling has stopped.

I lie wearily.

My leg feels stiff and I try and move it but it is trapped by something heavy lying across it. It seems like I wasn't the only one to take a fall. I move my leg a bit more and am surprised at the weight of my puny so-called son. Surely he can't have knocked himself out? The floor's only about five feet lower than his head.

I can now hear breathing, which would be a relief if it wasn't so laboured, and coming from directly above me.

"Sarah?"

I stay quiet, refusing to take the bait. Who knows what menacing trap I could be talking myself into?

"Sarah is that you?" I feel a foot tapping impatiently against my side. Andy?

The lights come on again and I see Andy towering over me, breathing hard and holding a bottle. Oh good.

"You found some wine then. Excellent."

"Well you seem to be alright. I wasn't sure if you'd even remember who I am. Do you know him?"

I manage to sit up and swivel my head towards the lump lying across me. It's Uncle George.

"Is he dead?"

"I don't think so."

"Well you can't have hit him that hard, the bottle didn't even break!"

"What? No I didn't use this, I used this. Lucky thing I'm a bus driver."

Andy holds up the taser thing that I last saw in the attic.

"My best friend, the Tommy Swift got him."

I wriggle a little more to see if there's any reaction. Nothing. Damn, what if this man really is dead? And what about me? I'm hardly in a position to make a quick exit.

I look up and grin nervously. I'm pretty sure Andy isn't going to attack me. He's already had plenty of chances.

"What happened? Why did you attack Uncle George?"

"He's your uncle?"

"I asked first….wait no you asked me but never mind…I don't know. He said he was my brother I think or at least he was Peter's uncle. Peter was supposed to be my son but he isn't because my son is called Frankie after his granddad and I don't have a brother; George or otherwise. But they said I had some kind of medical amnesia and that I was always blacking out and they showed me photos of my family and notes that were written to myself to help me remember. Except they didn't."

"They didn't help you remember?"

"No. But I don't think there *was* anything *to* remember.

They were trying to convince me I was ill and that I had to go to Peterborough…"

"You had the ticket."

"Yes. Some of it did sound convincing, but why would anyone go to so much trouble? I'm not special."

"Maybe you're more important than you think."

How sweet, but not very likely.

Andy kneels down and slides his hand into Uncle George's thick plaid jacket.

"Let's see if we can find out who he is then."

I watch him broddle about a bit which gives me chance to release a leg from under George's extraordinarily heavy torso.

"Doesn't seem to have anything," Andy, apparently oblivious to my undignified struggling. I finally make it out as Andy concludes his search.

"No money or wallet, only this business card. *Reliability Is Our Reputation!* Now where have I heard that before?"

What? Who's stolen my slogan?

"That's *my* slogan. Who's sto…."

Andy thrusts the card at me.

"Is this your card?" asks Andy.

"Why has he got your card?"

How would I know?

"You sure he's not your uncle?"

For the first time, I see Andy a little panicked.

To make him feel better I change the subject.

"So what happened to you? I woke up this morning and you were gone. Next thing I know you're standing over a dead body wielding a bottle of red wine."

"He's not dead – he'll be fine. He's just knocked out and it wasn't me who disappeared was it? I woke up and *you* had gone. I looked all over the cottage and was just locking up when this guy," he pokes a foot at Uncle George, who reassuringly lets out a small groan, "comes at me with this bottle."

Andy holds the bottle up to the light to see the label more clearly.

"That's odd, I could understand why someone would falsify a label to make a wine seem older than it really is but according to the label this wine hasn't even been made yet. Bet it doesn't taste very good."

Bet it's worth finding out. Unless it's been made with a special type of grape juice, that somehow matures into wine whilst it's in the bottle. Or even worse – it's non-alcoholic.

"Did you see the boy?" I ask.

"The boy you thought you saw last night?"

"Yes I think it was the same boy. Peter."

"Your son?"

Is he listening?

"No. He isn't my son. Though he…" I give Uncle George a little kick of my own but immediately feel very guilty, "…. told me he was."

I turn to check and see that I'm back in the flowery cottage. Andy was right, it *was* me that disappeared. And now it seems, so had Peter. But this is what I was hoping for, minus the unconscious body of course. I feel the letter in my pocket, would it still be admonishing? I get it out to see.

Hello.

I expect you're still wondering what is going on, right?

Right.

And I'm guessing you're expecting me to tell you, right?

This isn't going to end well.

Although I expect by now you're starting to have doubts?

You know me so well.

Well tough. And this is where you get *going! See what I did there?*

Now that's more like the inappropriate flippancy I'm used to.

Well done, by the way, for working out *the secret writing on all the letters. I thought if I went a bit over the top – "This is not a game- it's deadly serious!" you'd realise something was up; I hope it didn't take you too long.*

Is five years considered long?

Nevertheless, if you want to get *Frankie back …*

What? Frankie is alive?

…you need to put up with the confusion – I promise that if you carry on – eventually you will find him. Don't give up – and don't forget to break the coal.

How am I supposed to do that? I'm still puzzling over the letter trying to work out if it actually helped or not when I realise Andy is standing at my shoulder, trying to muscle in on my private correspondence.

"What's that?" he asks.

He's evidently waiting for some information. I suppose I should give him something.

"It's just a note that I found."

Should I mention where?

"Another one. Your pockets must be like the Tardis."

Excellent deduction Andy. That'll do for me.

"What does it say? Does it help?"

"I'm not sure. But at least I think I know *why* I'm here."

"Which is?"

"I think I've come to find my son."

"You mean you came for that boy, Peter was it?"

"No. I realise it's a bit hard to keep up but *once again*, Peter is not my son, he just said he was to make me think I was going mad."

"Going?" Andy grins.

"Not helping. Frankie is my son but he disappeared."

"When?"

"I guess it must have been a little over six years."

"So just over a year before you say you lost your memory."

The "you say" isn't lost on me but I let it slide. Seems Andy still isn't convinced by my story, which probably indicates that he's saner than he looks.

"That's correct."

"So what happened?"

"He left for school one day and never came home. By the time anyone realised he was missing he'd been gone nearly eight hours."

"How come the school didn't get in touch when his fingerprints weren't scanned at registration?"

"What now?"

"All kids get registered electronically by touching a screen as they enter the building, even toddlers. If they fail to register, then a guardian has to explain and confirm the absence. Maybe they didn't have it six years ago."

"I've never heard of it. Very Big Brotherish."

"Lots of people objected to it, but it's rather difficult to win an argument against child safety."

"I guess – anyway someone would have called, but Frankie had been off sick for a couple of days, so the school didn't realise he was supposed to be back."

"That's incredible bad luck. So what happened next? I presume there was a search."

"Of course. It was all over the news for ages because he was only eleven. There were local and international searches and loads of people tried to help. The school were very kind and the head kept in touch for a while – they even let off balloons and a held a bake sale but apart from some false leads there was nothing. He just seemed to vanish."

"But someone must have known something."

"The police went through hours of street surveillance but he never appeared on any recordings. Then they thought he couldn't have even left the building and for a while I think they thought me, or someone in the flats we lived in, had taken him, but they went through the entire block and found nothing. One of the neighbours, a spinsterish woman who poked her nose into everyone's business, said she saw him going into the lift but even that couldn't be confirmed. She would have said she'd seen him entering a spaceship if she thought someone would have paid her attention. Maybe I wish she had done because eventually everyone became more interested in other tragedies and it was almost as though he hadn't existed at all."

"Could he have reappeared in the time you can't remember?"

"How would I know?"

"Sorry, of course not. But we could try and find out."

"Obviously, although this note says it's up to me to find him."

"If it's genuine," Andy says unhelpfully.

"Obviously. But it's the only thing I have at the moment and it's a lot more than I had five minutes or even five years ago."

"So what do you think you should do? Go to the police?"

I look down at the body of Uncle George and quickly run through a version of my potential statement. Normally I am a very law abiding citizen, at least I remember myself as being one, but these don't appear to be normal circumstances.

"Maybe later. I wouldn't know what to tell them and unless they have a department specialising in weirdness…"

Uncle George groans again.

"I think we ought to go," I say, "he's waking up. But where? The only clue I have is this ticket to Peterborough which I presume is now out of date."

I look at the date which I am still getting used to and the destination which means even less to me. Why were Peter and George keen to get me to Peterborough? I don't know it, but it must be a large place, too large to be looking for something or someone that you don't even know is there to begin with. No wonder Jane Marple limited her investigations to small villages or big houses.

"What we need is a big house in a small village," I say.

"We need what?"

"Well obviously a full explanation and a detailed map indicating the whereabouts of my son is what I need but just ignore me – I was just thinking aloud."

"I can't help with the map but I think I might know where there might be an interesting place to visit – and it's in a village."

"What are you talking about?"

Perhaps my madness is contagious.

"Remember the address I saw on that bit of paper, the one I think belongs to Simon Greave's family? Well it's in a village quite close to here and it's bound to be a huge house, after all they must have got millions in compensation."

"And we should go there? Why? An autograph perhaps?"

Andy's mouth tightens as though resisting a reply.

"He's dead, remember?" he says.

I feel myself colouring again. He has a knack for making me feel ashamed.

"Sorry. So why would we go to his house?"

He looks up and stares into my eyes as if to emphasise the importance of what he's going to say.

"I think the question you *should* be asking is why are his private details written on magic pieces of paper and lying in a mysterious cupboard in your house?"

Should I?

"And also it's the only lead we've got, unless you want to go to Peterborough?"

"Nah."

"Let's go then."

Sleuthing seems to have livened him up no end.

"I'll follow you out. I'll just pop to the loo."

You never know when you'll get a chance again when you're on the road.

I avoid stepping on Uncle George and head for the toilet.

I hear the front door slam. I said I'd be out in a second

I switch on the light but the room looks wrong without the *Star Wars* poster and more annoyingly, there isn't any toilet paper. In the search for usable scraps of paper on the floor I notice my shoes have left footprints in an otherwise thick layer of undisturbed dust. It looks like nobody has been in here for months.

When I leave the toilet I glance into the living room – the lights are off but I can tell the room is completely stripped bare. No wallpaper, no carpets, no furniture, flowery or otherwise, nothing, just empty, neglected space. I'm pretty sure Uncle George hadn't had time to hire and fill a removal van, never mind arrange for a billion particles of dust to be delivered and distributed. Is that even possible?

I'm tempted to rouse George and find out but the bit of floor on which George was lying is now empty – apart from a thick layer of dust. I turn nervously around but there's no sign of him. I guess the slamming door must have been him leaving. At least I can presume he's O.K.

Maybe I should call Andy back and show him what's happened? Maybe he already knows. I step carefully across the bare boards and reach to open the door. Under the handle a key chain is swaying. So that's how they got in – they had a key. I wonder if he took *my* key. For now, instead of an ammonite, there is a balloon-shaped key fob on which 'Field View Cottage' has been scribbled by hand underneath the name Brightstone and Nephews, same as on the For Sale sign.

I take the key and leave. Andy waves at me from his car. Where have my relatives vanished to? I lock the door and instinctively feel drawn to the daisy-rimmed plaque that is hanging from the wall. I guess I could hide the key behind it, just like I used to do at my flat in my old life. I put my hand out but am jolted by the sound of the car horn. I change my mind. I think I should keep hold of this key just in case. I don't think this will be the last I see of this strange cottage.

CHAPTER ELEVEN:
"…to be…"

The car has a neglected feel to it. The tartan upholstery is threadbare in places and although it's not sticky I don't really trust it as I put my full weight down. Not that I know how long I've been wearing these clothes I'm in – if I've had them on for the last five years I should really pity the plaid.

I'm sure they are mine – a dark durable skirt and suit jacket with a multi coloured flowery blouse, all carefully chosen to hide casual staining and perfect for meetings. I'm almost certain I was wearing them as I was driving along the M1 – and according to the photos George showed me I was wearing them then too. I take a subtle sniff – they smell okay. Perhaps soon I will come across a wardrobe full of identical outfits.

I turn my attention back to the car and remember that Andy said it wasn't his.

"Didn't you say you borrowed this car? Won't they be wanting it back?"

"Maybe," he replies.

"What does that mean?"

"I didn't exactly speak to the owner."

"You mean you *stole* this car?"

"Of course not. It belongs to a passenger."

"Right, that sounds more reassuring. So how did they get it on to the bus?"

"Get what on?"

"The car."

"Obviously the car wasn't on the bus. It was lucky actually. The passenger was supposed to be getting off at the stop close to where we broke down, to meet her sister. When it became obvious that we weren't going anywhere I radioed for another bus to take over which they said would take quite a while.

"That's when I started to panic about you missing your train. The girl overheard me arguing with the station about having to get somewhere and she offered to let me borrow her sister's car."

"I assumed it must have belonged to a friend. I can't believe some stranger, a girl, just gave you a car."

"She only loaned it and she wasn't particularly young, early twenties maybe."

"That's okay then. But don't you think she might have expected you to have returned it by now? What did her sister say?"

"Well we walked to the next stop and her sister had gone but her car was parked nearby. The passenger, Mary I think her name was, rang her sister who said the car was open, the keys were in the glove compartment and that she didn't need it in the next couple of days. I just had to make sure the tank was filled and take it back by the end of the week."

"So she never even saw you and yet she just handed over the keys to her car?"

"Well I did say it was important and it's not like it's a new car or anything."

"That's the most ridiculous thing I've ever heard."

"Really? More ridiculous than suddenly appearing five years into the future and a cottage that changes its interior at the click of a switch?"

"Fine. But it's still ridiculous. Shouldn't you at least call her?"

"I haven't got a phone signal remember. Anyway it's not your problem."

"It is if the car is reported as stolen and the police stop us. Also, there's the small matter of a recent assault and battery that we just ran away from. Remember the previously-unconscious body that you beat over the head with a bottle of wine?"

"It was a taser and it was self-defence and what do you mean previously?"

"What I say. He was previously unconscious and then he must have not been because when I came out of the toilet, he'd gone. Or at least he wasn't there anymore."

"What do you mean?"

Should I mention the total disappearance of the furniture too? Maybe later.

"There just wasn't any sign of him at all. I'm guessing you didn't see him leaving the cottage?"

"No. Well at least that's one less thing to worry about."

Is it? Surely a walking, talking adversary is more dangerous than an unconscious one.

"Anyway, Mary insisted that I take the car to come rescue you. It was very romantic."

Andy blushes a little as I glare at him. How can he be so relaxed and flippant? None of this is romantic.

"Sorry, I didn't mean *romantic*, chivalrous perhaps."

So he fancied himself as my knight in shining armour. I feel inclined to challenge my status as a distressed damsel but if I'm honest I don't know what I would have done if he hadn't come to find me, so I change the subject.

"So what about your other passengers? Are you allowed to just dump them while they wait for another bus to arrive?"

He colours again and I'm guessing this wasn't the most tactful change of subject.

"Probably not, which is why there's probably not much point in rushing back."

"And you probably shouldn't have taken the Tommy Swift with you."

"Probably not."

"But at least it meant you didn't have to waste the wine."

"True – I thought we could take it as a gift for Simon's parents."

That's not what I had planned for it.

"Sure. Wine not?"

My attempt at lightening the mood appears to go unnoticed. I guess these windy country roads require a lot of attention, though you would assume he was quite accomplished at driving.

"So you never did explain what the killings thing was that got all the drivers armed."

This at last seems to get his attention.

"The Manchester City bus killings? Yes it was awful. It was supposedly a gang from some religious cult who decided to cause as much chaos as they could by getting on buses and stabbing people at random."

"How many died?"

"Six I think. What happened, was one of the killers got on a crowded bus, sat behind a passenger, stabbed them and then got off. The first time it happened nobody even noticed anything was wrong for ages, I think they assumed the passenger was asleep. People only started to panic when a toddler slipped on some of the blood."

"Yuk."

"Mm, but after a second stabbing, everyone who travelled by bus became more wary and anxious."

"I bet the back seat was popular."

Andy tuts and I feel shame at my insensitivity, even though I know nothing about what happened.

"Do you want to hear about this or not? Anyway people get jumpy and the bus company is losing money because fewer people are using the buses. So the bus company comes up with the idea of issuing tasers to reassure people. Naturally there were some objections but the hysteria at the killings managed to get the decision passed quickly through."

"So were you trained? As far as I remember bus drivers weren't particularly associated with physical prowess."

"Charming!"

I glance mischievously over to him and am sure I see his paunch being sucked in.

"But true I suppose. To be honest, I don't think anyone expected us to use them, they were really given to us as a deterrent. And most of the drivers I spoke to felt it wasn't their job to catch criminals, although giving the odd drunken yob a jab would be tempting."

"Did it work?"

"Yes. Gradually more people started to use the buses but when everyone felt more relaxed, which I guess was about a month later, the killings began again. Four times in one day and then it stopped."

"So did the bus drivers manage to taser the killers?"

"No."

"Did the killers get caught though?"

"Not exactly. Someone sent letters to the police and the press saying this cult was responsible but nobody was arrested."

"But there must have been loads of witnesses if it happened on a bus?"

"They only targeted full buses. Nobody reliably saw who had done it. Nearly all the eye witnesses had different ideas as to who the killer was. That was another reason why the case was so famous, because all of the witness reports describing the killer were so wildly different, like different genders, nationalities, heights and ages, you name it. So nobody was arrested."

"What about the cult. Surely they arrested the leader?"

"One, the police couldn't find the cult, never mind its leader and second there was no way to find out who sent the letters."

"So why did you say it was the work of a cult if it wasn't proved?"

Andy's brow furrows.

"You're right. It was talked about in the papers so much and because nothing else happened after the letters, everyone, or rather most people, just accepted that it was the truth. It's easier to come to terms with when you can put a name to your fears."

"But not a face. Doesn't sound like detective work has improved much."

"At least it stopped."

"What about justice? I bet the bus company had to pay out millions."

"Not a bean. I remember there *was* a court case. One of the drivers was hoping to reopen the investigation by trying to sue. He argued that he and the victims should get compensation because of the trauma they went through and that he couldn't work in the city anymore."

"And he didn't get anything?"

"No, an expensive defence team was able to convince the jury that the victims were unreliable because of the wildly differing evidence and it was this cult that was responsible, even though there was no evidence. He didn't stand a chance, the case collapsed and the driver was offered a new job or something and that was that."

"Shame I wasn't around to help."

"I thought you just tried to catch people out."

"Not always. You think he should have won?"

"I think he should have tried harder."

"Harsh. What about the other victims? Did you say they were targeted at random?"

"Apparently. Again all different. Different ages, sexes and races."

"Nothing connected them at all?"

"Still no. Not that anyone found out. Just random killings."

"I don't understand that. Just killing someone like that. I mean how can you just go out one day and pick someone to end. Obviously when Frankie went missing I had to consider the fact that he was dead and you just think how stupid that is. I mean the chances of anyone even being born in the first place are like trillions of billions against. I used to think about it a lot in the days and weeks after he went missing.

"I used to walk around town and look at people and think how everyone in the world seems so temporary and fragile, living one of billions of insignificant lives on one of billions of planets in one of billions of galaxies. And then I'd think about all the accidents and wars and diseases that all their ancestors had to survive and all the combinations of luck and chance from their parents meeting and their grandparents and great, great, great, great, great grandparents. And then there're all the eggs and sperm that were rejected – yet that one egg and sperm from two unlikely strangers get together and finally they get to be born. And then someone comes along after that amazing piece of luck and just ends it with one stab of a knife, just because you are sitting in the wrong seat."

"So you're saying life's a bit of a paradox – meaningless and miraculous at the same time?"

At first I think he's mocking me, but when I glance at him, he looks rather thoughtful. He'd summed up my thoughts rather well and I am a little impressed. Maybe he lost someone too.

"Exactly so, and I can't work out which one is right."

"I know which one I prefer. I don't want to think of myself as meaningless. Anyway I helped you didn't I? So I can't be entirely pointless."

"Yes, although so far it has just led to some strange events and a disappearing body."

"And a lovely drive in the country."

So far I have been largely ignoring all the squares of varied greens and yellow as we rapidly make progress down the deserted roads. I never have this luck when I try to negotiate these country roads – the only view I usually have is the back end of a long trail of cars.

"Lovely. I wonder what would have happened if you'd left me to wait for the bus."

"Maybe you would have got a chill and died or got attacked by wild dogs."

"Or maybe I would have found the station, recovered my memory and gone home."

"I don't see how me helping you could affect the state of your memory, and by the way you're beginning to sound rather ungrateful. I may have lost my job looking out for you."

"I thought you were leaving?"

"I still want to be paid."

"Sorry." I'm on the verge of pointing out that I hadn't asked for his help but don't. "It's just the thought of those poor people on the buses. It made me think about Frankie and all the hours I spent imagining the million different scenarios that could have resulted in his disappearance. All the abductions and accidents and murders. Like the people on the bus who just assumed their day would be the same as any other, but then they're gone and no one even knows why."

"Some people would say that all things are done for a reason."

The car swerves as Andy momentarily loses concentration.

"I guess that's true," he agrees, steadying the wheel.

"I remember, about a month after Frankie disappeared, someone from a local church turned up uninvited at the flat and said similar things to me about destiny and God's Purpose. The vicar talked about testing faith as though it would reassure me to know that my son's fate was a good opportunity to show off how mentally strong I was. How egotistical is that? Can you imagine the families of your bus killings being grateful for a chance to have their faith tested? What about the faith of the victims?"

I don't know Andy well enough to be pouring all my frustrations to him.

"Maybe the victims get their reward in heaven."

"Do you believe that?"

"No," he replies bluntly.

"Me neither. And anyway – there is no proof that Frankie *is* dead."

I look out at the scenery again to try and allow a little peace to flood back into the car. The greenery is finally tapering away and being replaced with the some buildings that steadily increase to form a village. The car slows down and I look expectantly at Andy.

"Yes," he says in response to my expression, "we are indeed here."

He passes me the paper that contains the address and asks me to repeat it.

With it being a small village there doesn't appear to be any need for numbers and instead we are just looking for a name which is 'Ivy House.' I envisage a large Edwardian country house with swirling tendrils of ivy and beautifully-kept lawns leading down to shaded, lily littered ponds.

Andy drives around the village unsuccessfully until we come to the end of a small row of terrace cottages.

"This can't be it," I argue. "I thought you said Simon Greaves' family was rich."

"Well they certainly got enough money from the court case. Maybe I've got it wrong. There must be hundreds of Simon Greaves' living in Britain. I don't know why I would assume that the address we found belonged to the famous one."

I'm thinking life would be simpler if this was just an anonymous person's house when Andy pokes me in the ribs. The door of the little house has opened and a young man is standing on the front door step.

"It's him," Andy says quietly, but a little too excitedly.

"I'm sure you told me he was dead."

"I did. He was!"

This Simon Greaves looks like a regular teenager in jeans and a white granddad shirt.

He turns his head towards us and I can see why he would make a popular choice for the finals of a music competition because even in casual clothes he looks quite mesmerizingly stunning with thick brown hair and matching eyes in a perfectly-chiselled face.

I realise he is looking directly at me smiling and starts to walk towards the car.

"Sarah," he beams, "how lovely to see you again."

CHAPTER TWELVE:
"…any place…"

"Just passing through," I say helplessly.

What else am I going to say? That he is supposed to be dead and I only just heard of him yesterday because we found his address on a magic piece of paper?

"Well great, do you want to come in?"

I look to Andy for guidance. Unable to talk, he just shrugs in dubious approval.

"This is Andy," I say. "He's a bus driver."

"Hello Andy the bus driver, nice to meet you."

"So how have you been?" I ask as we get out of the car, hoping for some kind of explanation of his recent and remarkable improvement in his health.

"Oh, you know, fine I guess."

He looks directly at me with large chocolate-button eyes and I feel an inappropriate warmth that makes me want to giggle. He must be at least twenty years younger than me. I can also feel a glare from Andy. Surely he can't tell what I'm thinking – would he be jealous or just disapproving?

We follow Simon up the path towards the cottage which doesn't look too dissimilar to my own. Before we go in, Andy pulls me back.

"What do you think is going on?" he asks.

"How would I know? I didn't even know his name before yesterday."

Andy grabs my jacket.

"Really? Well he seems to know you. How is that possible?"

I try to shrug him off. I don't like being man handled and I try to sound as irritated as possible.

"Again, how would I know? Memory loss, remember?"

"Fine. Okay, but can you think of any reason why a man who is seen killed by a worldwide audience of millions is now inviting us into tea?"

Having not watched this momentous event, as far as I know, but having just met Simon Greaves, it seems clear to me that the millions of people who thought they saw him die were all clearly wrong.

Andy, apparently in a state of mild shock, is still refusing to let go of my clothes.

"Maybe he didn't really die."

"You think?"

"So you met him through work because..." he pauses to think, "…you were hired to investigate the possibility that he was guilty of insurance fraud."

"You seriously think someone paid me to follow Simon Greaves around to prove he wasn't dead? Even if I had managed to cleverly catch him out and got evidence of breathing do you think he'd still be living anonymously in a little village in the middle of nowhere?"

"Maybe."

"Surely if what you said about him bankrupting an entire TV channel and getting billions in damages is true then why hasn't he been exposed and put in jail?"

"Maybe no one knows except you."

His face contorts, trying to will some sense out of it.

"You're in on it," he exclaims. "That's why you could suddenly afford to buy a cottage. You were bribed."

I'm rather taken aback by Andy's delight in exposing me as someone who would be so easily corrupted and bought off with a cottage. Even though my memory is still flawed I am quite sure that I have great integrity. Why else would I have the motto 'Reliability is Our Reputation'?

Before I can make this point and defend myself, Simon reappears at his door.

"All okay? Aren't you coming in?"

Andy lets go of my coat and I follow him in but not without first making my feelings clear to him with a purposeful glare.

Simon's home is well lived in; a tumble of books and guitars which lie haphazardly over and around most surfaces.

"So you like music?" asks Andy as he pushes one of the many guitars to one side before sitting down on one of the comfier looking armchairs.

"How did you guess?" Simon says, oblivious to any potential barb. "Would you like tea?"

Too early for wine I suppose.

As soon as Simon heads off to the kitchen, Andy starts looking around the room, probably in search of traces of extreme wealth or clues relating to the huge success and acclaim that comes with being a finalist in one of the biggest talent shows in the world. But if there are traces of this life, they are well hidden.

"So, do you still think that this is the famous Simon Greaves who died on TV?"

"Maybe," he replies weakly.

"Well let's ask."

Andy looks horrified, as though I've just ordered an exhumation.

"Well, obviously I'll miss the dying bit out unless you think he's a zombie or maybe a vampire – they both seem quite trendy these days."

"Actually vampires aren't that popular anymore."

"Aren't they?" asks Simon as he re-enters the room.

"Apparently not."

"I shan't miss them," Simon says before sitting down next to me and patting me on the leg.

"So what have you been up to?"

"Actually, we were just asking ourselves the same of you. Entered any talent competitions lately?"

"She's funny, isn't she?" Simon says, turning to Andy.

I hope he doesn't think we're together. Not that I've got anyone else, though Simon is cute. I try to stop myself from thinking further inappropriate thoughts and instead concentrate on what is being said. Am I funny? I'm curious to hear Andy's answer – he seems to be giving it a lot of thought.

"I don't know," he says finally, "more enigmatic I'd say – but I haven't really known Sarah long. How do you know her?"

Good question Andrew.

Simon looks a little startled as though he's been accused of some wrongdoing. He quickly looks to me.

"I'm sorry, doesn't he know?"

Know what?

"What do you mean Simon?"

Simon looks unsure as to whether to continue. Whatever it is I am definitely keen to find out.

"Don't worry about Andy. He's very discreet."

It can't be anything more sensational than coming back to life – unless we met at something like Zombies Anonymous.

"The therapy group. I wasn't sure if you wanted me to mention it." He gets up. "I'll go finish the drinks."

Andy looks inquisitively at me. I shrug. I hope it wasn't Zombies Anonymous.

"Doesn't ring any bells."

"What can therapy have to do with entering talent competitions?"

"What indeed," Simon says as he returns with a tray of mugs.

I think me and Andy would both appreciate a more enlightening response.

"As Sarah knows it was my dream to become a professional musician and I even got through to the final boot camp stage of Star Maker before I had to pull out."

Because? I give an appealing look to Andy because obviously I can't ask the question; apparently I already know.

"Oh, that's a shame," mumbles Andy, "what happened?"

Now we're getting somewhere.

"I had a stroke."

"A stroke, but how?"

Simon looks at me puzzled. I'd forgotten I was supposed to know.

"Sorry, I should have said straight away that I've been having trouble with my memory. To be honest I don't remember you at all."

"So why did you come here?"

"Good question. We found your address at my cottage and Andy thought he'd heard of you so we decided to come along and..."

Simon turns to Andy.

"You say you've heard of me?"

Whoops, probably should have left that bit out. Andy reddens again.

"I thought I recognised your name from one of those talent shows; must have been someone else. I'm sorry, I didn't even realise someone as young as you could have a stroke."

"Me neither," Simon agrees solemnly. "Apparently I was born with AMV or at least with the potential for it. I was lucky it happened when I was around people and I was given steroids to block the inflammation. So after two and a half years I'm sort of back to normal, but…"

"It's a shame Star Maker isn't on anymore, you could have gone back on; I'm sure you would have done well!" says Andy in what I think is an attempt to change the subject. The explanation of Simon's illness is making him feel uncomfortable.

"Thanks Andy, though I'm pretty sure it's still on TV I just don't want to do that kind of thing anymore. Anyway, ever since I had the stroke I don't feel I need other people's approval anymore. I believe it's quite commonplace to feel more peaceful and content, as though the lack of reality experienced after a stroke made us realise that we are all integrated parts of one universe."

Andy rolls his eyes – so much for lightening the mood.

"And actually," Simon pauses and turns dramatically towards me, "it was Sarah who encouraged me to be more confident in myself and made me realise I didn't have to be rich and famous to be fulfilled."

I didn't realise I was so philosophical.

"Really?" Andy probes, staring at me intensely. Did you? That's interesting. So Sarah actually persuaded you *not* to re-enter Star Maker? Very interesting. And is that how you met then – in hospital – some illness that causes you to keep losing your memory?"

Simon laughs.

"It would make sense I guess, but Sarah wasn't a patient, she was only waiting to pick someone up."

"Who was that?" I ask.

Finally I might get some clue as to what has been happening to me in the last five years.

"Frankie of course, your son."

CHAPTER THIRTEEN:
"…or person…"

So he's alive.

An immense sense of joy and relief floods over me. I must have found him after all.

I feel the tears coming.

"Is he okay?" I ask Simon.

"As far as I know, but why are you asking me? Don't you know?"

"I can't remember. Do you have any idea where he is?" I can barely wait for his answer.

"No."

My temporary elation is numbed. I put my head in my hands.

Simon comes over and sits next to me.

"Wait," he says, "I don't know where he is but… I almost forgot and actually after the initial surprise of seeing you I got to thinking that must be the reason why you came."

"What?"

Simon gets up excitedly.

"A package arrived a few weeks ago. I put it away because I didn't know what to do with it. I presumed you must have come for it."

"Me, why?"

"It was addressed to you. I've no idea why it was sent here, you never even came here – but maybe it's got something to do with Frankie."

"You think he sent it? Maybe there's a return address?"

Simon's colours slightly.

"Actually, after a couple of weeks I thought about that myself. It seemed pointless it sitting on top of the bookshelf, and I didn't really expect you to turn up, so I opened it."

"And?"

"I think you'd better see it for yourself, maybe you can make some sense of it. I won't be a minute. It's upstairs."

I look at Andy to see what he's making of it all.

"Don't ask me," he says. "I'm still reeling from the resurrection of Simon Greaves. Great news about your son though – it looks like your note seems to be right about being led to him."

We'll see. I haven't found him yet.

I sit very still, staring into a rare clear area of grease stained carpet as I strain to listen to each clunk of Simon's footsteps gaining volume as he brings the parcel increasingly closer.

Finally he returns and thrusts the package into my hands. I delve greedily into its contents; inside is another sealed envelope, a sheet of paper and something small, rough and hard. I remove this first. It seems at first to be a small rock but then I see the familiar swirls and coils that identify it as a fossil.

"Does Frankie collect fossils?" asks Simon.

Someone does.

"Not that I know of."

I pass it over to Simon who is hovering next to me.

"Some kind of ammonite," he says helpfully.

The envelope is marked with a letter S – for me? I decide to leave it hidden for the moment and instead pull out the paper.

"Weird eh?"

"Mm," I mutter, as I turn the paper over several times before finally accepting the fact that nothing is actually written on it.

"Weird eh?" repeats Simon. "Who on earth would send a fossil and a blank piece of paper?"

Andy has got up and is trying to look over my shoulder at the parcel's contents.

"A blank piece of paper eh?"

I turn and catch his eye, willing him not to say anything more but I can tell he's looking at the top right corner of the paper at a now familiar yellow smudge.

"Maybe there's a clue in the postmark," he says trying to cover his complicity.

I replace the paper and fossil and look at the writing on the front of the envelope. I realise I might know who the package came from – it isn't the post mark that reveals the clue but the scrawled handwriting below it, which I recognise as my own.

Do I own up or keep the revelation to myself?

"Well?" Andy asks, a little irritably.

I decide to keep quiet for now.

"It's hard to work out."

"Peterborough," Simon announces unexpectedly. "It took a while to make out but now I'm pretty sure.

Andy snatches the envelope.

"He's right, I think it does say Peterborough."

"I've never been there myself," Simon says, "except when I went through on the train to London. For the Star Maker boot camp auditions actually. So Sarah, any idea who sent it? Do you know anyone who comes from there?"

"Funnily enough when I found Sarah she was trying to get to Peterborough," Andy answers. "Isn't that where Uncle George lives? Maybe he sent this."

"But it's odd," Simon, adds, "because it didn't arrive with the regular post."

"It was hand delivered?"

"Maybe, but then why was it franked?"

Good question.

"Simon, is it okay to take this with me?"

"Of course, it's yours after all – you can leave me a contact in case anything else turns up if you like."

"I don't have a phone at the moment but I can leave you this."

I search in my pocket and fish out the address for the cottage at Field View.

"Apparently I live here."

I'm about to hand it over but reconsider – there is still the possibility of finding myself sitting clueless at the side of a road again

"You can make a note of it."

Simon searches out a pen and tears a scrap of from a paperback. He sure looks like he spends a lot of time reading.

"Do you have a phone?" he asks Andy.

Andy fumbles in his pocket, pulls out his phone and starts tapping at it.

"I don't know what's wrong with it. It's got charge but it's not connecting, sorry."

Simon turns back to me.

"What about your cottage, does it have a phone?"

"I didn't see one. I don't suppose *you* ever went to the cottage, maybe with Frankie?"

"Sorry. I seem to think you lived in a flat but I might be wrong."

I did once.

"Simon, have you got a phone I could borrow?" After all this, Frankie could be sitting at home, waiting for me to come back and make his tea.

"Sure."

He reaches into another pile and hands me a mobile "You can remember the number?"

Like it was yesterday.

"Yes, if it's the same flat I'm thinking of."

I dial the number. What if it's a stranger? What if it isn't?

There is a momentary and momentous delay as the numbers dance on the screen ready to connect with the relevant signals. And then a further pause and a disheartening combination of three notes, spiralling downwards in a depressing, dejecting arpeggio followed by a cold voice: "The number you have dialled…"

I redial, smiling tightly at my two onlookers, but I'm greeted with the same three depressing notes and hang up.

"Disconnected."

"I suppose it has been for a while. Is there anyone else you can try?" Andy asks. "Any number you can think of?"

"Not by heart."

Anyone else's numbers are stored in my indispensable mobile, the whereabouts of which remains unknown.

I pass the phone back to Simon who takes it and tuts. I can't tell if this is out of sympathy or irritation.

"What about the envelope? Maybe there's something in there?"

I want to wait until I'm alone but Simon is looking at it eagerly so I carefully open it. As I lift the flap I see something written on the inside of it, just two words in small capital letters: LEAVE NOW. I glance inside and see that it contains some newspaper cuttings.

"It's empty, must be someone's idea of a joke."

"Not very funny," Simon says suspiciously and tuts again.

I don't know why I would be telling myself to go but there seems little point in staying.

"Well thanks for the coffee Simon and thanks for keeping hold of this."

I slip the envelope back into the package while making for the door.

"No problem. I hope you get your memory back soon and find Frankie of course."

They follow me out.

"I can't believe that old thing is still running," Simon remarks at the car.

"This? It's not mine. Andy borrowed it from some girl's sister when his bus broke down."

"I could have sworn it was the same old rust bucket you used to turn up to therapy sessions in. You used to get a lift from a girl whose sister sometimes went to the sessions. She used to leave her keys in the glove compartment because she said she was always losing things – and why would anyone want to steal her car anyway? She had an old fashioned name, Amelia I think. She and her sister were gorgeous but a little odd. They used to wear bright dresses with coloured tights and dangly necklaces, a bit like 1920s flapper girls. I really liked the sister, I hinted about going out together a couple of times but although she was friendly, she was always too politely busy. Shame."

I can't believe anyone would be too busy to make time for the gorgeous Simon Greaves.

"Ring any bells?" Simon asks.

"I find it very unlikely that this is their car," Andy replies, looking embarrassed. "I only met one of the girls but the keys *were* left in the glove compartment and Mary *was* wearing a colourful dress. Lemon and red roses."

Lemon?

"Mary! That was the sister's name. It has to be the same sisters, did they know you were using the car to come and see me?"

Oh so now we get a glimpse of why he might have been suited to the egotistical world of a pop star.

"Hardly," Andy replies. "*I* didn't even know I was using the car to meet you."

"So you do think it was them? Maybe they know where Frankie is."

Now I'm interested.

"Why might they know that?"

"They used to be particularly friendly towards him and I remember they'd sometimes take him to the pictures."

"Really?"

I feel somehow slighted.

"Yes, he was always going on about the movies but you hate going to the cinema."

It's true I can't stand being forced into the presence of a crowd of unpredictable and potentially annoying strangers but I don't like it that he knows that, and yet it feels strangely flattering that Simon should have some information about me. I realise this is what it should have been like for him not me. Would he have enjoyed strangers knowing what his favourite flavour of ice cream is? Was it really partly my influence that prevented him from performing and why would I do that? It doesn't sound at all like the kind of thing I could or would do. I hardly had much influence over my own life, never mind those of others. It's ridiculous to think that the gorgeous, talented Simon would listen and act on the words of some kid's mother. But nevertheless I feel bad.

Simon asks if I'm okay. He looks concerned, as though worried that the mention of me hating the cinema has stirred up some uncomfortable memories.

"I was just thinking about ice cream," I say. "What's your favourite flavour?"

His concerned expression turns to puzzlement.

"Don't know, chocolate maybe, why?"

I can't really explain how this is meant to lessen my guilt over his lost aspiration to become a rich and famous pop star. And I can't even explain why I should feel this way – after all there's clearly no evidence to support Andy's claims about Simon's fame and misfortune being true. It's all beginning to give me a headache and I hope we can finally actually leave.

Simon seems to have given up on getting an explanation and is now talking to Andy about the lovely Mary.

I am jolted back to the relevance of Mary and her possible knowledge of Frankie's whereabouts.

Andy appears still unconvinced by the possibility of their two Marys being one and the same, and as Simon launches into the subject of serendipity, I butt in.

"Can you give us Mary's address?"

He doesn't look best pleased at being interrupted and I get the feeling he doesn't get the opportunity to chat very often. Why do I feel so responsible for him? Surely it can't be my fault he lives this isolated life, how can it?

"I wish I could," he replies with a sigh. "Heaven knows I tried often enough to get it but she always managed to change the subject."

Of course, why would I think it would be so easy? And poor Simon, no wonder he seems so miserable. What a waste.

"Sorry, I didn't mean to be insensitive but do you have any idea how we could get in touch with her?"

He shrugs.

"I only ever knew her through the therapy groups. I suppose you could try there. You really don't remember ever going there? That's really crazy. I'll get the address – it's only a couple of miles away. They held the sessions locally, which is partly why I decided to live here. Though presumably they would have lived near to you if they gave you both a lift."

He goes back inside.

"What do you think?" I ask Andy, trying to gauge his reaction.

"About what, exactly?"

He seems surprisingly tetchy. Clearly he hasn't enjoyed our visit to Simon. Apparently it often happens when you meet a celebrity in the flesh – it's not as exciting as you'd expect.

"I mean do you think it's worth going to the therapy place?"

He screws up his face. I think he's still annoyed about Simon saying he recognised the car but I'm not sure why. Maybe he doesn't want Simon to be proved right about the girls. I hope it's not me he's annoyed at; he can't possibly have guessed my silly attraction to Simon.

Simon returns.

"Here you go," he says, handing me the address, "I hope it helps."

"Say hello to the girls for me if you find them," he says to Andy, "and tell Mary I'm still available."

He almost smiles for the first time.

"We will," I says, "and you know, maybe you should give that Star Maker show another go."

"Maybe," he says. "Oh wait, there's this too, here." He hands me a photograph. "This is Frankie – it was taken at Barton last Christmas."

The picture is of a group of four young people sitting at a table wearing paper crowns. I recognise Simon immediately. He isn't smiling at the camera, but staring somewhat begrudgingly at a young boy who is being hugged by a couple of pretty girls – one of which I'm guessing is the object of his unrequited affection, Mary.

But the boy with whom they are protectively entwined isn't Frankie – it's Peter.

CHAPTER FOURTEEN:
"…yet…"

Andy twiddles with the keys and I worry he's going to desert me. I know he's feeling confused and shocked and it makes me wonder why I am not in a similar state of mind. As the car stutters off I look at the package again and wonder how and when I came to send this to Simon. I know the date from my unused train ticket and work out that this was posted about a month ago. Did I know what was happening to me then; did I have my memory?

I take out the envelope containing the clippings and put it into my pocket. I replace it with the photo that Simon gave me and put the package down on the floor.

Andy still hasn't spoken.

"Are you okay?"

"Of course," he replies, "but it feels like I'm in the middle of an elaborate hoax."

Really?

"Why would anyone go to the trouble of impersonating a dead man – especially one who is famous for *being* dead. And now this car possibly belongs to the same people who might just happen to know where your son is and who might just have happened to give you regular lifts. Could it really be a coincidence that this is the very same car you used to travel in?"

"Well we don't know that's true, do we? And maybe this was a different Simon Greaves, one who just looked and acted a bit like yours. This one didn't even get to the final round of Starmaker."

"So you really think it's all just a misunderstanding?"

I don't know.

"Yes."

"Okay, but you must admit it would be very weird if it turns out that you know the owner of this car."

"Well, only one way to find out and that is to find them and hopefully Frankie."

"So you want to go and find this therapy place do you?"

He was so excited about this adventure before. Please be enthusiastic again.

"We've come this far, surely you don't want to give up yet?" I say. "And if we do find the owner of the car it will save you having to return it later."

"So you *do* think it's the same car! But I suppose it is intriguing and I did say I would help you find your son – it's not like it can get any weirder can it?"

Probably.

"Of course not."

"Okay then, let's do it."

I read out the address that Simon gave me.

"That's an odd place to have a clinic."

"Why?"

"Well, Simon's right about it being close by but it's not in a town, in fact I don't think it's near any populated place."

"But you've heard of it?"

"Well I am a bus driver round these parts remember."

That I do. For once.

"If I'm right, it looks like we'll get our mansion after all. This place, Barton Hall, is an old country house a couple of miles away. I didn't even realise it was inhabited, never mind it being used as some as some sort of medical centre."

"Sounds nice."

"Sounds expensive."

Last time I remember, the NHS didn't stretch to refurbishing old country halls for its treatments and I certainly didn't have private insurance.

"It doesn't sound like your typical NHS premises or somewhere that I or non-dying Simon could afford."

"Maybe you can now. You managed to acquire a nice little cottage in the last five years, so you must have got money from somewhere."

"Yeah, but that was a bonus for doing some work."

"A bonus for what though?"

I hadn't really thought about what I had been asked to do by the mystery 'clients' for a while – I've been so focused on the possibility of seeing Frankie again.

"I know, but there's nothing I can do about it at the moment. My only chance is to find people who have known me in the last five years and then start to piece it all together."

"Or we could go back to the cottage and find out what the blank pieces of paper actually say."

He pauses for effect.

"The yellow smudge," I say, equally dramatically, as though it is some deadly pirate curse.

"Yeah, alright," he replies sourly. "But maybe the letter will help, perhaps even tell you who you were working for."

Were? That's an interesting point. When did I stop working for them? Did I stop? I decide not to raise this point. Things are complicated enough already.

"I hope it might provide some answers but so far all the notes we've seen haven't exactly been explicit, especially the ones supposedly written by myself."

"You think you wrote this letter?"

"I don't know. Maybe. It looks like my handwriting."

"I take it you don't remember writing and sending it though? B it looks like you did get to Peterborough."

"Unless it wasn't me who posted it."

Sometimes I surprise myself with my insight. Hours of reading Agatha Christies were not wasted; now all I need to do is look for someone with an unusually pale complexion or a limp. Except I should really discover a crime first; maybe there will be a dead body or two to be found at Barton Hall.

"Didn't Simon think it might have been hand delivered – could have been anyone."

"Like who?" I ask.

"What about Frankie?"

"I've only got Simon's word that he's been at Barton, but hopefully it will have some records of him."

"Well we'll soon find out, it's just around the corner.

The fields here seem just that bit more lush and fresh and are divided into perfect squares by regimental lines of the most wonderful golden bejewelled oak trees I have ever seen. And in the middle of this landscape, settled like a nest, is the outline of a rust coloured building which I presume to be Barton Hall.

"Impressive eh?" Andy says unnecessarily, as we turn onto a beautiful tree-lined road.

"A nice place to get better. Do you think it's residential?"

"You'd have thought so, given the size of it."

It only takes a few moments to reach the front of this commanding building. The house is at least three stories high and two large central windows take on the resemblance of sad hooded eyes which are framed by trails of ivy curling down like locks of seaweed hair. The main feature though is a large wooden door, the frame of which is carved in large swirling spirals, resembling the ammonite attached to my key ring.

The Ford casually spits stones from under its tyres as it slides to a stop on the gravelled drive alongside a dark transit van.

"Doesn't look like there are many patients in today," Andy says.

"Unless they all came in the van," I add inanely.

"So what should we do? Covertly tip toe round to the back of the house and slip in through an open window or brazenly walk up to the door and knock?"

"Well, given the number of cameras trained on us," I say, indicating the army of small security cameras all simultaneously twisting towards us, "I think we can rule out clandestine option one and just go for the traditional knocking on the front door."

However, as we get out of the car and approach the large wooden door, option two becomes redundant.

The door swings open and in the entrance stands a tall, thin middle aged woman, wearing an expensive looking green suit; like a humanised version of a praying mantis. She has very short hair, a sharp, slightly hooked nose and eyes that look like they have pierced through a thousand suffering fools. I am instantly intimidated.

"Sure we can't just sneak around the back? She looks very scary; does she look familiar?"

Luckily not. The insect woman comes striding over to us as we get out of the car.

"Hello Sarah," she says in an icily cold voice.

Is there anyone who *doesn't* know me?

I don't want to get myself into the same pickle of misunderstanding that occurred with Simon, so I bluntly announce my amnesia.

"Yes, so I gather," she replies unexpectedly.

"Hello, my name is Andrew Porteus,"Andy says. I realise this is the first time I have heard his full name and feel a little jealous that this woman, this stranger, has managed to elicit such information so very easily. He extends his hand – which is ignored – but rather than dropping it he reaches up to scratch the back of his head as though this was his intention all along.

"Nice to meet you Mr. Porteus," she replies, without appearing to move her mouth. "I presume you are accompanying Ms Norton?"

Andy nods vigorously. He turns happily towards me.

"That's good – so they know you here?"

"Apparently, and Miss…" I deliberately pause hoping the woman will fill in the gap but she remains stoical, allowing me to flounder.

"And Miss...well, she already appears to know about my problems with my memory."

"This isn't the first time it's happened is it? When I used to pick you up on my bus you never remembered the way to your own cottage from one trip to the next. So it figures that you must have forgotten everyone else quite regularly as well."

"I suppose so."

I look at the insect woman for confirmation but even after such a short acquaintance, her reluctance to comment comes as no surprise. I decide that a more direct approach is required.

"Do you know if I've had memory loss before?" I ask her.

"How would I know?" she answers abruptly.

"Sorry." Here I go again with the apologising. "But you know my name and know that I have …."

Before I can finish she cuts me off, as though I am not even speaking.

"I presume you didn't come here to chit chat, you'd better follow me," she says harshly.

Without waiting for a response, she turns and heads towards the building; her long insect legs, elongated in polished lime green heels, step gingerly over the gravel as though picking her way through a field of cowpats. We're left standing in the car park like school kids, clueless as to what to do, other than follow her instructions.

The foyer is magnificent. This was clearly once a home of significance and although the original decoration and furniture has been replaced by anachronistically modern desks and notice boards, the marbled floors and ornately plastered walls still retain the imprint of past grandeur. We walk through the reception and enter a hallway. It is huge – its ridiculously high ceiling is dripping with cascading chandeliers casting light over original wooden panelling. The effect is only spoilt by the inexplicable presence of stackable blue plastic chairs which have been placed at regular intervals down the corridor.

I wonder who used to walk along this hall when it was a home. Would they have taken all this extravagant beauty for granted – skidding along the floor in muddy boots or ripping careless fingernails into the shiny chestnut walls? I wish is had been me, gliding along in long flowing petticoats oblivious to any uncertainties and responsibilities of normal life. Belonging so totally in a place that it was never necessary to leave; it wouldn't matter if you lost your memory because everything you ever knew would appear immediately again in front of you. Nothing would have changed; nothing would ever change.

This lovely house is making me homesick – though there is precious little here to compare with my small and cluttered, two-bedroomed flat. I remember the book cases that were shoved up against the wall of my bedroom, towering haphazardly with increasing numbers of books that I fully intended one day to read.

Would all my stuff still be there, keeping a silent guard over my place? There were none of my belongings at the cottage. No wonder I couldn't feel comfortable there, or here now, walking, bereft of any recognisable memories and possessions, behind this cold woman walking down this equally cold hallway. Leading to what next?

Standing in the doorway of what looks like a treatment room is the forbidding presence of Uncle George.

CHAPTER FIFTEEN:
"...ultimately..."

I glance anxiously at Andy. There were no police cars in the car park when we arrived so I'm hoping we're not about to be arrested, although technically it was *Andy* who attacked him.

What does he want? To go to Peterborough?

He doesn't say anything and neither do we. They're not big on conversation around here, maybe it's catching.

Instead of speaking, he turns and walks into the room.

"In here please," the insect woman demands. She gestures into the room that George has just entered and then carries on down the corridor.

"That's him isn't it," Andy whispers. "The old guy who came at me outside your cottage?"

"Yes, the man you tasered – George – but it doesn't look like he's called the police, in fact he seems particularly calm."

"I know. And he's wearing a white coat."

"Maybe he's a doctor."

"Maybe he is, but here? Really? This can't be good. Shouldn't we just leave?"

The insect woman has returned carrying a folder.

"I thought I told you to go in Ms Norton," she says, "is there a problem?"

"I'm just not sure what is going on," I say. "Why am I going in here? And who is that man?"

The insect woman looks annoyed.

"It was you that came here, Ms Norton, nobody made you. And as you said yourself, you're having trouble with your memory. Why else would you be here? You're lucky Doctor Franks has agreed to see you at such short notice. Now, if you mind *not* wasting any more time, please follow me. Your friend," she indicates Andy as though he is some dirt that I have failed to remove from my shoes and have unwittingly trailed in behind me, "can wait for you outside."

"Do you mind?" I ask him.

Perhaps I will be more likely to find out what George is up to if I speak to him alone.

"I guess not," he replies with a wink. A wink? Somehow I feel flattered and emboldened by it.

"I'll wait for you here," he adds.

Andy heads towards one of the plastic chairs as I am shepherded inside the room.

It's small and artificially lit despite sunshine streaming through a partially-open window taking up the top half of the back wall. There's another plastic chair, a bed covered in disposable plastic sheeting and a desk, behind which sits Uncle George.

"Won't you take a seat," he asks, studying the document the insect woman has given him. I sit down uneasily on the chair, wriggling in an attempt to find a position that isn't entirely uncomfortable as George continues to study his notes.

Finally he looks up.

"I hope you don't mind if Ms Malone stays with us? She is curious about your case."

My case? I thought it was Frankie who was a patient here, not me. And why is he ignoring the fact that he was at my cottage earlier?

"I'm sorry Doctor…?" I pause once again but as with Ms Malone, he doesn't take the hint to fill in the blank. Instead he continues looking at me with a half-smile.

"I'm sorry," here I go again apologising – and to him of all people. "I don't know what you mean about my case. I only came here today to find out about my son and hopefully to get some information about another patient here who was a friend of his."

"Your son?" he asks gently.

Why is he doing this? Ms Malone has moved away from the door and is now standing at his side as though she is his head henchwoman.

"Yes, I was told he was a patient here."

"You were told? Don't you know?"

"No, at least I don't remember."

"Ah. Of course," George looks down at his notes and starts reading.

I don't know whether to tell him about Simon. I don't even know why I'm talking to him at all. I want to shout at him and ask him what's going on but I feel like I've already missed the opportunity to expose him and am now complicit in his charade. It reminds me of a time when I went on stage after volunteering to take part in a hypnotist show. All the volunteers were told to close their eyes and then asked to try and pull their clasped hands apart. I did what I thought was expected of me and tugged hopelessly away but when I opened my eyes I realised that there were only a handful of people left on the stage. So, despite not feeling in the slightest bit hypnotised, I felt obligated to go along with the rest of the show, pretending to see elephants and the like stampeding through the theatre, just to cover up my embarrassment for my initial lie. Is this how conmen work? Is George a conman?

"Miss Norton, the doctor asked you a question." Ms Malone says. I feel as though a spotlight and an unrolled set of torture instruments wouldn't be out of place here.

"Sorry?"

"Miss Norton, the doctor asked you how you knew to come here?"

"I recently met an ex patient who told me he had undergone some therapy sessions here with him."

"And this ex patient," George stresses the words, "told you to come here? For what reason?"

He knows the reason.

"I'm trying to find out where my son is."

"And you think he's here?"

I hadn't done. But looking at this gruesome pair I wouldn't put it past them to have Frankie locked up in the cellar.

"No. At least I presumed that he had been discharged. I just came here to find out if there was anyone who knew where he is or maybe get the address of someone who does. Is that my son's file?"

I point to the file in George's hands.

"Do you think it is?"

Why is he being so cryptic? I feel as though I'm in a therapy session myself. Why can't he give me a straight answer?

"Yes. Can I have a look?"

Ms Malone shifts a little as though any sudden attempt by me to retrieve the file would be met by an equally sudden preventative manoeuvre; probably a karate chop.

"I'm very sorry Miss Norton."

For what? Is it Frankie's file or not? I'm confused.

"Well could you just tell me when he was discharged?"

"We never fully discharge people from here Miss Norton; we take a particular pride in always being available to our patients whether they have been with us for months or even years."

He looks purposefully into my eyes and raises a particularly grey, hairy eyebrow.

I get the distinct impression that we are not talking about Frankie.

When I first 'met' George, which was only this morning, he spoke to me about having a doctor. Why didn't he just introduce himself as a doctor then? Why would he pretend to be my uncle and the following day act as though he hardly knows me?

"Tell me doctor, have we met before?"

I sense Miss Malone bristling again. Why would this upset her?

"Do you remember something?" he asks.

Maybe I'm not the only one with – what did he call it – amnesia epilepsy?

"Yes of course I do. We spoke yesterday at my cottage when you introduced yourself as George – and you brought along a young boy who you said was my son!"

He just looks blankly at Ms Malone and scribbles something onto the notes.

"You said I was supposed to meet you in Peterborough on the train," I continue, "but that I must have blacked out because obviously I didn't and that it was because of some epileptic fit that made me lose my memory."

"Ah," George nods slowly in that supposedly empathetic way that only makes you feel infuriatingly patronised.

"You said that I had been seeing a doctor," I push on, "because I kept forgetting things but I would have remembered if I had a brother or if that boy was my son."

"And you think this man you met yesterday was me?"

Yesterday he almost convinced me that I really did have these 'relatives' and that I was going mad and now he is implying that I'm making it all up. He even tried to prove it by showing me the photographs.

"Wait," I say. "I have proof – photographs that you knew I was carrying, of you and Peter with me at the cottage."

"Interesting," says George, with a look of concern. "Excuse us a second."

While the doctor and Ms Malone huddle whispering in a corner I take the opportunity to stand up, instantly feeling the relief of moving off the hard, plastic chair. I begin to search my pockets; I can feel bits of paper and there's still some money but no sign of the photographs. After I looked at those unfamiliar faces posing by the cottage what did I do with them? I don't remember. Could I have put them down before going upstairs? I remember being more concerned about leaving to check if my amber necklace was still around my neck. Anyway, they weren't in my pocket now.

George told me I needed them to remind me who I was; so why didn't he make me put them back? Though to be fair, the next time I saw him he was unconscious.

"Yes Miss Norton? We don't have all day."

Ms Malone is back, tapping her long fingernails impatiently against her thumbs.

"I must have left them at the cottage but it doesn't change the fact that you and Peter were there."

"I see. But I don't understand why you've come here looking for your son if you were with him only yesterday."

"But he wasn't my son."

He's doing it again, making me feel like I'm making it all up. Maybe I should have insisted that Andy came in with me after all.

"Look, if you just tell me where I can find someone who *does* know him, then I'll get out of your way."

George nods at Miss Malone who takes a step towards me.

"I'm sorry Miss Norton," says George, rather seriously, "I don't think that is going to be possible. You're clearly not well enough to be allowed out at this moment. You're lucky you have friends who care enough about you to bring you back here before you do any serious damage to yourself."

What does he mean? Who is he talking about? Not Andy? He didn't bring me here to admit me; that's ridiculous.

"What friends? Nobody brought me; I keep telling you I just came here for information. What is she talking about – that I can't leave?"

George looks at me gravely.

"Ms Malone is only pointing out what is best for you. It's obvious that you're confused and that your problems with your memory have not improved."

"Are you saying that we didn't meet at my cottage yesterday?"

"Of course not."

Of course he's not saying that or of course he didn't come to my cottage?

"Ms Malone will confirm that I was at work yesterday if you think it's necessary."

Of course I don't expect Ms Malone to contradict the good doctor. And as if to confirm what I was thinking, she smiles slyly at me.

"I'm sure she will," she says. "And what about your nephew Peter, are you going to tell me that he doesn't exist either?"

"Of course he does. It's true that I have a young nephew called Peter and you've met him many times when you were here."

"When I was with my own son you mean?"

Silence.

"Why can't you give me a straight answer?"

I can feel my face redden with anger. Why are they behaving like this? Ms Malone bristles again. She doesn't like me asking questions.

"I'm very sorry, Sarah that this is so distressing for you. We had no idea that your problems had returned."

"What are you talking about? Why won't you listen to me? I'm just here for information. You seem to be deliberately misunderstanding me. I'm not here for myself. I'm not the patient here."

I can feel myself beginning to tremble with frustration and an increasing fear that this isn't going to turn out well. I have to calm down and leave. There must be other ways to find Frankie.

"Please sit down Miss Norton. You're getting yourself worked up."

Ms Malone takes a step forward and looks towards George eagerly as though she's waiting for a signal. He nods and Ms Malone reaches into her pocket.

"Now then Miss Norton, Doctor Franks is just doing what's best for you."

Doctor Franks? He's called George Franks?

I have little time to think about this as I see the syringe Ms Malone is wielding.

"What do you think you're doing?" I cry.

"Just a small sedative to calm you down and then we can see about getting you better again."

"But there's nothing wrong with me!"

I move towards the door; it is slightly open and if I can get to Andy, maybe he will be able to help but Ms Malone and the doctor have anticipated this move and have already blocked the exit. Ms Malone's face contorts with a determined pleasure as she raises the syringe. The only way to get Andy's attention is to scream. I am not a natural screamer but I can feel real terror as the syringe plunges towards me.

I take a deep breath and just as I am about to produce the loudest scream I am capable of I hear an even louder noise.

An alarm.

The screeching is enough to momentarily unsettle the doctor and his accomplice and I sprint through the door slamming it shut behind me and run.

CHAPTER SIXTEEN:
"…be plagued…"

The corridor is dark and deserted. Where is Andy? I daren't stop and look for him. The lights are off but the red flashing glow from the alarms above my head provides enough illumination to allow me to see. But as I charge towards the main entrance, I am surprised to see that the hallway remains empty – even emptier than before – the horrible plastic chairs have all disappeared. Where are the patients and the rest of the staff, why aren't they scrambling towards the safety of the car park like me? Not even George and his bad lieutenant are following me or trying to prevent my escape from this mad house.

With relief, I reach the door and twist the handle. Nothing. It doesn't move. It's locked and I'm trapped. I turn and check the reception area but the desk is unmanned. There doesn't appear to be any smoke either, so for the moment at least, I am unlikely to be burnt alive. Even so, I need to find an alternative way to get out.

There are doors on either side of the front desk that are all closed. I attempt to listen at the first but I don't think I'd be able to hear a rave party above the screeching siren.

Cautiously I try it but it's locked. I go to its opposite number and again discover it won't open. Rather less cautiously now I move back down the hallway trying more doors; all locked. I'm now in danger of returning to the treatment room which presumably still contains the doctor.

I try one more door, not really confident of gaining entry and rightly so. But why *are* all the doors locked? If there is a fire, you're not going to deliberately prevent people from leaving a burning building.

What to do? I stare up and down the corridor with only the blaring alarm for company, having no idea how to get out of this pickle.

I cautiously head back towards the reception where luckily I see the handle to the main door move.

I rush over to take advantage of this opportunity to leave, but judging by the excess movement of the dancing handle, it would appear that whoever is on the other side of the door is having as much luck getting in as I did getting out.

The movement at the door and the alarm both cease at the same time.

The foyer is now dim – except for the tiniest pulsating red light that seems to be glowing on to my wrist. A laser gun?

I stand completely still. I can hear someone breathing. It is steady and calm – not coming from someone in a hurry to leave or capture a wayward patient. I think I can make out a shadowy figure –too short to be either the doctor or his assistant.

"Sarah."

Do I know this voice? It seems vaguely familiar – a young woman's voice – but I can't place it.

"Sarah," they repeat. It's not a question – more a statement of resignation.

"Why are you here?"

If she turned on the lights she would be able to see that I am in fact trying to leave.

"Is this how you want to remember him?"

I stay quiet – feeling cornered. Who is she talking about, Frankie? I want to ask her but she speaks again in a sterner tone.

"Are you really sure that you want to find out the truth? Stay focused Sarah, find Andy and finish the job."

Before I can ask her anything the lights come back on and I find that I am alone. The stillness and relief to my poor ears is short lived as they are now they are being assaulted by loud banging.

"Hello?" I venture.

"Sarah, is that you? You need to get out of there!"

"I can't, the door's locked."

"Just hang on, the doors should be unlocked in a moment."

How does he know that? Has the fire gone out? Still can't smell smoke – luckily.

"How do you know?"

"The alarm's stopped."

Does he think I'm stupid? What has that got to do with the doors? They're hardly likely to *lock* the doors in the event of a fire.

I pull hopefully at the handle but Andy's optimism that the door will become suddenly unlocked seems sadly misplaced.

"I don't know why the door's still locked, unless they're scanning the building first."

What? What is he talking about? Scanned? How?

As if to answer my question I see a red band of light sweeping down the corridor towards me. It looks like a laser and I try to duck but there is nowhere to hide. I crouch down with my hands over my head as the light crosses harmlessly over me. It then disappears with a loud clunk. As I uncover my eyes I notice a faint green glow on the back of my right hand, but before I can work out what it is, I hear the doors being opened.

Andy is standing agitatedly in front of me.

"Come on, we need to hurry." He grabs my arm and we head for the car.

From behind me I can hear a voice calling my name. I turn and see Ms Malone emerging from the hallway, her face finally leaking some composure as she tries to regain control.

"Sarah, come back!"

She must be joking. I keep going.

"Sarah, wait, you need our help. Sarah, listen to me, we can help you. You can trust us."

Strange choice of word, *trust*, a few minutes ago she was trying to hold me against my will.

"We have to get out of here," Andy as we reach the car.

Why is he in such a hurry? It wasn't him who was just about to get stuck in the arm with a needle. I didn't even manage to get any of the information we came here for, so it doesn't make any sense. I look back again, expecting security guards or at the very least, Ms Malone to be scampering towards me with a restraining jacket.

But instead, Ms Malone is just standing at the entrance, her face not showing anger but pity. It confuses me for a moment and I pause. She has stopped shouting and her lips are tightened as though there is something she desperately wants to say and can't. Perhaps this sympathetic demeanour is just a final ploy to get me to return. Fat chance. But there's something genuine in her expression and as I turn she calls softly so I have to strain my ears to hear:

"Sarah. Good luck."

Was it her voice speaking to me in the darkness?

At that moment George appears alongside her and Ms Malone's face immediately reverts to a steely gaze.

"Sarah, get in the car!"

Andy has started the engine and is beginning to reverse so that the passenger door is directly beside me.

Ms Malone calls out but I can't really hear her over the sound of the car. Something like escape the fold – or was it break the coal? I don't have time to find out as the passenger door swings open, nearly knocking me over. I barely touch the seat before Andy completes his reversal and spins the car into a rather dramatic wave of gravel before heading off down the drive.

"Whoa!" I squeal as I attempt to get on my belt before Evel Knieval propels me out of the windscreen.

"What's with the dramatic exit? I don't think there really was a fire."

"True," he replies before slowing down a little. He pauses.

I recall the green glow on the back of my hand. I turn it over on my lap and am relieved to see that the throbbing green light has gone. It must have just been a light reflecting on my hand from the ceiling.

"What did you mean about the place being scanned?" I ask him.

"Mm," he responds enigmatically. "Remember I told you about how schools electronically register kids now?"

"What? Oh yes, something to do with fingerprints."

"That's right, but there's a bit more to it than that. When each kid is registered, a microchip is activated which can keep track of them."

"A what? Where?"

"Right. You know how dogs have microchips?"

"Sure."

"Well, in a nutshell, they do that to kids now, so they know who's in the building."

"And how do they do that?"

"Did you notice a red beam, sweep over you?"

Indeed.

"I did."

"Well if you were a schoolchild then it would be like having an emergency registration."

"Would it cause a physical reaction?"

"No. It's supposed to be completely harmless."

"I mean something like a light."

"Yes, how do you know that? Did you see someone's hand glow? There's a small light that emanates from the chip to show that you are entitled to be there. But you'd have to have been chipped for it to happen."

Am I chipped? Why would I be chipped?

"And why would someone in a place like Barton Hall need to be chipped? I can't imagine why it would need to keep track of its patients; especially when there didn't appear to be any. Maybe they don't come in on a…"

It never occurred to me to wonder what day it was. Normally I wouldn't even be able to get out of bed without mentally setting my head for the appropriate day and now I am even functioning without my watch. I wonder how long I have been living without this knowledge; maybe I'm used to it.

"Tuesday."

It doesn't feel like a Tuesday.

"No one shuts on a Tuesday."

"My Chinese takeaway does," he adds unhelpfully.

"But seriously – is it usual for a place like that to scan people?"

"Well maybe. If they treat children, like your son."

"But what about adults?"

Andy glances at my hand – could he know?

"I'm not sure. As far as I know only adults in secure units like prisons are allowed to be chipped. Why?"

That can't be right. Surely I can't have been engaged in criminal activity during the last five years – I won't even drop a piece of litter.

"I just wondered why we were locked in. Not convenient if there actually was a fire."

"You weren't in any danger."

How does he know? He wasn't the one threatened with a syringe at his throat.

"It was me who set off the alarm."

"On purpose? Were you listening at the door?"

Had he done it to save me from being sectioned?

"No. But I'm keen to find out what your Uncle George had to say. He looked well at least."

"More than well. It was as though the incident at the cottage had never happened. He barely seemed to know me, though he hinted that it was me and not Frankie who had been a patient at the hall. I tried to find out about Frankie and the others but he kept avoiding my questions. One thing was the same though; he still seemed to think I was mad."

"So he didn't mention being attacked by a taser?"

"Not once. I thought he was trying to play mind games at first but honestly it was like the doctor was a different person. By the way, the woman called him Doctor Franks. That's a bit uncanny don't you think?"

"Why?"

"Frankie of course, the similarity in the names? It seems an odd coincidence."

"I guess."

Clearly he doesn't think so.

"Fine. So if it wasn't to rescue me why did you set off the alarm? Where did you go?"

Andy pats his breast and looks like the dog with the largest bone.

"For this." He pulls out a file.

Very *Mission Impossible.*

"This is why the alarm went off? You were stealing files? Blimey, yesterday I catch you fighting and now you're sneaking around soliciting confidential material from mysterious and probably top secret filing cabinets. You've come a long way since your bus driving days don't you think?"

"Yes well, and again I'd like to remind you that it's for your sake I'm doing this. Anyway I don't think it's too top secret; the file wasn't hard to find."

"But you still set off the alarm. How did you get past the lock down?"

"Jumped out of an open window; you can't lock something that isn't already shut."

"That sounds very profound. And lucky!"

"Not if you open the window first."

How did he know to do that I wonder.

"So what's in the file?" I ask him.

He passes it over.

"Be careful not to let anything spill out."

I take it from him and open it hoping it will be more revealing than the contents of the note sent to Simon.

Well it might have been. However it is now empty.

"A bit late to caution me on keeping the contents intact."

"Huh?" he replies.

"There's nothing here. Oh wait – sorry there is something – surprise surprise! Another sheet of blank paper – just what we needed."

"What?" Andy brings the car to an abrupt stop.

"Ow!"

Just as well I was wearing my seat belt.

"Sorry, but I just risked my skin to get that list."

"Here, see for yourself."

He takes the file back and jiggles it impatiently.

"So what was in this?"

"It was a sheet of hand written names, a bit like the sheets I saw briefly in the cottage. I think it might have been a list of the clients registered at Barton."

"That would have been interesting. But why would the lists be written by hand? It doesn't sound very professional. Did you happen to recognise anyone – Frankie for example? Or memorise any useful addresses?"

"I was in a bit of a hurry, remember. I didn't have time to look through them -though I did spot one familiar name…"

"Simon? Mary?"

"Nobody you would have heard of but a very famous name for a couple of weeks."

He pauses.

"Go on then," I prompt.

"Like I said it won't mean much to you. It was the name of one of the victims in the bus killings. It doesn't mean it has to be the same person; probably just a coincidence."

Another one. I fold the piece of paper in half and lay it on my lap.

"There was also a…." He taps at his jacket pocket again, and like a successful magician triumphantly pulls something out.

"Yes!"

"What's that?"

"This," he declares proudly, "is a computer memory stick, which with any luck will provide us with all the answers."

"What makes you think this will have anything interesting on it? It could be just an inventory of bed linen for all you know."

"I suppose it might, but why would a list of bed linen be labelled with the initials 'F. N.'?"

"A new line in funky nylons?" I joke lamely to cover the lurching in my stomach that happens every time we seem to be getting closer the truth about Frankie.

"I thought you might be more excited."

"Sorry, I am, it's just a shame we don't have a computer."

"Mm. Anyway, at least we have it in case we find one. We just need to keep it safe."

He passes it over as though I am likely to be a more reliable custodian. I can't even keep my own memories.

It doesn't resemble anything I remember as being a memory stick, but it does look familiar.

"Are you sure this is a memory stick? It has a very odd shape."

I turn the strange shaped object around and lift it up to the light.

"Of course. Technology has come a long way in the last few years, though I think it has more to do with getting the customer to keep spending. Pretty though."

"Yeah, it looks like a key."

I press my hand against my neck to feel for the amber necklace. Interesting. So maybe my intriguing little surprise doesn't just unlock a door after all.

I slip the file and memory stick into the package from Simon and drop it back on the floor, earning myself a disapproving tut from Andy.

"What's the matter?"

"Maybe it will be a little safer in the glove compartment."

"Fine," I sigh.

I pick up the package and click open the glove compartment.

"But be careful, it's…"

"Rather full by any chance? Great idea."

The compartment door drops down allowing a torrent of paper to spill out.

"I don't think there's much chance of getting this in there."

I grab a handful of paper and realise the trip to Barton Hall was completely unnecessary.

It looks like our detour to see the sisters will bc going ahead after all.

CHAPTER SEVENTEEN:
"…by dissatisfaction…"

"Actually it wasn't such a bad idea after all," I say as I pass him an envelope. "We had Mary's address all along"

"Right… oh. Actually, if I'd used my head we might not have even needed this."

"What do you mean? Do you know this address?"

"Not especially, but I'm pretty sure that this is exactly where I got the car from. It was obviously parked outside her house!"

"No kidding Sherlock."

"Well it wasn't like it occurred to you either. And anyway it's her sister's car, not hers."

True. And yet now it seems the most obvious thing in the world that this would have been a good place to begin looking for Mary.

"So is it far from here?".

"Not at all. I told you that Barton Hall was on my bus route, it's just the other side of these fields on the outskirts of town."

"I wonder if your bus is still there."

"Highly unlikely don't you think?"

"Highly," I agree.

Which doesn't rule out that it is.

Andy takes one last look at the address, starts the engine and passes the letter back to me.

"Off we go again then."

I bend down to collect up all the paper that is lying on the floor of the car. I don't like to think of myself as nosey but nevertheless I am. Instead of shoving it all back in the glove compartment I make a pretence of arranging the paper neatly on my lap. There's a lot of advertising material and invitations to take up cheaper car insurance and local gardening services and at least two offers on half price circus tickets.

The past might be another planet but the junk mail-based future seems rather familiar. I never took Frankie to a circus, although I remember being taken myself and have a vivid memory of staring through the high seated benches at the popcorn-strewn grass far below. The sudden erection of this enormous canvas structure was always far more magical than what happened inside the tent. Anyway, me and Frankie didn't go.

"You allright?" Andy asks.

"Sure, just tidying up the mess I made."

"Yeah, well don't tidy up too much. I don't want her to think we've been rifling through her personal stuff."

Good point. I'll mess it back up in a bit – once I've finished rifling.

"Don't worry it's mainly just advertising leaflets."

"And at least one letter."

Yes, the letter. I pull the envelope to the top. It couldn't do any harm to take a peep – it wasn't as though she'd left it somewhere private.

The name on the front is M. Brown. Mary Brown, hardly an inspiring or imaginative name – certainly not one that commands secrecy. I slip out the envelope's contents and have a little look.

'*Dear Martha*' it begins. So this must be written to the sister, not Mary. Still, Martha is likely to know the whereabouts of Mary; or, even better, maybe Martha knows the whereabouts of Frankie.

Dear Martha,

Please excuse this rather old-fashioned means of communication, but the staff are still refusing us access to anything vaguely technical and the monstrous Malone is still insisting that the police have my mobile.

Ms Malone?

Why they should have any interest in my limited number of friends and family I have no idea.

Anyway, it doesn't look like I'm going to be getting out of here any time soon – not like you, you lucky soul!

They're still doing tests and I have to sit through those long terminal talks with Dr Franks. I wouldn't mind, but they never seem to have any point to them. We just go over and over the days before the accident – like it has any bearing on what happened.

Anyway I shouldn't be writing to moan – but I miss our little chats and there's no one else in here that I have anything in common with at all…especially that weird woman …in fact you couldn't even imagine such a diverse bunch of people. So I was just hoping that you might have time to reply, or even visit? Sometime soon? This place is driving me mad!!!

Anyway, hope everything is okay with you,
Your friend forever,
Jakob

I feel a bit ashamed reading this obviously private letter but am nevertheless thrilled by the connection with Barton Hall – given my limited knowledge – it's almost like talking about an old friend. I look at the date and work out that the letter was written only a week or so ago. Where are all these patients? Have they all been released? It didn't sound like Jakob was going anywhere soon. No mention of Frankie though, but he probably left long before this Jakob arrived. Strange spelling though – German perhaps?

"Interesting leaflet?"

I'm suddenly jolted by Andy.

"What? Yes…. The Chinese acrobats look amazing."

"Don't lie. I know what you're doing."

"You do?"

"Yes. Go on then. Tell me who it's from."

"The letter?"

"Of course. Yes."

"Well first of all it was written to a Martha, not Mary."

"Mary, Martha," he sings as though adding a melody will make them sound indistinguishable. "It's not that different," he adds for further clarity.

"Or it could be her sister, the car owner's."

"Maybe," he concedes.

"And secondly it appears to be written by an inmate of Barton Hall."

"Really?"

"Yeah, it doesn't say much only that he's bored because he has nothing in common with the other patients and that he hopes she – Martha – will get in touch soon."

"Who is it from?"

"Someone called Jakob. With a k," I add helpfully as though this will help him distinguish this particular Jacob from all the other Jacobs he knows.

"With a K?"

"Yes."

Maybe it makes a difference after all.

It certainly makes some kind of difference as Andy suddenly pulls onto a grass verge and takes the letter from me. I let him read in silence for a few moments unsure of what he could possibly make of such a bland note.

Finally he hands it back to me and sighs.

"Well Sherlock, what have you deduced?"

"Nothing really. It may just coincidence…"

There he goes again, believing in coincidences. When will he learn? Nevertheless I can sense a 'but' coming.

"But?" I prompt.

"But do you remember that I recognised a name on that list before it mysteriously disappeared?"

"Yes, you thought it was the same as one of the people involved in the bus killings."

"That's right. A young American woman called Cindy Romero."

"Sounds like she should be a Country and Western singer."

"I think she might have been, but even so I bet there can't be many people in the UK with a name like that."

"You would hope not. But what has she got to do with this letter?"

"It's just that another of the victims was a young bus driver."

"A bus driver was attacked?"

"Yes I'm sure he was called Jakob Werner."

"With a K?"

"Exactly."

"So?"

"Well, what if there's some connection?"

"How is that possible exactly? If they were both victims in the city bus killings, then they are now both dead and hence unlikely to have been admitted into Barton Hall over two years later."

"There is that. But being dead hasn't stopped Simon Greaves from living in a little cottage down the road."

"Or from being a patient at Barton Hall?"

"Exactly. So let's see if we can find out anything else about the residents of Barton Hall. Or how they are both involved with this Martha – although I'm not sure what happened to Jakob, I don't remember if he actually did die."

Andy starts the engine again and pulls back out into the road.

"You don't suppose they've got some voodoo thingy going on in there do you? Some reincarnation project?"

"You'd better hope not. You were a patient there yourself once."

"Apparently, and so was Frankie."

Though, according to Simon, we weren't there at the same time. I feel my hand again but there is no visible or physical sign of the chip device.

"You know those security chips? Can they be used to track people?"

"You think it might help you find your son?"

"So are they traceable?"

"Sort of, but as far as I remember you have to be scanned to show any signs of the chip."

"But can the chip be detected outside? Like if a pupil wasn't in school could they still be scanned in a different building?"

"Technically yes, but you would have to be registered with that building for it to care if you were there or not. Some places like museums will register kids as they go in and a lot of public places have to do this to satisfy their insurance requirements."

"So they can tell the fire brigade how many burning children to look for?"

Another tut, another sidewards glare. He thinks I should be more sensitive about misplaced children, and he's right. But if kids' hands can glow in different places then so can mine, which means I didn't have to be chipped specifically at Barton Hall. I'm unsure whether this is a good thing.

I study my hand again but see nothing.

"So how do they put it in?"

"It's injected and…"

"What?" I can't believe something so monumentally intrusive has been allowed to happen in such a short time. "Surely there must have been huge opposition to it – human rights and what not? You can't go around injecting kids like that."

"Doctors give kids immunisation jabs all the time in school and most parents are happy to protect their kids from disease."

"But this isn't even a disease!"

I am, often to my shame, the last person to start protesting over anything, but even I would have plenty of objections to tagging Frankie.

"No, but it could help protect kids from much worse. No parent wants to go through the nightmare of losing their chil…."

Andy breaks off his sentence and gives his bright crimson look an airing. Obviously he gives me some credit for being sensitive about the absence of my own child.

"God, sorry," he adds.

"It's fine. He's fine remember." I hope. "But how would this chip have helped Frankie if he wasn't abducted from school? I thought you said you have to be activated for it to work?"

"Yes, exactly, and if a child goes missing then the information on the child is shared out and activated by every surveillance system in the country."

"In schools and hospitals?"

"Not just there. If you're activated you can be detected by almost any cameras – on the street, in shops, even some homes."

"Wow. I wish this had been around for Frankie."

"You've changed your tune rather quickly haven't you? A second ago you were up in arms about the wrongs of injecting kids."

"Yes well. I can see it might have a few benefits."

"But what happens when they leave school – is the chip removed?"

I look tentatively around the car for something like a nail file that might be used to gouge the chip out.

"You can't remove it. For a start it's tinier than a grain of salt. I'm sure it's supposed to just disintegrate or something after a few years."

"Like radioactive tracers with short half-lives?"

"Get you!"

"I'm not completely clueless. I know that the point of a short half-life is so the tracer in your body decays quickly so you don't die of radioactive poisoning."

"I guess they aren't radioactive then."

"Let's hope not."

"I'm pretty sure the human rights protestors would have had some objections to the mass murder of the nation's children."

"Let's hope so."

"So there's no way to get rid of it until it just goes away by itself?"

"As far as I know. I'm no expert."

And yet he seems to know quite a lot about it.

Andy looks at me looking at my hand.

"I'm guessing that the hand that glowed back there was yours?"

Do I deny it? What would be the point? I settle for cagey.

"Why do you think that?"

"Oh let's see. One, the mini inquisition, two, the possibility of you being a former patient and, oh yes three, the fact that there was only you on the other side of that door."

Show off.

"You're wrong."

"Really?"

"Okay, fine. You're right – but why would a former patient still have a chip? If I or any other patient was discharged shouldn't the glowy thing dissolve or disappear or something?"

"Ha. I knew it was you!"

"Yes. Well done. But seriously…why am I chipped? I don't want to be chipped."

"No idea. But you weren't necessarily chipped at Barton Hall you know."

"I did think of that but I'm worried that an alternative could be worse."

I look out of the car window and see that the fields have been replaced by increasing numbers of houses. No broken down buses though. Yet.

"I see what you mean. Though I must say that you're the only adult I've met that has ever been chipped."

"That you know of. *I* didn't even know I was chipped until I was under that scanning thing. For all you know, you're chipped yourself!"

"Yeah sure. I think I would notice if a needle had been inserted into my arm."

"Yeah, well I didn't. And I'm not happy about it."

Andy laughs.

"It's serious!"

"I know," he agrees, "it's just…. sort of typical of you. And it's just the way you said you weren't happy."

"I'm not."

"I'm sorry. It must be awful to discover you've been tagged, but it's not very likely that you're being followed or watched or anything."

The camera!

"There was a security camera in the cottage," I tell him.

"Really? I didn't see one."

"It was upstairs during the time you went missing. I went upstairs to get away from George and that boy and I found a safe which was being monitored by a little camera."

"A safe? Did you open it?"

"Sort of. You remember that note that told me Frankie was alive? That's where I found it."

"A letter written to you in a locked safe, was it locked? Safe in the attic of a mysterious cottage. How thrilling! Who wrote it? Might they be a better source for information than the girls?"

"Afraid not. Apparently I wrote it."

"So that means you must have known you would lose your memory. But why put the letter in a safe? Did you have a key?"

"It was a combination lock and opened using the date Frankie disappeared."

"Interesting. That must be important then."

"Yeah but what I'm saying, remember, is that there was a camera pointing at it."

"So?"

"So – you don't have a camera without someone to operate it and observe what's being filmed? Who was on the other end or the camera?"

Andy shrugs. I didn't really expect him to know. But typically he answers anyway.

"It might have been there for years. Maybe the previous owners never bothered to take it down."

"But it's still an odd place to put a security camera, don't you think, in an attic? And why would it be conveniently pointed at the only object in the room?"

Andy shrugs again.

"Don't know. But what I do know is that we are here."

Andy slows down and drives up to the curb.

I take a deep sigh and tremble slightly with the nervous anticipation that my search for Frankie could almost be over.

CHAPTER EIGHTEEN:
"…disappointments…"

The street on which we are parked is deserted. Its rural appearance is tainted by the presence of menacing rows of bare, gnarled trees that point like the fingers of witches to a cauldron of a sky. Not the best omen then. I look for a couple of magpies, always guaranteed to provide me with false confidence, such as during Wimbledon or less hopefully before one of Frankie's tennis matches, but the sky, like the street, is bare.

Andy leaves the car first and I watch him walk towards a gate covered with swirls of peeling white paint. He stands before it, presumably waiting for me, but I am temporarily paralysed, caught between hope and impending disappointment.

"Are you coming?" he asks.

I guess it would be absurdly pointless to stay in the car. Unless – could one successfully avoid a lifetime of disappointments by doing so? I suppose so.

Also I need the loo.

"Yes."

I kick the package under my seat and get out.

"She's very nice you know," Andy assures me, as though my reluctance to get out of the car is the result of being scared of young women.

"I'm sure she must be, to go lending out cars to strangers."

"Oh sugar, I was supposed to put petrol in it."

"You're returning the car? How will we find Frankie or get back to the cottage?"

"Bus?"

I'm tempted to head back to the car and try our luck at the cottage and I'm about to suggest this when the door opens.

Standing there is a strikingly beautiful young woman wearing a colourful shift dress of orange and green swirls that skims her thighs over purple stork legged tights. A severe dark bob swings fluidly past her ears and her face suddenly crumples and she starts sobbing.

Andy and I gawp with astonishment.

Abruptly, she stops and two large, plum smeared eyes look imploringly at Andy.

"Has something happened to her?" she asks in a sweet, voice which make her words sound more like an invitation than a question.

"Her who?" asks Andy, which seems a reasonable thing to discover, but clearly not to the girl standing in front of us, whose features once again transform, as though a string has pulled away the softness of her features, leaving a hollow, hardened face filled with dark, angry eyes.

I have to look away to stop myself from sniggering. But the quick turning of my head seems to have drawn her attention and I can feel her eyes penetrating into me.

"You're not the police!" she accuses sharply.

I smile, hoping she'll still let us in so I can use the toilet.

"I know you," she adds angrily.

She pushes her face towards me and I suddenly feel a flash of familiarity. Could I be remembering something?

"What are you doing here?" she asks.

Replying would probably make the situation worse so I attempt to win her over with my warmest smile. Bad move.

"You think it's funny?" she snarls.

I really need to work on my smile. I wonder what I've done to upset this woman. Clearly something unforgivable.

"Is this your doing?" she asks Andy. "I can't lose her again."

And then it comes to me – where I've seen this woman before. I'm sure she was in one of the photos that George insisted were mine, posing outside the cottage.

Before I can make sense of this, the girl looks beyond us and sees the car.

"My car! What the…?"

"Did you steal my car?" she says, turning on me.

I look again towards Andy. I'm pretty sure the car business is all his doing and I'm tempted to say so, just to shift some of her venom away from me. But there's something about this woman that is preventing us from responding – as though she's some angry, inhuman spirit that has been summoned to protect the entrance of her house.

"Did you steal my car?" she repeats. "Or shall I call the *real* police?"

I feel inclined to point out that neither of us claimed to be police. But I don't.

"We didn't steal it," Andy tells her.

We? Again I want to point out that I had nothing to do with the acquisition of the car.

"You don't call taking a car without the owner's consent stealing?"

She looks as though she's about to swallow Andy's head and I rather shamefully back away. Am I the type of person to sacrifice my comrade to save myself? Unfortunately I have no time to find out as her neck suddenly swivels towards me.

"Well?" she spits. "What are you doing with my car?"

I see tears once again brimming in her eyes and wonder which might be worse – to be eaten alive or drowned.

"Your sister said it would be okay," Andy tells her. "She said you wouldn't mind."

"You've seen my sister?"

All at once her face softens as though the string restraining her features has been released and the tears that have been held in check begin flooding out again. We seem to be back to stage one and all this water isn't helping with my little problem. But at least she's not quite so scary now.

"Do you think I could use your loo?" I ask.

She looks at me in astonishment but then gestures behind us to the loo.

The toilet is small and thankfully furnished with toilet paper, nothing else. No magazines or funny posters to help while away the time, but there is a small montage of photos in a frame on the wall above the sink. Why is a toilet an appropriate place to display personal photographs? I guess you might have a captive audience for a while but, unless you have a regular flow of visitors, it is rather narcissistic. Maybe as a reminder that amongst the humdrum of life there are moments of pleasure? I wish I was in my own toilet; I could do with being reminded of some pleasurable times.

As I wash my hands I take a closer the look at the photos. The girl who opened the door, who I assume is Mary's sister, is there, obviously in happier times. There are several of her in different poses, mostly with the same happy expression. In almost all the photos she is hugging different young and very beautiful people and I prefer to see this as a sign of her insecurity rather than popularity. The centre photograph is of large group of unreasonably chipper youngsters, circling a large cake, possibly celebrating a birthday. I look closer at the group hoping to see someone I recognise, hoping to see Frankie beaming up at me, happy and alive, but unless he's the photographer he's not there.

I am enjoying the solitude and realise that this may be a good opportunity to have a closer look at the newspaper clippings that were sent to Simon Greaves' house.

Andy was right.

Or at least, according to this news article – Simon Greaves has at some point died. There is a photo of a stretcher about to be lifted onto a helicopter and another of the collapsed stage and above them both in huge letters is a headline questioning whether the Star Maker TV show was responsible for the tragic death of its young contestant.

Another article, taking full advantage of Simon's surname, shows hundreds of sobbing fans placing flowers outside what I am guessing is the studio in which he died.

I can't see how or why all these pictures could have been faked – but judging by the photos of Simon it is definitely the same person who served us tea a few hours ago. If it was a trick it would have been a very sick joke to play on the young lad, especially after his stroke. What kind of person would send someone such disgusting images – surely not me? I glance at a few more headlines and realise that although they are all writing about the same person there are some strange irregularities. I know newspapers can be liberal in their interpretation of the facts but while one story has Simon dying from falling stage scenery, there is another in which Simon is stabbed by the fan of a fellow contestant and another which has Simon dying from food poisoning from meals provided by the show's catering company.

What is the point of this? I look at the top of the paper clippings and see that both the name of the newspapers and the dates are all identical. Ridiculous.

I'm guessing that I've been in the toilet longer than is socially acceptable, especially as an unwanted guest, and decide to ignore what I've just seen. The newspaper stories must obviously be fakes.

Andy and the girl who is yet to be confirmed as Martha are now sitting amicably at a kitchen table.

"Tea?"

"Love some please."

I realise I am gasping for a drink but need to be careful – you never know when the next toilet will be available.

Martha is like a different version of the girl from the doorstep. This one is calm and sweet looking, as though she's stepped out of a 50s advert for baking powder.

"Cake?"

"Love some please."

I realise I'm also rather famished. I expect the cake to appear freshly topped with pink icing and strawberries but instead she pulls open a Quality Street tin and pulls out some Jaffa Cakes. Personally I would class them as biscuits but decide against beginning our re-acquaintance with a debate on the relevant criteria for baked goods.

"So, small world eh, Sarah?"

I smile and nod, unsure what has brought about this sudden change of heart. She looks genuinely friendly but the speed of her transformation and her inability to distinguish cake from biscuit make me wary.

"This charming young man here tells me you've lost your memory, do you know who I am?"

Blimey Andy, I've only been in the loo a minute. I wonder who's charming who. And again the question sounds ever so slightly menacing as though she's testing me.

"No."

She looks at me closely and gives a little laugh.

"Well that would explain why you came here."

How would it?

"We came here because someone told us you know my son. I was hoping you might know where he is."

She laughs again.

"Looks like we've something in common after all, Sarah – we both seem to have misplaced someone."

"Mary?"

"I thought you said you couldn't remember anything?"

"I can't. As far as I know, we've never met. I'm just assuming that because you said the car is yours that you're Mary's sister."

"You've seen Mary?"

How come Andy didn't cover this while I was at the loo?

"No, I haven't. Andy here borrowed your car from her after his bus broke down. Didn't he tell you this?"

The girl's face spreads into an expression of awe as stares at Andy as though she'd just been introduced to the queen.

"You're Andy? The bus driver?"

Well I know I've been out of the loop for a while but I can't imagine the new darlings of society have been replaced by bus drivers.

She looks back at me and raises an eyebrow. What does that mean?

Andy is utterly charmed and doesn't seem at all surprised by this strange outburst of admiration.

"So Mary *did* tell you she lent the car to him? Apparently she said you wouldn't mind if he borrowed it for a couple of days."

A flash of anger returns.

"I haven't seen or heard from my sister in over a week."

Really? So how does she know who he is? Was Andy's improbable explanation for turning up with a car improbable after all?

"Andy? Tell her about Mary," I prod, thinking it's high time he did some explaining.

"Nothing much to add. The bus broke and Mary offered to let me borrow your car. I wouldn't normally take advantage but I was in a hurry."

"You were driving the bus?"

"Until it broke, yes."

"So you just left it."

"I know it sounds bad but I needed to pick up Sarah."

"While you were at work?"

"She was waiting at a bus stop."

"So she's just a passenger?"

Harsh.

"Well, I know it sounds strange."

"Something strange happened?"

What is she talking about?

"And you Sarah – did you lose your memory before or after you were picked up?"

"Of course I remember him picking me up."

Martha sighs and starts to laugh.

"Anyway, that certainly sounds like Mary, she's always been quite free with my belongings. Did she say where she was going?"

"To meet you she said. After I contacted the station we walked together to the next bus stop and then – I remember – she rang you!"

"Are you sure?"

"Yes. Don't you remember?"

"I have no problem with my memories."

"But we were standing almost outside this house!"

"So, let me get this right, you were with my sister, standing almost outside my house and yet, rather than walking two yards actually to my house and personally asking for my help, she stands outside my house and calls me on the phone. Is that right?"

Andy's face starts to redden again.

"Yes," he says. "Except I didn't know then, that this was your house."

"So how come you're here now?"

She looks suspiciously at me as though this is all my doing. I shrug innocently, grateful that this particular problem isn't mine.

"Sarah found your address in the glove compartment – we're assuming that you are Mary's sister, Martha?"

I thought I was being safely left out of this one. Thanks Andy. And again she studies me as though she's waiting for something; maybe to catch me out or to look for some clarification. I smile.

"Mary's sister, yes. But coming here has nothing to do with Mary?"

Andy is conveniently chomping on a Jaffa Cake, reminding me of a dog I once who always ran to his food bowl and pretended to be ravenously hungry whenever he was unsure what to do.

"Well sort of," I say. "I told you we're looking for my son and I hoped you might be in touch with him."

"Why do you think that?"

"I heard you were friendly with him at Barton Hall."

"What do you remember about Barton Hall?" she snaps.

"Nothing!" I snap back. But clearly there is something I ought to be remembering.

What did Simon say about it? Nothing much really beyond his infatuation of Mary and that her sister sometimes gave me a lift there. But then it clicks – he didn't call the sister Martha, it was something equally old fashioned but a little more unusual. What was it? Amelia! Blimey that was easy – usually I have to go through the alphabet a couple of times to pluck out the right name.

"Did you say your name was Martha?"

She narrows her eyes.

"Not once."

"So who's Martha?" Andy asks.

"A good question. And I've been wondering how you came to hear about her?"

"I'm not sure," says Andy unconvincingly. "Is she here?"

"She's wherever Mary is."

Huh?

Andy was right after all.

"Mary and Martha are, is the same person. Along with Miriam, Moira and probably some I've not yet come across. You don't need to look so surprised. I thought you knew she was a patient at Barton.

"It's not that unusual for trauma patients. Mary likes to be as generous with personalities as she is with belongings. I thought she was getting better, it's been quite some time since our accident, but it looks like we both need to go back"

"I'm sorry, I didn't know about any accident. When you say 'we' – were you a patient too?"

"The accident was years ago but unfortunately Mary still finds it hard to adapt. At least I still have her. And no, I'm not a patient. You really can't remember me? I work there. I'm Nurse Amelia Brown and you were my patient. Perhaps I'd better explain."

CHAPTER NINETEEN:
"…and despair…"

"You work there?" Andy asks unnecessarily.

"Yes."

"So, you *do* know Frankie?" I ask her.

"Sort of, you too," she adds enigmatically. It's annoying how people I meet know more about me than I do. And why never any straight answers? I look expectantly at Nurse Amelia but she just looks quizzically back.

"So," I prompt, "can you tell me why we were there?"

She screws up her eyes as though thinking something through.

"I think you should go back to Barton," she says finally.

"What? Why?"

"You're clearly not well."

"I feel perfectly fine."

"I don't mean for your physical health."

Not another diagnosis of madness. But at least she doesn't know I've just escaped from there.

"I'm fine." I repeat. "Or I will be if I can just get some answers and find Frankie."

"Mm, perhaps, but I'm not supposed to talk about patients outside the hall."

"It's hardly breaking confidentiality if I'm the patient."

"It is if I'm telling you something you don't know."

"Please?" I abandon reason and try good old fashioned begging.

She pauses and inspects my pleading face; is it pathetic enough to win her over?

Unfortunately it only reproduces a look of disdain. Clearly Nurse Amelia is not so easily swayed. And clearly there is something I've done that's bugging her. Not enough petrol money perhaps?

"What is it I've done to upset you?"

"I suppose you're just going to say that you don't remember anything," she replies.

"Only because I can't."

"Very convenient."

I hope this isn't a professional diagnosis.

"I'm not lying."

Amelia looks at Andy who is enthusiastically nodding.

"It's true. Every time I picked up Sarah up from the train station she would have to ask me which stop she needed to get off at. She never remembered me or even where she lived."

"So that's why you went to pick her up when the bus broke down?"

"Well. Even though I didn't see Sarah very often I knew her routine well enough to know that by the time the bus had done its circuit she would be anxiously waiting to be returned to the bus station."

"But this time she wasn't there?"

"I was," I add helpfully, not wanting to be excluded from this touching story.

"But *I* wasn't which is why I took up your sister's offer of your car so I could...."

"Rescue her." Amelia interrupts.

"Yes. I suppose so."

"Why?" she asks, looking at me as though the very idea of anyone helping me is ridiculous. And maybe she's right.

"I didn't really have time to think about it. I wouldn't have been able to help her if it wasn't for your sister."

"Very convenient," she repeats "and yet also very ironic."

"Why's that?" Andy asks, but I can sense the answer – whatever I did to upset Amelia, clearly involved Mary.

"If my sister is missing, then it's Sarah's fault."

"Really?" asks Andy.

Not knowing what else to do I pick up a Jaffa Cake, but under Amelia's glare, I put it down again. Fine. Tell me what I did.

"Yes. Your damsel in distress persuaded my sister that she didn't need to stay at Barton where she would be safe and where I could look after her. Told her that she would be better off trying to sort things out for herself."

"Oh," says Andy sheepishly. "But she seemed alright."

I know he's only trying to be reassuring but it's not helping.

"So where is she then?"

"I don't know," Andy replies even more sheepishly. Why would he? He only met her for five minutes. Five minutes which led him here.

"What about you?" she turns accusingly towards me. "You claim to know what's best for Mary, so where do *you* think she is? Well?"

She raises her hand and I think she might be going to hit me. I push my chair back, ready to move. What's wrong with her? Once again she's spitting venom.

"I'm sorry you think I've done something wrong but I honestly have no idea who she is let alone where she is!"

Nurse Amelia looks behind her and I hear a door opening.

"Who's that?" Andy asks.

I'm hoping its Frankie, but I'm thinking it's Mary.

Instead of responding Amelia sits calmly back down.

"When you both arrived I genuinely thought something must have happened to her and when I saw Sarah I just assumed.... well it was a shock."

She looks at me again as though my arrival was orchestrated simply just to annoy her. But it's Andy who is annoyed.

"So your sister isn't missing?"

"Apparently not. Though she's not exactly all there, does that count? I mean you must have known something was wrong with her, who in their right mind goes lending out other people's cars to strangers? "

The relief in her face is evident.

"The bit about Sarah persuading Mary to leave Barton was true. I couldn't believe that you would dare come to my house. I was just angry. I was trying to make you feel guilty. Anyway, I just have to pop to the kitchen a minute."

Amelia gets up and walks out of the kitchen leaving me and Andy to smile nervously at each other.

I have no idea what to make of her. Even if I had persuaded her sister to leave Barton there must have been a good reason. I'm sure I haven't suddenly transformed into the type of person who goes around changing people's minds just for the fun of it. I suppose there was Simon, who it seems I persuaded not to enter Star Maker, but that's only two. I'm sure there have been countless people I haven't intentionally influenced. Andy, for example. I didn't make him come and rescue me or make him stay and help me.

"Well that was a bit disturbing," comments Andy finally. "Do you think she's even a nurse?"

"Well she'd fit in well at Barton, from what I've seen so far of the staff, but there's no denying that was a bit over the top. I thought she was about to hit me."

"I still don't get it. Even if you had persuaded her sister to leave Barton, which at the moment seems like a very sensible move, it still doesn't explain all the theatrics. Why pretend to be distraught and then be as sweet as apple pie?"

"And what's all that about an accident and Mary being Martha… was she making that up?"

I can however, hear muffled talking in the next room but not the voices of two young women as I had expected.

"I don't think that *is* Mary out there," I whisper to Andy, "it sounds like she might be on the phone. I'll try and hear what she's saying."

I put my finger to my lips; although why Andy would suddenly start shouting I have no idea, and begin to creep stealthily towards the door.

I can make out certain words and am surprised to hear Andy's name being repeated frequently.

What has he got to do with all this? I hear something about something not going to plan. She's talking about her car and wishing she hadn't allowed Mary to get involved and then she gasps. I hear Doctor Franks mentioned and she seems to be repeating something about Andy getting hold of an…Alternator? Has he done something with the car's engine? The tone of Amelia's voice changes as though she's preparing to say goodbye. I scurry back to Andy. What plan is he involved in? Is he involved with these people?

Andy raises his eyebrows at me. He looks so trustworthy with his innocent curly hair and his honest chestnut eyes. How could he be part of some sinister plan? Bus drivers don't have sinister plans.

"I couldn't hear anything in particular but I think we should leave."

"So soon?" asks a voice from behind me. Amelia is standing in the doorway, alone.

"Yes, things to do..."

"But I thought you came to see Mary. Don't you want to speak with her?"

"So that was Mary?" I ask.

"Well I suppose she might be Martha today, in which case you would be wasting your time," Amelia laughs. "Although it would be funny, both of you not knowing who the other is, like two farcical amnesiacs!"

"Which girl did *I* meet?" asks Andy.

Before she can answer, the kitchen door opens and a girl, who I presume to be Mary, enters.

"Amelia's just being facetious. I don't know why she likes to do that."

"I was worried about you Mary. I thought something might have happened."

"Like what?"

"Excuse us a second will you?"

Amelia takes hold of her sister's arm and guides her to the back of the kitchen where she starts to whisper.

I gaze awkwardly at the new arrival. She could almost be Amelia's twin with the same thick black hair swinging effortlessly around her long neck and a similar round face that could easily belong to a child. Her shift dress is also similarly vibrant as though it too had been salvaged from a 1960s wardrobe. I'm also sure this is the other girl from the cottage photo.

I watch as Mary shoots a look of anger towards her sister before nodding and turning to look uncomfortably at me and Andy. She then smiles and comes towards us.

I'd love to know what they've been whispering about.

"Sorry about that, just sister stuff. I'm Mary, hello Andy, I see you managed to find Sarah and of course I already know who you are – you're Frankie's mum."

My heart jumps at the sound of his name.

"She's looking for Frankie," Amelia tells her, "and she wants to know what happened at Barton. She's forgotten. Again."

What does she mean by again?

"Have you?" asks Mary gently.

I nod. Mary definitely seems to be the nicer sister. She sits down opposite me and smiles serenely.

"What is the last thing you remember?" she asks.

I don't know her, and she can't be more than twenty years old, yet I feel compelled to answer.

"It was five years ago. I was driving along a motorway, going to meet some new clients." I pause and Mary nods encouragingly. "That's it. Then suddenly I was standing alone on the side of a country lane in the middle of nowhere. That's when Andy arrived and helped me."

"That's lucky," she smiles.

Yes it was. Very lucky. And then he brought me here. Could it possibly all just be a coincidence?

"And now she's here looking for answers," Amelia says.

"I really don't think it's our place to tell her Amelia."

"You don't have to, I'll do it, and anyway it's more than likely she'll have another blackout and forget, so what does it matter? She might as well hear it and I think Andy the bus driver deserves to know something about his damsel, seeing as he's gone to all this trouble."

Mary sighs.

"Are you sure you want to hear what Amelia has to tell you?"

"Absolutely, especially if it helps me find out what's happened to Frankie and helps me find him," I say.

"Well that's the thing," Amelia interjects. "What we're about to tell you might make that harder."

CHAPTER TWENTY:
"…how marvellous…"

What's that supposed to mean? How can I *not* hear what she has to say? To learn anything at all about Frankie will be marvellous.

"So?" she asks.

"I'm ready."

Mary looks towards her sister and nods.

Amelia lowers herself onto a stool like a nesting stork.

"I think it is best that I start at the very beginning. I first came across you almost four and a half years ago. For six months before that you'd been lying unconscious in a hospital ward suffering from multiple injuries. Scans had shown unusual activity in your brain which made you of particular interest to the doctors at Barton Hall. You were transferred, without regaining consciousness, to Barton where you were hooked up and constantly monitored to try and work out what was going on."

"To see if I was brain damaged?" I ask.

"It was a definite possibility of course."

"But not true, seeing as I am fine, obviously." I wait for them to agree but nobody says anything. "So when you say I was unconscious was I in a coma?"

"Well that's the conundrum, because your EEG scan wasn't consistent with typical coma patients. Yours behaved as though you were just asleep, but you couldn't just be asleep since nothing would wake you up."

"But I must have woken up eventually. I'm awake now aren't I?"

I have a moment of doubt as I visualise myself in a cold white room lying on cold white sheets attached to wires that perpetually mimic the desperate fluctuation of my eyelids as I attempt to re-emerge into reality.

Surely not.

"Anyway," Amelia continues, "you remain unconscious for a further six months and all that time your brain has been showing a variety of hectic patterns that you would normally only get from a stimulated brain, i.e. belonging to someone who is awake and engaged in a mentally-taxing activity."

I smile smugly as though I've been awarded A's for tests in exams I've not had to study for.

"And then I wake up?" I prompt hopefully.

"For a little while, yes."

"And what? I go back to sleep?"

"Yes. But not before you cause quite a stir. That's why I know so much about you. You're quite famous at Barton, you know."

First I'm a genius and then I'm a celebrity. I should knock myself out more often.

"You kept ranting about having been on an underground tube train which was taking you to the future and that you needed to be released straight away because you had work to do and that 'reliability was your reputation.' Then you handed out these business cards – goodness knows where you got them from – and tried to convince people that you needed to be somewhere. And that's when I first heard about Frankie."

"How? Was he there?"

"No. Again, it was *you* shouting about having to find him. You said that he'd been abducted but that you had information that he was alive and that you needed to go get him before it was too late."

"Too late? What do you mean? How too late? Too late for what?"

"Calm down," Mary interrupts, "you'll get yourself into a state. Maybe this isn't such a good idea."

They can't stop now. I look calmly at Amelia who is wearing a faint smirk as though she is enjoying my reaction. Could she be deliberately trying to wind me up?

"I'm calm," I insist. "Tell me what I said."

"Obviously no one knew what you might be too late to do," Amelia continues. "And as you only stayed conscious for a few hours it wasn't really relevant that you would be going anywhere."

"So when did I wake again?"

"Usually you woke every few days but occasionally it was a little longer; one time almost a month went by. I remember some of the staff held bets over when you would regain consciousness; that four week period was a very tense and exciting time for us."

"Amelia!" Mary scolds her sister.

"Fine. So every now and then you would wake up and we were all keen to hear what you had to say. That was also unusual because most people would be groggy after being unconscious but you acted as though you'd just been having a nap."

"So what was it you were so keen to hear?"

"Well mostly you just insisted that you should be allowed to leave and go find Frankie but sometimes you'd talk about the magic underground train with strange people on it; including a young boy who we thought must be the son you were looking for. One time you talked about going to a strange museum of stuff that sounded like something out of a science fiction story."

"Amelia, that's not funny."

I glance towards Andy but he doesn't come to my defence about this supposedly-imaginary museum.

"And did anyone ever come to visit me?"

Who would that be? Frankie was gone and there was no one else really; no close family or friends; it's a wonder I bothered to wake up at all.

"Just one."

"Who?"

"I can't quite remember what she was called; the name of a river perhaps? Anyway she only came the once and you weren't awake; in fact that was during the time you were unconscious for the longest. Maybe someone was supposed to let her know when you woke up but forgot."

She likes to poke the knife in does Amelia.

I wonder who it was? Maybe an old colleague, or a school friend?

"Smallish woman, not very remarkable. She spent quite a long time talking with the doctor so she may have just been there because she had connections with Barton, unless maybe she knew you when you were a child. Ring any bells?"

Not a tinkle. It's rather embarrassing to realise that basically there's no one who would notice if I were alive or dead, a fact no doubt realised by Amelia. Indeed, I seem to have more acquaintances now than I ever did.

"Anyway, she never came back. So you just had to make do with telling the doctor your mad ramblings."

"Amelia, there's no need to be rude."

No *need* perhaps but she certainly has a preference for it.

"Which doctor was that?" I ask hopefully.

"Doctor Franks of course. He's always been your doctor, very patient if you ask me. Every time you woke up you'd fling one of those cards in his face and tell him that you had a reputation for being reliable and that you would lose work if you weren't."

Yes, my reputation relies on it. I know. Probably got no clients left now though.

"One other thing that kept cropping up was that you needed to get to Peterborough. You said you had a ticket and that you needed to meet someone there, but there was no ticket in your belongings. In fact you had very little in the way of possessions, just an old folder with some blank bits of paper inside."

I sense Andy bristle at this bit of information but he remains quiet.

Peterborough was where 'Uncle George' said I was supposed to meet him and where the letter delivered to Simon might have been posted.

"And I told this to Doctor Franks?"

"Of course. You talked a lot."

"Did you know he pretended to be my brother?"

I look directly into Amelia's eyes expecting some sign of discomfort or shock; instead she laughs.

"Maybe he felt sorry for you because no one visited. Except that little woman. Sorry."

"Are you sure?" Mary asks, a little more sympathetically.

Of course I'm sure.

"How can you remember?"

"It was yesterday at my cott…."

I feel a sharp kick under the table from Andy.

"What?" Amelia asks.

"Nothing, you're right everything is a bit confused. That sounds crazy right? "

Andy looks puzzled but still remains silent.

"Anyway you still haven't told me about Frankie."

"I suppose," says Mary softly.

Amelia smiles and continues.

"You'd been at Barton for nearly a year and you were waking up more frequently but you weren't becoming any more rational – no offence – so it was suggested that you should be allowed to join other patients in the therapy sessions. You weren't very happy about it and you were still insisting that you should be out looking for your son and it was causing some upset with some of the other patients. One day you had several of them in tears, demanding they should all be released. So Doctor Franks eventually decided you should be told how you arrived in hospital."

"I was wondering when you'd get to that," Andy says suddenly." Why did Sarah have extensive injuries? Was she in an accident? Apparently you were driving along the motorway."

"The M1?"

It's the last thing I remember. I was on my way to a meeting with important new clients which, according to the letter I wrote to myself, I did actually attend.

"I think so. Nobody knows what happened, the weather was fine and no other vehicles were involved; perhaps you fell asleep at the wheel or had had a drink or…"

"But surely I would have remembered that, and how come I don't have any scars?"

"It was five years ago," Amelia says. "They did a good repair job on you."

"And you say no one else was hurt?"

"I said no other car was involved."

"What do you mean by that?"

"You had a passenger."

"Who was it?"

"You really don't know? It was a boy around the age of twelve? Ring any bells now?"

"Amelia, stop it," Mary says. "Sometimes it's hard to believe you're supposed to be in a caring profession."

"Well," Amelia presses on, ignoring her sister, "did you know any twelve-year-old boys five years ago?"

I can feel heat spreading across my face.

"What do you mean? Why are you doing this?"

Andy shuffles in his seat, his face showing concern but he doesn't say anything.

"You know exactly what I mean. You'd told yourself and everyone around you that your son had mysteriously disappeared but it's not true is it? I bet you knew all along that he hadn't been abducted, you were just trying to block it out because you couldn't bear to face the truth."

"What truth?"

"That it was your son in the car with you when it crashed. That you were responsible for what happened to Frankie."

"No. It's not true."

I turn to Andy to see if he believes this ridiculous story but he's clearly in shock.

"Andy, she's lying."

"Really? And am I lying about the alcohol levels that were found in your blood? If you hadn't been unconscious you would have been in prison. Why do you think Barton has so much security? Do you think it's to keep patients out?"

I instinctively touch my hand.

Amelia reads the gesture.

"See, you do know what I'm talking about. Why do you think you've been tagged? Surely you can't think it's normal for law-abiding adults to be monitored?"

"What you're saying is wrong," I say. "There was no one in the car."

"How do you know? You're just selecting bits of memory to suit you."

"I'm not. Frankie had been missing for months and I would never drive over the limit, never."

"So you don't like to drink, eh Sarah?"

What's that got to do with anything? Sometimes after work, well nearly always after work, but never if I knew I had to drive.

"Sometimes, but never if I was going out in the car."

"What if you didn't think you were going to have to drive? Say for example if your son suddenly took ill and you needed to get him to a hospital? Would you drink and drive then?"

"Amelia, stop it. You've made your point."

Mary turns gently towards me.

"It seems as though your son was suffering some kind of fit when you were driving. Anyway you lost control of the car and you both ended up in hospital."

"You're saying Frankie nearly died while I was drink-driving? It didn't happen."

Amelia is clearly enjoying the impact she's having.

"You may have convinced yourself of that, but everyone else knows what happened. You're lucky you were so badly damaged or you would have gone to jail."

"So Barton isn't for criminals?" I ask Mary.

"It's not a prison. But some potential offenders are allowed to be treated there as an alternative to prison if they are not deemed dangerous and agree to be tagged."

I agreed? Unconsciously it seems. And it looks like I was oblivious during my so-called trial and sentencing as well.

I can't believe it. I look at Andy to gauge his reaction. Surely he must believe in me after all he has done?

He looks at my hand and sighs.

"There must be another explanation for the chip – I wouldn't put my son or anyone else's life in danger. They must be lying. They are lying."

Andy looks uncomfortable,

"I don't know what to believe," he says but then turns determinedly towards Amelia. "Whatever happened is in the past and Sarah came here to find out information about her son. You still haven't told her what happened to him."

"Yes," says Mary staring, with what looks like a warning look, at her sister, "and I'm still not sure what you are doing is a good idea. I agree that Sarah needs to return to Barton but it would be better to wait and let Doctor Franks speak to her."

That's not going to happen.

"Oh for goodness sake," Amelia shouts as she gets to her feet, "what are we pussyfooting around for, just tell her."

"Tell me what?"

"That you'll never get to see Frankie again."

"Why not?"

"Are you stupid as well as mad? I thought you would have worked it out by now. He's dead."

CHAPTER TWENTY ONE:
"…and comforting..."

Now I know she's lying.

Amelia is exultant. I expect Mary to scold her sister but she closes her eyes and stays quiet.

It's actually Andy who speaks first.

"So if Frankie is dead, why were we told that you and he used to attend sessions in Barton together?"

Mary mulls over an answer. It can't be that hard, she either did or didn't.

"Who told you this?" she finally asks.

I'm reluctant to tell these girls anything. They are clearly not to be trusted.

"Simon Greaves," Andy tells her.

The girls look at him, puzzled by his apparent glee at knowing Simon.

If he was hoping that they were going to be impressed by his association with his version of a miraculously resurrected, formerly mega famous Simon Greaves then it looks like he is going to be disappointed.

"You've seen Simon?" asks Mary. "How is he? A bit better I hope."

Andy tries to recover from his embarrassment at having failed to impress, by nodding vigorously.

Not that he would have any idea if he was better or not, or indeed what he was better than.

"He seemed very well," I answer for him.

"Why wouldn't he be?" asks Andy. He still seems to have a bee in his bonnet about Simon unless he's casually probing into the circumstances of his reincarnation.

"No particular reason," Mary replies, taken aback by the force of Andy's question. "I just remember him as being a bit sad and lonely."

"Only because you wouldn't have anything to do with him," Amelia interrupts with a smirk.

"Well I'm not the sort to mess around with people's feelings am I? You used to tease him about his music as well; telling him he could be a big star one day. Poor Simon, at least Sarah had the sense to tell him not to waste his time with those moronic TV shows. Sometimes I think they deliberately target vulnerable contestants like Simon, just to exploit them. "

So apparently I *did* stop him from going on the Star Maker show. But why? I never used to have a problem with that type of show.

"I don't remember doing that," I say.

"Naturally," Amelia sneers.

"But it doesn't sound like something I would do. I quite like TV talent shows but Simon did say something about me persuading him against entering."

"Of course," Mary says gently as though she is soothing me but I ignore her attempt to distract me.

"And he was also quite certain about the fact that I used to visit Frankie at Barton; in fact he said you often used to give me lifts there. Now I'd hardly be visiting a corpse would I?"

"Poor Simon," she repeats, "he'd get things into his head and then you couldn't get them out."

"So you're saying I didn't go to visit my son in Barton?"

"Not really."

"What do you mean not really? I can hardly partially visit him."

"Amelia did occasionally give you lifts but it was for appointments with Doctor Franks."

"But why would Simon say I was visiting Frankie?"

"Stop messing her around Mary," Amelia snaps.

She turns to me and smiles; this isn't going to be nice.

"Remember we told you that you were upsetting other patients with your outbursts? Well, one day when Doctor Franks arrived for work he wasn't alone. A close friend of his was involved with some family crisis and couldn't look after her son and as the doctor was his godparent, he offered to look after him for the day."

I don't like the sound of this. Is this Peter?

"Anyway, he gave the child to one of the nurses, to look after – not me I might add – I don't agree with being taken advantage of or used as a babysitter…"

"I'm sure it would never have crossed his mind to impose on you Amelia," Mary cuts in.

Amelia scowls.

"But after a couple of hours the boy must have got bored and decided to explore," she continues. "Eventually he found the doctor who just so happened at that moment to be working with you."

I don't like where this is going. She smiles and I look hard at her, daring her not to say what I know she will.

"So, you're talking to Doctor Franks when his godson comes bursting in followed by a very flustered red faced nurse," Amelia tells me. "The nurse starts apologising and tries to grab the boy who pulls away and begins to howl. The doctor gets up to comfort his godson but is beaten to it by you." She looks directly at me. "And apparently you start crying too and begin saying stuff like 'you're safe now' and 'no one will take you away' and you keep holding on to him and the boy looks shocked but then starts howling louder."

"And you know this how?" I have to stop her before she turns her tale into an epic of hysterics. "You made it quite plain that you weren't the nurse involved in the supervision of Doctor Frank's godson."

"I know I did, but the staff do talk to each other you know, especially when something interesting happens and of course there's always the cameras. There's not much privacy at Barton Hall."

"So what are you saying? That I thought this stranger was my son? That I suddenly imagined that he was my missing Frankie?"

"Well first of all, you *did* think that the boy was your son and at least it stopped you carrying on and attempting to organise the other patients into search parties. And for some reason the doctor decided to let you carry on believing it and arranged for you to see the boy on a regular basis."

"Ridiculous."

"I agree. But ridiculous or not it happened and it carried on happening for quite a long time, even after you left Barton. I think you were waiting to see him once after we'd taken him to the pictures with Simon, which is probably why Simon remembers you visiting your so-called son. We were all instructed to go along with it but a lot of the staff thought it was wrong, or even cruel."

"And what about you?" Andy asks her.

Surely he can't be taken in by this ludicrous story? But I can't help feeling uncomfortable when I think back to the photo Simon showed me.

Amelia turns towards Andy.

"Me? I thought it was stupid at first, but it seemed to keep her calm and the doctor said it was safer for her than being given large doses of sedatives. The lying just becomes normal after a while and anyway, I knew she'd forget anything I said as soon as she had her next blackout."

I can't believe she has just admitted her lies. I turn to Andy,

"See, she's just confessed to telling me lies, why would you believe her now?"

Andy lowers his eyes and I can't tell whether he is trying to decide what to make of it all or too ashamed at what he thinks to look at me.

"You asked to be told the truth," he mumbles. "You've never asked that before – you used to be more than happy to accept lifts to visit the boy. Perhaps you didn't fully believe it then, I don't know, maybe your subconscious knew the truth but your brain was telling you something else to protect you. I expect that's what Doctor Franks thought and felt you would heal quicker if you were happy."

"Maybe, but what about the boy? For one thing he sounds too young to be Frankie…"

"Exactly," Amelia agrees. I ignore her.

"But more importantly how could the doctor convince Peter to pretend to be my son for all that time?"

Amelia and Mary exchange a look and I think I've finally caught them out.

"The boy treated it like a game and it wasn't like you were the only one to act strangely at Barton."

"And you're saying the doctor kept up this charade even after I left Barton? Surely if I was well enough to leave I was well enough to know the truth?"

"See, you don't even believe it now," Mary says kindly, "and if you're still having blackouts you need to go back to Barton. Amelia has arranged for a car to take you back there."

"Mary!"

"Well, she'd find out soon."

"When?"

I look at Andy who looks as alarmed about this proposition as me.

"When did you arrange this? You can't make those decisions for me, I'm fine. I only came here because I thought you could help."

"And we can," Mary replies "by making you better again."

"We know you've been to Barton today," adds Amelia.

How can she know this? The phone call perhaps? Was all this 'info' just some plot to keep me occupied before my extradition back to Barton Hall?

"Doctor Franks is sorry if he frightened you but he just needs you to return for a little while. He promises you won't be sedated but he wants to do a few tests to make sure you're well."

I touch my hand. I bet I wouldn't be so lucky escaping the place a second time.

"No thanks."

Amelia stands up.

"I'm not going back," I say, "and you can tell the doctor that I don't believe the story of Frankie's death or that I could or would ever accept that someone else was my son. I don't know what happened to me or him but I would know if he was dead – and he's not."

I can feel my neck tightening with anxiety and anger and I know that I have to leave. Quickly.

"Perhaps we should go back," Andy suggests.

Is he mad? Has he forgotten the circumstances of our departure an hour since? I glare at him and he glares back.

"Perhaps Amelia won't mind us borrowing her car again," he suggests, "it will be a lot quicker, and anyway I said I would fill the car with petrol, so what do you say?"

Andy stands up and rattles the car key in his hands. Bless him. Does he really think this will work?

Amelia laughs.

"Do you really expect me to believe that you're voluntarily returning to Barton?" she says. "The car will be here in a second and if you even think about trying to stop her from going then I will get the sensor on her hand authorised for immediate activation; and maybe this time she'll go to prison where she belongs."

"You can't do that!" Andy shouts. I'm not entirely sure what they're talking about but it doesn't sound good.

"Of course I can. Sarah must still be on a positive behaviour bond and I'm pretty sure that car theft doesn't come under the heading of positive behaviour."

"I had nothing to do with the car – you know that!"

"The police don't," Amelia adds coldly.

"Why would you do that?"

"Just doing my job. Doesn't matter now – I expect they're just about here."

What job? Nursing?

Mary remains silent. Is this what she agreed to, stalling for time?

"Then we'd better be off," Andy says forcefully and grabs my hand. "Come on, though I doubt anyone really is coming to get you."

"You're right," Amelia agrees as she throws out a surprisingly strong arm to stop me from getting up. "It's actually you, Andy, they're after, a little matter of some stolen files. Quite a serious offence. I wouldn't be surprised to hear that you're carrying a chip anytime soon."

Andy tugs me again and I am able to push past Amelia.

"So why haven't you called the police? Got something to hide?"

I am pulled half walking, half dragging towards the front door. I'm rather impressed by this forceful version of Andy but I am rather fearful of what to do next.

"We need to get the stuff from the car."

The file and key thing might be my only hope of finding out the real truth. I certainly didn't get it here. And the wine!

Andy opens the car door.

"Just get in!"

"You can't be serious," I say. "We can't just take Amelia's car again."

We get in anyway. Andy fumbles with the keys, trying to get them into the ignition.

"Come on," I urge, "if we're going let's go."

Amelia is at the side of the car. I push down the lock a second before she begins tugging frantically on the handle. Amelia thrusts her contorted face against the window-. Andy looks determined but is still unable to fit in the key successfully. Amelia's face disappears and I think, for a second that she is giving up but her head re-emerges like a swooping eagle. She lifts up her hand and I see she is armed with some kind of large rock which she swings back behind her.

"Hurry," I scream and Andy shoots me a glare that confirms he is already aware of the urgency of our exit. The key is finally in the ignition and I think we are going to make it when a thunderous shattering of glass proves otherwise. Andy tries to twist the key but Amelia lunges her arm though the shards of glass, stretching past me, and grips onto Andy's shirt. I become fixated for a moment on the repercussions of him returning to work with a damaged uniform, but then refocus on more immediate worries like how, at any moment, reinforcements from Barton could arrive to brutally remove us from the car and drag us back to Barton. I think for a second about getting out and pulling Amelia away from the car but before I can perform any heroics Amelia screams and loosens her grip.

The taser.

Andy is pressing the weapon against Amelia's arm.

"Where did you get that?" she asks.

Andy ignores her question and tells her to move away from the car. I would have thought this would be enough to encourage her withdrawal but she is still fixated on the taser.

"Where did you get that?" she repeats, more urgently now.

"He's a bus driver, remember?" I shout hoping to clear up the matter quickly and make our escape.

Amelia looks at me with a puzzled expression. She's about to say something else when she's distracted by footsteps. Andy tugs his arm away, but instead of pulling back from the car Amelia transfers her grip onto my arm. She's stronger than she looks.

"Fine – take the car but leave the USB stick."

Mary appears at the side of her sister.

"Come on," says Mary to Amelia, "Let them go."

"But look," replies Amelia, nodding towards the taser.

"It'll be fine. It looks like you were right about George but it can't hurt me if you let them go, it's probably empty anyway," says Mary, "just let go."

"Maybe, but we can't be sure, and what about the stuff on the data stick?"

Suddenly the silence of the deserted street is broken by the sound of approaching cars. Amelia still has her hand gripped roughly on my elbow. I panic and do the first thing that comes into my mind. I grab the taser that Andy is still aiming at Amelia and jab it into Amelia's arm.

"Stop!" Mary shrieks, "It's not what you think!"

I'm pretty sure I haven't fired it but nevertheless it has the desired effect of forcing Amelia out of the car. She screams, stumbles and sinks to the pavement.

"What have you done?" Mary shouts, but we are clearly not staying to find out. Andy finally presses hard on the accelerator and we head off.

CHAPTER TWENTY TWO: "...would..."

"What did you do that for?" Andy says as we speed off down the street.

I don't think Andy has any right to judge. I thought he was just some ordinary, pudgy, curly haired bus driver with a heart – but in just over a day he has committed theft at least twice and assault. I only accidently maybe hurt someone once.

"I didn't do anything with the taser," I say thrusting it back at Andy, "Amelia just knocked into it. I didn't do it on purpose, it wasn't like I deliberately stole a car or anything."

"Nice deflection. But thank you would be nice. I don't want to point out the obvious but you didn't want to go back to Barton did you?"

"Of course not, but why didn't you just hand over the memory stick? She said she would let us take the car."

"I know what she said," Andy replies rather tersely, "and how does she know about that? They might have noticed some files were missing but I don't know how anyone could tell I'd downloaded information; at least not that quickly. And doesn't it make you wonder what's so important about the information on it?"

"Well of course if it has anything useful on it, but it could just be confidential stuff that we're not supposed to have access to. I just hope we haven't got ourselves into more bother."

"If you mean Amelia, I'm sure she's fine. The taser didn't even have a cartridge in it."

"So why did she scream like that and fall over?"

"Don't know. I suppose she just expected it to hurt. The brain is a funny thing; it can fool the body into reacting strangely to all sorts of things."

"And Uncle George? Was it loaded then?"

"I think so."

"You think? I thought you'd been trained!"

"Well it must have been charged then. I don't believe the body can be fooled into staying unconscious, although now you mention it I don't remember any sparks. I can't remember."

"It was only this morning."

"It's been a busy day."

"Yes, it must be hard to distinguish it from all your other crimes."

Andy pulls up the car.

I suddenly feel nervous.

"Look," he says turning towards me, "I've no idea what is going on with you and these people but something's definitely wrong. I said I would try and help you but if you don't like it then you're welcome to get out and I can get back to the station."

"They won't be happy about your torn shirt." I say in an attempt to lighten his mood.

Andy looks at the rip on his sleeve and sighs.

I wait a second and wonder if I should add that they might also be more irritated with him for abandoning his bus; but this probably isn't as funny.

"No," is all he says. Maybe he really does want me to get out. Better proffer an apology – why haven't I yet? I used to be so generous with them.

"Sorry. It's just been a strange day and I'm not used to being in trouble or even doing anything slightly frowned upon."

At least I hope it's unusually strange. I still can't vouch for the last eighteen hundred or so days but I am reassured that it doesn't *feel* normal.

"It's not exactly my typical day either," Andy retorts.

I think he feels a lack of appreciation for the disruption to his life, which I should remind him was of his own choosing. Instead, I attempt to flatter his ego.

"Of course not, but look how brave you got to be." I wait for him to colour and grin modestly, but he merely tuts. "I guess you're staying then. Any suggestions?"

"The cottage?"

"You *do* know that will be the first place they'll look?"

"Then we'd better get a move on."

"Fine. Let's hope it proves less eventful than the rest of the day so far."

We can hope.

We're now winding down familiar country roads.

"So why do you think you're so popular?" Andy asks eventually.

"You mean why am I being pursued by psychotic sisters and a doctor masquerading as Uncle George?"

"*Your* uncle?"

"No, Peter's uncle, which means he's got to be the boy who was pretending to be Frankie at Barton."

"This explains why he said he was your son at the cottage."

"Are we nearly there?"

I don't feel like we're being followed. But I'm not sure if that makes me feel more or less safe.

"We are indeed. Have you noticed that most of our stops have been on my bus route? "Here we are, home sweet home. Oh."

Andy pulls up outside my cottage, but I can't be certain it is still mine, for outside, thrust into the small patch of grass beside the front door, is a sign declaring that the cottage is up for sale.

"I'll take a wild guess," says Andy, "that you didn't know about this. Do you know of anywhere else you might live? I suppose you must live somewhere else if you only visit here occasionally."

True, Peterborough perhaps? Or my flat?

"No clue," I answer. "You know as much as me, well more actually, but the notes in my pocket only ever make reference to here. So if this place is gone I have no idea *where* I'm supposed to be."

"Do you think your clients have reclaimed it?"

"You mean I might have done something wrong; like break the terms of my contract?"

"Well you haven't exactly been too reliable lately."

"There goes my reputation." Andy laughs but it's not really funny. "Do you really think that in the short time we've been out someone has decided to make me homeless and arranged to repossess my cottage?"

"They'd obviously have to be more efficient than you."

I shrug and get out of the car.

"There *was* a for sale sign at the side of the house, I saw it when I was locked out, but it was old and dirty," I tell Andy. I look down the gap at the side of the cottage but it's not there. Granted this one looks all shiny and new but it wouldn't take much effort to give it a scrub and place it in front of the cottage. But why would someone do that?

"You don't suppose the locks have been changed?" Andy asks.

As I stare at the sign I begin to feel confident that it wouldn't matter, because it's emblazoned with the same yellow balloon as my latest key.

"Well let's find out shall we?"

"Where did you get that key?" asks Andy as I pull out the balloon key.

"It was in the door."

"Of course!"

And of course it unlocks the door.

Maybe now I'll be able to find out if there's anything to be discovered from the latest acquisitions.

"The package," I say, but Andy just nods and continues to walk towards the cottage. I'll get it myself then.

Andy brushes past me and opens the door.

"See," he says as though he has been the one to achieve this seemingly unlikely result. Wow!"

Now what? Maybe it's turned into something handy like a wine cellar.

Andy has his head inside the cottage. He pulls it out again.

"Blimey it reeks in there and I can't see a thing."

"Just hang on a second."

I go back to the car and grab the package from under my seat. Andy has already gone into the house when I get back. Couldn't he wait a second? Inside, the cottage smells of damp and dust.

"Andy," I call.

No answer. He can't have got far; the cottage isn't exactly what you'd call expansive. I stand still to try and determine his whereabouts but I can hear no noise at all. It is also very dark. Early afternoon light is pouring through the open door but it is not enough to illuminate the room.

There is a light switch by the entrance but, although I am tempted by the desire to see, I think I will take the precaution of not using it for the time being. I don't want to lose Andy again.

After a few seconds my eyes adjust to the gloom. The cottage appears to be in the same state as I left it this morning, with dust liberally covering bare floor boards. I look for footmarks but can only make out one set heading towards me from the small toilet. Where are Andy's prints? I head towards the kitchen but again there is just undisturbed dust and grime on old linoleum.

Where is he? I have an awful feeling in my gut that I have indeed misplaced him. Why didn't he wait? Idiot.

Maybe I should turn on the light after all.

"Hello!"

Thank goodness for that.

I turn towards the voice but from the thin, lanky silhouette I can tell it isn't Andy. It doesn't sound scary but I nevertheless hesitate.

"Miss Norton?" the lanky man enquires.

Who is he and more importantly, how does he know me?

I push myself back into the shadows – although it seems clearly too late to pretend I'm not in – and try to get a good look at him. All I can make out is that he's wearing a suit; not very thuggish attire but it could just be a ruse to lull me out into the open.

Could he be one of the people Amelia said was coming to take me back Barton Hall? Have they already got Andy? Should I push past him and make a run for it? Could I just stay here forever asking myself questions?

"Miss Norton?"

The lanky man takes a step inside the cottage. I take a step back.

"Miss Norton? Hello? I'm sorry if I startled you. I think we agreed to meet at two?"

For what? Who on earth could I have arranged to meet here? For a start, how would I even know I'd be here and yet I can't deny that I am, in fact, here. So who is this lanky man, another doctor perhaps, or my parole officer?

"Miss Norton? Are you okay? I'm here about the sale of the cottage?"

That was quick. It can't have been on the market for more than a couple of hours.

"You want to buy the cottage?"

"What?"

He laughs. What's funny?

"Of course we haven't actually met in the flesh but I'm John-James Brightstone from 'Brightstone and Nephew's' estate agents. I'm here to sell *you* the cottage."

CHAPTER TWENTY THREE:
"…it be…"

"You're what?"

"Well to be more accurate, I'm here to show you around the cottage that is being purchased for you."

I shove my envelope inside my jacket and step into the light to get a better look. He is even thinner without his shadow and his grey suit hangs very loosely over his gangly limbs – perhaps trying to give the impression of having a few extra muscles. He also has a small amount of dark hair that is sculpted to a point at the top of his forehead – maybe he's hung up about his height too – but it just makes his long head look even thinner. The overall effect is quite comical.

He shoots out one of his long arms and I feel obliged to shake it.

"John-James Brightstone," he repeats brightly and points to the For Sale sign outside the door. I hope you got past the sign alright. Though I'm certainly not saying it isn't spacious out there – of course a compact lawn has a lot of potential. I just wanted the sign to be noticeable – prominent. Do you like the logo? It was my idea? It's supposed to show that moving house with us is as effortless as letting go of a balloon. Do you get that? Anyway I'm one of the nephews, though my brother doesn't actually work with us anymore. He moved down south and doesn't even work as an estate agent. Can you imagine?"

I open my mouth to speak but he doesn't require a response and carries on.

"He's married now so we don't get to see him very often. He says it's much nicer down there, but I can't imagine it, can you? I suppose you're one of those people who like the city life. I expect you have to go down to London a lot with your job but you must crave the peace of the countryside or you wouldn't want to have this place to come to. Is it going to be a holiday home this then? Silly me, of course you probably have lots of places dotted around the world."

That's interesting. Why would he think I own several homes? I don't even appear to own this one any more, or is it *yet*?

"It's a little dark in here Miss Norton, shall I turn on the light?"

"It's fine thanks. You'll get used to it in a moment."

"Of course. Always better to have natural light if possible. You'd get on with my uncle, Mister Brightstone, he can't stand to have electric lights on in the daytime. He's forever going round the house or the office turning off unnecessary lights. Says it's bad for the eyes having all this artificial light on all the time. It drives my aunt mad, she's the opposite, "Let's put a little light on the subject," she says as she wanders around after him; she can't stand the gloom. Says it makes her depressed, especially in winter or autumn or when it's raining. She's sad quite a lot of the time actually."

I wonder why?

He walks past me and heads towards the kitchen

"Oh dear, I think you might want to rethink the décor. Formica, yuk , and such a small fridge. Do you mind if I put my packed lunch in it? I've been carrying it around all day, not had a minute to eat it and this milk will go off if I'm not careful."

I don't think he has stopped speaking since he arrived. Once again he doesn't wait for an answer and I hear what I assume is the sound of a fridge opening and shutting. I haven't had anything decent to eat in ages. I wonder what he's got in there, but first I need to find out what job he thinks I have. It certainly can't be deduced from my appearance.

"Any idea when you might be moving in?" he's says. "The paper work is only a formality with employers like yours."

"Mister Brightstone!" I shout to get his attention finally, "What do you mean my type?"

Finally he takes a breath and turns to me.

"The rich," he says simply. "Is that being indiscreet? I am sorry – my mouth does tend to run away without me sometimes. I didn't mean to be vulgar – people don't tend to talk about their money do they, unless they don't have any like me. I wish my employer would buy me a lovely cottage – well lovely-ish – but I still have to pay rent for mine; although I do hope to have my own place very soon. Oh and please call me John-James."

He beams.

"So have you worked with my employers often?" I ask.

"Not as often as we'd like obviously. Some buyers are more reliable than others and don't make such a fuss about the price, though you'd be surprised how many rich people do haggle a lot over costs. I suppose that's how they stay rich!"

John-James lets out a high squeaky laugh.

"I guess so," I agree, "so have you met them personally?"

"Who?"

"The buyers, my employers?"

Extracting information is not proving easy but I can hardly ask him outright who I am supposed to be working for.

"Dear me no, of course not – I expect they are far too busy with their work to be bothering personally with a little sale such as this. You do like it don't you?" He shifts a little and raises a long hairy eyebrow. "Do I detect a little dissatisfaction with the property madam? I can assure you it is very quiet and discreet and with just a few minor cosmetic touch ups you could have it looking fabulous. Perhaps you need to have a better look around? The kitchen obviously could do with a little updating but the lounge is a very generous size and once there are a few rugs and a few choice pieces of furniture in here it will look very lovely.

"In fact I believe a few items may already have been delivered, not sure what or where but maybe we'll come across them. Anyhow, this way…"

I follow him, curious to see how the cottage looks now.

"Right, just before you get to the lounge you'll notice a little room to your right – a very convenient downstairs toilet – a convenient convenience if you like!" He squeaks again. "Very handy if you get caught short while cooking or watching the television. Not that I see you as someone who watches much telly, far too busy I expect."

He seems to be blurting out everything apart from anything useful. What does he think I'm so busy doing? I certainly wouldn't mind watching a bit of TV right now; I could do with a bit of relaxation after the day I've had.

"Do you mind if I take a look?"

I head towards the toilet and hopefully a moment alone, but John-James is on my tail, probably to draw my attention to some superficial defect. Does he ever manage to sell anything?

"Do you mind? A little privacy would be appreciated."

John-James colours and steps back.

"I'm sorry, I didn't realise…"

I enter the toilet and sit down on the seat lid. Who knew how useful toilets were for enjoying a bit of peace. Now for the file. It feels like I've been waiting for ever to find out what was written on the sheet.

I take a deep breath and slip the piece of paper out. The computer key thing falls into my hands, I'd forgotten about that; I hope the safe is still upstairs. I put it into my jacket pocket.

The paper looks very new and very white. I turn it over and it is still blank apart from the small yellow smudge. I feel overwhelmed with disappointment. Why didn't it work?

I shove the paper back angrily and feel the folded paper that Andy stole from Barton Hall. I pull it out and unfold it. There *is* something on it. In scribbled, almost illegible writing, I can make out a list of about half a dozen names. Most of the words are hard to decipher but there are three names towards the bottom of the list which stand out, probably because I recognise them – Amelia Brown and George Franks and Sarah Norton.

Is this part of the list of Barton's patients Andy saw? If so, why is it so short and why are Nurse Brown and Doctor Franks on it? Andy said he recognised at least one of the names – a passenger involved in the bus killings – I'm sure he would have mentioned it if he'd seen my own name on the list. At least I presume he would.

I scrutinise the other names – the letters are tall and bunched close together as though hurriedly written – but no matter how hard I try they don't stir even the most distant of memories. Some names have a swirly design against them, including George and Amelia, but mine doesn't. I look for some explanation for the symbol but I can't see any key. What could connect us all? And what could set us apart? Could they both have once been inmates at Barton?

"Are you okay in there Miss Norton?"

"Fine," I say. "Just trying to visualise how it might be redecorated. I won't be long."

What does this all mean?

I stuff the sheet back in the package, fold it and shove it into the inside of my jacket. I open the door to be greeted by an anxious looking John-James.

"Is it all okay? I think everything works, just needs a spot of paint or a few posters perhaps to brighten it up, don't you think? We have photographs in our downstairs toilet. It starts many a conversation with visitors. Though I don't suppose you'll have time for many visitors – not that you don't have friends – I expect you have more than you can shake a stick at. Which of course, you wouldn't do, if they were your friends.

"Not that I'm presuming, at least I don't mean to presume. Perhaps you'd like to look at the lounge space?"

I take a step forward and find myself looking into the lounge.

"The previous owners even left a few bits of furniture if you want them," he says. "Not that you wouldn't want your own but I think there's a leather sofa under here."

He tugs at a large dust sheet to reveal the hideous blue leather sofa. There's no way that's staying if I can help it. "Very stylish don't you think and very expensive?"

"Maybe but it doesn't really suit the cottage. I visualise something more cosy and floral."

"Quite right Miss Norton of course, that would be much more in keeping with the location. Very good. Any questions?"

Questions? Oh I know.

"Yeah. Where does one actually sleep in this place? Or what about a shower? And the boxes you mentioned?"

Acceptable questions I think, but by the look of John-James, you'd think I'd asked him to define quantum physics.

He's standing on one leg and is pulling at vigorously at his tuft of hair.

"Good question. Or rather, good questions. I'm sure they must be here. I mean who would live in a cottage without the means to wash and sleep. That would be ridiculous."

He pauses and looks around him as though he's looking for rooms to suddenly appear. Not entirely implausible. At last his eyes alight on the little door leading up to the attic.

"Of course! I believe there is also some space above which is also a lovely bonus don't you think to a cottage – somewhere to put your bits and pieces?"

"Or bedrooms?"

"Quite! Of course."

He cautiously opens the door and stretches his long neck into the new space.

"There's a narrow set of stairs, it's a bit gloomy but shall we take a look?"

Before waiting for a reply he springs upwards and I feel compelled to follow – curious as to how the upstairs looks at the moment – probably bare and dusty like the rest of the cottage.

"Come along Miss Norton the steps are perfectly safe. Like I said only cosmetic problems, easily fixed. Ah here we are – now if I open this little door then all will become clear. I'm not sure if there are any windows up here. No, it's all very dark but I'm sure there must be a light switch around somewhere. I mean you wouldn't go to the trouble of fitting stairs if there was nothing to go up to would you?"

I can hear him patting at the walls; very tentatively at first and then a more impatient slapping until he finally sighs. I suspect he found the switch.

"Here we go. I do apologise I should have got here before you and checked out where everything is but it's alright. oh!"

What's he looking at? I sprint up and follow John-James into the now illuminated attic room. Oh.

The room of surprises, surprises me once more.

John-James is leaning against the door post scratching the top of his head.

"Well I don't know what to make of this," he says, "very strange."

The attic is not dusty or empty, far from it.

The room now resembles some elaborate control centre, the type you see in movies whilst the hero is off saving the planet somewhere in space. There are rows of computers lined up along one side of the room with several large plasma screens above them – and above the screens there are a few cameras. One is pointing to the centre of the room where my safe used to be and where I am now standing.

For the first time John-James is lost for words.

"Well I've heard of people leaving old junk behind when they sell their house but nothing like this," I say. "Do you know who used to own the cottage?"

I look towards John-James who is still standing in the doorway; his eyes travelling wildly around the room with his mouth open and waiting to catch up with the information being sent to his brain.

"The cottage has been empty for over a year."

"Really? Well this doesn't look like the trappings of your regular squatters."

"I can assure you Miss Norton that there have been no squatters here. We take very good care of the houses on our books and we regularly check the properties for anything irregular; not me personally, I might add. Of course this might appear to be irregular but …well, I guess our employee didn't feel the need to check the attic for….this kind of thing. Most unusual. I can assure you that this is not typical."

"Well it's not as if there's a giant hole in the roof or anything. It is after all cosmetic." I look over to see if he is listening but his mouth is still agog. "And it looks like it's all new."

I walk over to one of the machines which is covered in protective plastic. I can't see any keyboards so maybe it's not a computer after all. Maybe they are all just stolen TVs stored here and waiting to be collected by hardened criminals when the heat has gone off a bit.

John-James walks over for a closer inspection. I bet he wishes he'd got here before me, he could have had the lot. I bet there's thousands of pounds worth of equipment here.

He looms unnecessarily close behind me and peers at the equipment. He moves along the line of TVs until he reaches the end and finally turns towards me.

"You've not seen this room before?" he asks.

Well technically I have but not when it's been like this – and I'm not sure which is more unsettling: this or the museum of weird exhibits.

"Why would I?"

"Well you did ask for the key and you were here before me. Are you trying to play a little joke on me Miss Norton?"

Seeing as there still appears to be no bathroom I fail to see what is funny.

"That," he says pointing to one of the stickers attached to the plastic covering.

I move over to look as he continues to jabber in my ear.

"I assume you found the packages after all. You know you only had to ask, after all, I did say the signing of papers was just a formality and if you wanted to keep it all hush hush, then I'm sure you could rely on me to keep my mouth closed. Captain of discretion, me."

I peer at the sticker but it doesn't mean anything to me.

'Spiral Industrials.'

I look to John-James for clarification.

"It's a bit late to look all innocent now Miss Norton. It's obvious that you've had this all set up. After all you are one of the senior directors of Spiral Industrials."

CHAPTER TWENTY FOUR:
"…if…"

A director, a senior director? A smug smile creeps onto my lips. My parents would have been so proud of this unlikely achievement and me too if I knew what this accomplishment actually was. Nevertheless it sounds good and it seems to impress John-James, who is nodding and smiling at me as though he has just been let in on a private joke.

"No wonder you asked to get a key in advance. This must have taken some doing. Of course, technically you should have waited for the papers to be signed but I'm sure it's not a problem with such prestigious clients."

Now that I've been established as important I feel rather annoyed by this comment as though he's morphed into some lackey who is impertinently questioning my methods. It's startling how quickly I adjust to this level of superiority; I've never had as much as an assistant, never mind a lackey. Could I be an ordering-people-about sort of person? Maybe I could.

"Perhaps, but as you rightly point out I am a very prestigious client."

Yes, I seem to be warming to this role.

"Of course, I didn't mean to sound rude. So do you think you will be able to sign the papers today?"

"Surely the lawyers will take care of that."

I hope I'm not supposed to be a lawyer.

"Of course Miss Norton, I realise you're very busy and clearly there must be lots to do here. And if you need any help?"

"You could help get me some nice flowery sofas."

John-James frowns. I don't think that was the kind of help he was offering. He takes a dramatic panoramic sweep of the attic before finally resting his gaze back on me. He then dips his head as though to pass on some conspiratorial information.

"I know it's none of my business but what exactly is all this stuff for?" he asks.

Good question. It might help if I knew what Spiral Industrials actually does. They sound very important but they can't be that big or I would probably have heard of them. Could they have been the clients I was supposed to meet on the day I lost my memory? I'm guessing we bumped into each other at some point in order to appoint me director. Director! It does sound good.

Luckily John-James isn't the type to allow dead air time.

"Of course I understand, very hush hush eh?" he says. "Top secret operations here in Field View – no one would guess! And here I was thinking this was just going to be a holiday home. Don't worry I won't tell anyone."

Yeah right. Though I'd be interested to know exactly what he *would* tell them.

"Yes very classified," I confirm.

"This must be the latest technology then. The screens must all be touch and wireless. I bet you just have to speak to them and they do as you ask. Am I right?"

He might as well be. He turns expectantly towards me with his extraordinarily wide mouth beaming as though expecting a reward. So he thinks they are computers; well you wouldn't need to talk to your telly – except to ask it to turn over channels or maybe to record something or…ok maybe you could but again why would I order a dozen of them to be delivered to my attic. Or a dozen computers I suppose.

So could I get the information out of Andy's memory stick in one of these? I take a look at the side of one of the screens to see if they have any USB ports. I'm no expert but disappointingly the ports look too intricately shaped for a normal memory stick. Before I can explore further I am interrupted once more.

"You want me to fire one of these up?" asks John-James enthusiastically.

I don't know. I have little experience with computers and although I can do basic things like write and send reports and even buy the odd trinket or two, I have successfully managed without touching or clicking on the majority of keys or menus. So how would I cope with something that doesn't even have buttons?

"Well I don't know if that's appropriate, although I can't imagine that there will be any confidential..."

"Great!"

Did I say yes? John-James seems to think so as he tears off the plastic covering of the nearest screen.

"Wow. This looks amazing"

He scrutinizes the screen, and the oohing seems to suggest he is making sense of his findings.

"I've never seen anything like this before – you are *so* lucky."

John-James pulls out something from the side of the screen which I am guessing is a remote control.

"This is cool. I really must get my Uncle to update our systems. Obviously we couldn't afford anything like this – I bet it has multi cores and hyper threading and has a fully unlocked multiplier."

What is he on about?

"I bet the download capacity is titanic."

He can understand all of this just by looking?

I watch in astonishment as John-James starts swaying around the room as though he is some demented Tom Cruise tapping at his arm and pointing to the screen.

"I've never seen one of these before!"

Me neither.

He bends down and flicks a switch and one of the screens powers into life. The screen turns orange and we both jump back when a voice booms out from nowhere and demands authorization.

John-James hurriedly removes the control and passes it to me. It looks like a keyboard fused into some strong type of material. I try not to look too surprised and take it from him.

"I'd better sort this out later."

But at least I now know how to switch the thing on.

I look at the armband control thingy carefully but I still can't see where the key thingy could be attached.

"Ow!"

Something on the not-so-soft keyboard thing scratches me, like a pin accidently left in a shirt.

The screen suddenly explodes into what looks like a thousand colours and a bright logo showing the words 'Spiral Industrials' appears.

'DNA recognition activated. Welcome Sarah Norton.'

"Wow," says John-James.

Wow indeed.

"How did it do that?"

Coincidence? I rub at my sore wrist. It is throbbing in exactly the same place as my chip. If I'm going to be probed I definitely prefer the scanning method.

"Like you said, very high tech."

'Command not recognised!'

It's only been on a minute and this thing is already getting on my nerves.

"Give it a command," suggests John-James excitedly. The computer is not the only thing testing my nerves and I give John-James a glare.

"Sorry, none of my business. Though technically this is…" He stops. The first sign of tact he's revealed. "Perhaps we'd better conclude things downstairs," he adds and turns dejectedly towards the stairs.

I feel suddenly guilty as though I've offended him.

'Perimeter breach!' barks the computer.

We both look towards the screen and see that it is showing what looks like a live camera shot of the front of the cottage. Someone is approaching the front door. Andy? The person has short dark hair and they are too slim and definitely too short to be him. I run through my small repertoire of people I have remembered meeting in the last five years: Peter, Uncle George, Ms Malone, the sisters and of course; Simon Greaves. But none of them fit the silhouette of the approaching figure. Whoever it is looks very determined. At the door the person stops and looks directly into the camera:

"I need to speak to you Miss Norton."

"Who…?" begins John-James but I have no idea. The face peering up at us does indeed seem vaguely familiar but all I can make out are two dark eyes burning into the camera, seemingly filled with anger.

"I think you'd better go." I say to John-James.

Suddenly the lights flicker on and off and my estate agent has disappeared.

Not possible.

I look at the screen and the camera shot has been slightly obscured by the word 'accepted'.

Accepted by or for what? Surely I didn't just facilitate John-James's sudden departure? No matter how irritating he is he doesn't deserve to be 'disappeared'.

The face on the screen suddenly pulls back and I see John-James scampering past and heading towards his car.

Thank goodness. Either this senior director thing is going to my head or all the comings and goings in the cottage are making me a little crazy.

'Property breach!' barks the computer once more.

This time the screen splits into several sections. Now I really do feel important, and a little scared. John-James' unprofessionalism in failing to shut the door behind him has allowed the angry stranger to enter.

Another movement draws my attention. Andy! My hero! Where has he come from? He's wandering about the kitchen – surely he must have heard John-James running past? Another screen shows the large unmistakable silhouette of Uncle George. What's going on down there? Another section of the screen is now showing my sofa – the flowery one. There are two figures sitting there but it's hard to make out who they are.

I touch my wrist remote but there are no useful buttons marked zoom. I feel a bit silly but if the controls are voice activated maybe I can just ask it to zoom in for me.

'Zoom in!'

The words: 'Confirm camera number.' flash onto the screen. I look closely and see each section is marked with a number.

'Camera three!'

The screen duly changes and the sofa and its occupants fall into focus.

'Stop!'

Downstairs might be becoming overcrowded but the two people I am looking at now can't be down there with them – although I can only vouch with any certainty for one of them-because I know *I* am standing right here.

On the screen are pictures of me, talking with Simon Greaves.

These must be archive films, but how can they be if I haven't even moved in yet? So what am I watching? I take a closer look and it seems that I am the only one doing any talking; in fact Simon is barely moving. I look to be gesticulating wildly and I have something shiny in my hand that I can't quite make out. Is it a knife? But there's no way I would ever threaten anyone and Simon, unlike Amelia, hadn't reacted badly to my unexpected appearance at his home. So what's going on?

"Sarah!"

I'd momentarily forgotten about the angry stranger; so there's at least one person downstairs. And it's hardly going to take long for them to find me.

"Sarah. We need it sorting."

We, now? Who's we I wonder.

And what is it that I need to sort?

Well if it was before yesterday tea time it could have been anything. And after? Well a lot has happened; I suppose it could be to do with the files or the memory stick, although as I like to keep pointing out, if only to myself, it wasn't me who stole these. Is possession a crime though? I am, after all, carrying them.

I can hear someone banging about downstairs.

I hope every day isn't as hectic as this. The little angry guy downstairs continues to bang and suddenly, rather than being scared, I feel like I've had enough and storm down the stairs to tell him so.

I feel decreasingly less confident as I descend the stairs and the violent sounds become increasingly louder. But I remember I am now the senior director of a fancy-sounding company and almost the owner of a country cottage and I am spurred on.

"How dare you break in and destroy my property," I cry, hopefully with authority.

The little angry guy, who was in the process of looking under the blue sofa, turns and lets it crash down with a thud.

I hold my nerve.

"What are you doing here?"

He turns towards me. Not a guy at all, but a rather attractive small woman with short, chestnut brown hair, probably in her early thirties. She is immaculately dressed in another expensive looking suit but she looks less intimidating than Ms Malone.

"Hello Sarah."

Are there *any* people who don't know me? I don't know whether to feel unsettled or flattered. But actually there is something very familiar about her. An old client perhaps?

"Should I know you?" I ask.

"You have known me," she answers cryptically.

"Right, well if you can't be more helpful I think you should go."

"Not yet. I need to put something right."

Well there are plenty of things to choose from – bringing back Frankie would be at the top of my list.

"Go on," I encourage.

The woman stands up and I take a step back. Do I know her? She seems curiously at ease with our awkward encounter which suggests she is used to being in control. And then she smiles and I can sense that she is used to being admired and obeyed.

"Well. You've got yourself into a pickle. Taking something you shouldn't?"

She needs to narrow it down.

Files, car, necklace? I put a hand protectively against my neck. Idiot! Now she'll know where it is.

"I've no idea what you're talking about," I try.

"I know," she replies unexpectedly.

"Well then. I'm sure we can sort out this misunderstanding," I offer.

She looks at me. "You're lucky it wasn't properly loaded."

"The taser? But I didn't steal that..."

"Taser? It's not..," she pauses as though changing her mind about explaining something. "We still have to reconfigure the coal,"

What does she know about the coal? Does she know it's broken? Even though I had instructions to break it I'm sure I wasn't supposed to lose its contents.

"Okay, well how about a nice cup of tea and we'll have a little chat," I suggest.

"Sit down Miss Norton," she says.

Who does she think she is?

"Well I'm having one," I say with as much confidence as someone who knows full well that there is no tea to be made can muster, and head towards the kitchen.

As soon as she is out of sight I feel around in my pocket for the bits of broken coal. Where to hide them? I can hear her moving around so I don't have much time. I choose the fridge which is empty except for the plastic tub containing John-James's lunch. It's highly unlikely he'll return for it so without much thought I quickly open it and stuff the pieces in amongst the cheese.

"Nothing to make tea with anyway," I say as brightly as I can as she walks through the kitchen door.

"I know," she says.

What the..?

She walks into the kitchen and I think I've been rumbled. Instead she leans forward and flicks a switch above the fridge.

"I always think a fridge is more productive when it's turned on."

She heads for the door but before she leaves she turns.

"I can go now. But first perhaps we should also shed a little light on the subject."

And with that she flicks on the light and disappears.

CHAPTER TWENTY FIVE: "…someday…"

"Ah there you are."

I turn around and there's Andy.

What happened to the woman?

"You were a long time getting the stuff from the car. You haven't lost it have you?"

I hope not. I feel inside my jacket. I really must get myself a bag. All this stuff is literally weighing me down, not to mention the responsibility involved in keeping it safe. The package is still there and now that the woman's left I can retrieve my coal.

"Just a second."

I run towards the fridge and open it. Nothing.

"Have you eaten anything out of the fridge?" I ask him.

"What?"

Andy looks bewildered. Again.

"I hid my coal in some cheese," I offer, by way of explanation.

"The piece in the museum?" he asks.

I'd forgotten that he was unaware I'd snuck the coal back into my pocket after he left. I don't know why I hid it from him or why he told me to put it there in the first place – it's not really his business.

"How did it get into some cheese?"

A very good question that would involve a very long answer involving a colourful estate agent and a small but rather aggressive stranger, which I think I'll skip.

"It doesn't matter."

And yet I suspect it does. I take a breath and consider what type of sofa I have today. My head hurts and I could really do with a sit down on a nice soft flowery one.

I walk past Andy back into the lounge. Flowery. Well done John-James.

Come to think of it, the sofa is always flowery when Andy is around and either he's been busy with a broom or the layers of dust have magically disappeared too.

I gratefully flop down onto the soft seat.

"What about the file?" Andy asks impatiently.

"What about it?"

Obviously I do know but I just need a couple of minutes.

"Come on. What if you have another blackout? You can't just be wasting time lounging on the sofa."

Sounds like his best idea so far.

"Anyway, you'd be here to remind me."

Or would he? He's right. He only has to go and turn on a kettle maybe and poof! I might wake up and not know that he'd ever been here. I'd just be left sitting here alone and clueless. Nevertheless, I'm still sorely tempted to give up and have a little nap on this wonderfully soft sofa.

"Sarah!"

"Fine!"

I pull out the package, remove the sheet and sit up.

"There's a short list of names on the sheet. Two of which I recognised, one of which was my own."

"Really? But I guess that's not surprising, seeing as you were an inmate at Barton. Who was the other?"

"George Franks."

"Doctor Uncle George Franks?"

"I presume so."

"Well that's interesting."

"I thought so too. Especially as you thought the list was of patients."

"Yes, but not your typical patients. I mean what hospitals keep confidential information lying around offices, handwritten and on bits of paper? I'm sure there's got to be something different about these people. And what is Uncle George doing on the list?"

"The inmates taking over the asylum?"

"It doesn't seem likely but we didn't see anyone else there at Barton."

"Except Ms Malone."

"Yes well, you wouldn't rule her out would you?"

"And Amelia, she's on the list."

"What about Cindy Romero?"

"No. I would have remembered a name like that."

"Let's see then."

I pass the sheet over.

"And when exactly did you see this list?"

"About quarter of an hour ago."

"When we were still at Mary's house?"

Okay so maybe it was some other time.

"When you went missing – I read it then – in the toilet. But the cottage was different again, it had the blue sofa but not the red armchairs –well I didn't see them – and I don't think I'd even moved in yet."

"I think you'll find *I* went nowhere. It was you who disappeared and I've never been privy to this blue sofa you speak of."

Andy looks carefully at the paper.

"Didn't you say there was a *short* list of names on this?"

Here we go again, the vanishing word trick.

"I promise you I saw them. There were about six."

He stares at the sheet for a few moments and then shows me the piece of paper. Instead of disappearing, the list has more than doubled, filling the entire page.

"That's clever. Anyone you recognise?"

Instead of answering he just passes it across.

There are now at least a dozen more scribbled names with more recent dates.

I look up at Andy to see what his reaction is but he's difficult to read.

I look back at the sheet. At once I see Frankie's name, written at the side of mine. That definitely wasn't there before. Above mine, Amelia has Mary's name against it and Peter is written alongside George's; both are marked with the swirly symbol I'd seen before. I glance up and down the list . A few of the new names have been crossed out and I try to see if I can still read them. I don't think I recognise anything until about two thirds down. Despite there being a thick black line through it I can still clearly make out the name of Simon Greaves. I already knew he was a patient at Barton Hall but why has his name been crossed out?

I don't expect to know any other names but near the bottom, next to some question marks I see a Jakob with a k and a Cindy Romero, and then one more name that I recognise.

"Looks like we're all members of the same gang," says Andy cheerfully.

There, at the very bottom of the list, is Andy's name.

He seems to be taking it very well. Did he already know it would be there?

"So do you have any idea what this list is about? Why our names are on it?" I ask.

"Of course not!"

"Only I thought you were a bus driver."

"What, and bus drivers aren't allowed on the list!"

"I didn't mean it like that! I didn't mean to insult you, I just meant that I thought you turning up yesterday was just by chance."

"Well I certainly didn't sabotage my own bus if that's what you're thinking."

"No, of course not." Or did he? "But it doesn't look like it was so random any more either."

"You think we were supposed to meet?"

"Well you definitely got some help. Mary's car, remember? Conveniently waiting near the very bus stop that you happen to break down at?"

"True. But how could she know I would break down there?"

"No idea. But I bet you she did."

"And she wanted us to meet for what reason exactly?"

"No idea. But if you hadn't come along I can't see how I would have found out about Barton and I wouldn't have met Simon Greaves or got the letter sent to him."

"Of course, your letter! Did that tell you anything?"

"Nothing more. If anything, the paper seemed emptier than before."

"But you said you thought you were reading it at a time before you lived here, perhaps it was also before you even wrote the letter? In which case there wouldn't be anything to read. If it's like the list of names perhaps the words only appear in the right time line.

"Maybe," I agree and scrabble in the package for the paper once more.

"Which means that by now I will have written it and I should now be able to.yes!"

It is another letter:

Hi Sarah,

Ok a disappointing start.

I know you'll be disappointed, but at the moment I have as little idea as to when we will find Frankie as you – but I hope that will change soon.

Which brings me to why I sent these letters.

Letters? I sent them to other places too?

If you're reading this, you have become distracted. Do not be tempted to try and discover what has happened to you since you took this contract. It will not help you to revisit the past or the people you have been 'involved' with.

Carry on with the task, it may seem strange to you but you should trust the decision you made to take part in this venture.

I stop reading for a second and see Andy once again looking expectantly. I don't know what to tell him because I don't really know what is going on so I just shrug and read the last bit of the letter.

It's important for you to focus. The Alternator (the thing that looks like a taser) will not cause any real harm so don't be afraid to use it.

The Alternator? Amelia mentioned that, just before she was freaked by Andy's taser. Coincidence?

Everything is tied up with Frankie and we will only get him back if you complete the tasks we have been set.

Trust yourself – even if you don't trust those around you. And importantly, in order for this to work you need to keep calm and break the coal. Good luck.

There we go with the coal again. Is that the best advice I've got? Keep calm and break some coal? I don't even have the blasted stuff anymore and even if I did it's too late, it's already broken. Does this mean I've failed, that I don't get Frankie back?

I pretend to keep reading while I consider the rest of the letter. The only person I trust is Andy but if he's been lying about his so-called taser can I believe anything he's said? Is he even a bus driver?

"Do you have to wear special ID when you're driving buses?"

"What?"

Ha, I've caught him out.

"What's that got to do with anything?"

"Well do you?"

"You're supposed to, yes."

And here comes the part when he says he's conveniently lost it or probably left it on the bus.

"You mean like this?"

He puts his hand into his breast pocket and pulls out a plastic laminated photo.

I take it from him and see his face smiling back at me with the bus logo watermarked across his chin.

"Why did you want to see it?" he asks. "What does the letter say? Does it suggest I'm an imposter or something?"

I feel my cheeks warm at the directness of his question. So now what? All I've managed to do is to annoy him.

I turn the photo card over. It looks genuine enough.

"It doesn't say you're licensed to hold a weapon though," I add tentatively.

"A weapon?"

"Your so-called taser."

"Right. You're right."

I'm not sure I want to be this time.

"We don't really get given tasers. I mean bus drivers aren't really issued with tasers."

"Oh, so what you said about people being killed on buses was just a lie? Why would you tell me that?"

"No," he jumps in quickly. "The city bus killings really did happen, but the bit about drivers being trained to use tasers wasn't true."

"So why did you say it and more to the point what are you doing with one then?"

"I had to explain what I was doing with one, so I made up the story of bus drivers needing protection. I didn't want to alarm you."

Alarm bells are certainly ringing now.

"So what are you doing with one?"

"I found it."

"Where?"

"Here."

"Here, where?"

"Behind the sofa."

"You're telling me that you just happened to find a taser lying around my cottage and you didn't think to tell me about it?"

"Well when you saw it you looked terrified, so I knew it wasn't yours, or at least you didn't remember it as yours. You assumed it belonged to me and at that moment it seemed the best thing to do."

"Really?"

"Yes! You were already vulnerable, not remembering anything and when some mysterious intruder knocked me out I thought it was a good idea to keep hold of it."

"But all that stuff about Tommy something or other?"

"Just because I don't take one to work doesn't mean I don't know stuff and anyway I thought it might convince you I was telling the truth."

"Well it worked then, except now I don't know what to believe."

"Sorry, I've never actually used one before."

"What about Uncle George?"

"It certainly had some effect on him."

"Do tasers usually make their target unconscious?"

And possibly disappear?

"Like I said, I've never actually used one."

"Are you sure it really is a taser? Can I have a look?"

Could this actuallybe the Alternator that my letter was referring to?

Andy delves into his jacket but I wouldn't know a taser from a toy gun. And rather than pass it over he stares at it.

"Although now I look at it properly," he says hesitantly "I must admit I've never seen a Tommy Swift quite like this before. I just assumed it was a taser."

"Except you don't think it acts like one."

"Yes, there is that," he admits.

He finally hands it over. There's something about it that is vaguely familiar and I try to wrest out a stubborn morsel of memory – maybe I've seen one in a magazine once or maybe it really is mine. It's as likely as me being a director of a global company, so frankly ludicrous. But then it comes to me. I have seen it before and it was in my own hands.

CHAPTER TWENTY SIX:
"…soon…"

When I was watching myself on the screen in the attic I was brandishing something shiny at Simon Greaves. Is this the same thing and what exactly was I doing with it?

"Have you heard of something called an Alternator?"

"In a car?"

"Not that apparently it's something that looks a bit like a taser, I think this is one."

"An Alternator? Sounds a bit weird. Can I have a closer look?

Andy takes it back and inspects it from every angle and then starts twisting different sections – what is it with men and wanting to take things apart?

"What does it do?

"Not sure."

He continues to prod and pull a little while longer having, I presume, failed to glean anything even vaguely useful before he finally gives in and shrugs.

"Any idea?""

Surely he must have deduced something from his lengthy inspection.

"I don't know," he sighs, "not without actually trying it out."

I grab the Alternator from him, pretending to look at it.

"I didn't mean it seriously," he adds quickly.

Maybe I should try it out on Andy. The letter didn't say what to do with it but there's clearly something I'm supposed to do. Apparently it doesn't cause any real harm, Simon's ok – at least by *most* accounts.

"So there's nothing on it at all?" I ask.

What am I thinking? A label with 'This is the property of Sarah Norton' on it?

"Just the manufacturer's mark on it, the ammonite."

I look at the swirly design engraved into the handle. It seems to be becoming a recurring image.

"Do you know what it represents?"

"Of course, it's the logo for Spiral Industrials, but there's nothing useful in that, seeing that they make practically everything nowadays."

Spiral Industrials. Should I share rumours of my new position with Andy? It was only a second ago that I was considering shooting him. I put the Alternator, if that's what it is, in my pocket in case I change my mind and decide to share.

"Apparently I'm a director of Spiral Industrials."

I wait for him to look impressed but he just laughs.

"Really?"

"Apparently."

"Apparent to whom? When did this become apparent exactly, why would you think that?"

I get the impression he's not taking this news very seriously. I use my sternest look but he continues to laugh.

"What's so funny?"

"Sorry." he gulps. "It's just out of all the unlikely things that you've said in the last couple of days this has to be the most farfetched. You are joking aren't you?"

"Well, until a half an hour ago I'd never even heard of Spiral Industrials, but I'm not joking. It would explain why I was given the cottage, if I'm so very important."

"So important that you've never even heard of them. What is your job exactly then? I thought you said you were some kind of insurance fraud detective. How did you suddenly get promoted to a senior position with one of the biggest companies in the world?"

"I don't remember do I? Maybe I just applied for it."

"And how did you find out about this promotion to, what was it, managing director?"

"I didn't say managing."

"Managing!" he roars. "You can't even manage to remember you have a job!"

I feel my face redden. He's right, but I feel hurt and he notices.

"Okay, I didn't mean it like that," he says. "It's not that I don't think you could. It's just...."

"It's fine." I cut him off before he manages to become even more insulting.

"So how did you find this out?"

Why didn't I just keep my mouth shut? Was I trying to impress him?

"An estate agent was here."

"Of course. Did you find out what the For Sale sign was all about?"

"I'm not sure, but I don't think it's for sale anymore. Anyway, he told me that Spiral Industrials had bought the cottage for me."

"Well it seems a little bit out of the way for an office."

"True. But it has proved very handy so far, for Barton and Simon and you I guess."

"Thanks. But why wouldn't an important director like you have a car or a chauffeur? Why would you be using public transport? Not many directors go to work by bus."

"And how many do you know? Never mind. So what do you know about Spiral Industrials?"

He frowns.

"What's with the face? What's wrong with them?"

"I don't know really. But any company that gets so huge in such a short time has to be suspect. They've only been in existence for a few years and yet everyone knows their name – even you – and nearly everything seems to have their name on it. I think they bought out hundreds of companies."

"So lots of people lost their jobs?"

"Actually I think it was the opposite, the company created lots of jobs. The press seems to treat it like some kind of philanthropic company – apparently giving good jobs to the unemployable and providing well-paid training to school leavers."

"What's wrong with that? We sound like the perfect employers. I'm sure I wouldn't have taken the job if they were dodgy. I do have principles you know."

At least I remember having some once.

"Yeah I'm sure, but it's still a bit of a stretch to accept you as a boss of the biggest company on the planet."

"Why? It sounds like they have very sound employment policies."

"Most policies don't include employing people in comas. Although they do say they give jobs to the unemployable." He thinks he's so funny. "Maybe you were a sleeping partner!"

I'm not laughing.

"I thought you didn't believe Amelia's version of events?" I say.

"It was just a joke. You can still trust me you know."

"Can I?"

"Why ask that? Why now? Did your letter say something about me?"

He waits for a confirmation or denial.

"Not especially. It did mention this Alternator, but no details."

"Anything else?"

"Not much, just to stay calm and break my coal."

"The same coal you hid in some cheese?"

"A cheese sandwich actually. It seemed a good idea at the time – but it was already broken anyway."

"So you *did* break it then?"

"I don't think so. Not that I remember."

"And when was this?"

"I found the broken bits of coal upstairs in the safe and then hid it in a sandwich but now it's not there and I think the content of the coal was important, maybe even leading me to Frankie, but now it's all gone."

"Are you sure it was the coal from the museum?"

"It had unusual indentations so why wouldn't it be? It's not like we're sitting in a coal mine. What are the chances of finding random bits of coal around here?"

"Well, the bit with the metal in is in the museum."

Now he'll really think I never trusted him.

"I didn't leave it there Andy. I know you put it in the exhibition but I took it out again."

"Yeah I know."

"How?"

"Well you know when you disappeared this morning?" When I was looking for you I found it."

"Found what?"

"The lump of coal."

"A whole lump?"

"Yes."

"Where? Behind the sofa?"

"No need to be facetious."

"Sorry. So where is it?"

"I put it back."

"What do you mean?"

"When I was looking for you I went up to the attic and when I was there I put it back."

"So it's in the museum?"

"I told you it was."

That's true.

"Why didn't you say anything before?"

"You never asked about it before."

I suppose it wasn't the most eventful moment of the day, finding a lump of coal on the floor, but it might turn out to be the most important.

"Let's see if it's still there."

Andy jumps up, eager to do something I think, rather than just sit around becoming increasingly awkward. Will the museum still be upstairs? When I think about it, the cottage really only seems different when he's *not* around.

At the top of the stairs I hold my breath before pushing open the door.

Darkness.

We both reach for the light switch at the same time and our hands touch. It's more awkward than Mills and Boon and we quickly pull them apart, luckily distracted by the sudden illumination of the room.

About half a dozen spotlights turn on in unison and to my genuine surprise we are back in the museum.

"It's actually still here," I exclaim.

"What were you expecting?"

If there'd been a large whale swimming around in a tank of champagne I wouldn't have been particularly surprised. So why am I amazed by the sight of the strange exhibition? And yet its presence is also reassuring.

But what about the coal? I hurry past the dinosaur footprint to where I first found the amber necklace. I quickly raise my hand to check it's still there. Yes – so that makes at least two things in their expected place. What's going on? Is my erratic existence becoming less chaotic? Surely this can't carry on, and yet there in front of me, nestling in its napkin is my coal. And it's in one piece. Does that count as predictable or not?

"Aha! I told you I'd found it," Andy says.

At last I get the opportunity to find out what happens when I finally get to break it.

Andy looks expectantly, keen to know what's going to happen next. He's not the only one.

I pick up the coal and turn it over in my hands, checking for the little shard of metal. Once more I'm not disappointed. The coal does indeed appear to be my very own miraculously rejuvenated little lump.

Now I'm finally back in a position to follow my own instructions I'm beginning to feel somewhat hesitant. It certainly doesn't help that a certain somebody is breathing down my neck and studying my every movement.

I turn and glare.

Maybe I just need a little privacy. After all I don't have a clue what might finally happen if I do decide to crack open my coal. Might I be transported somewhere else in time or space? Home perhaps? With Frankie? The letter I wrote to myself insinuated that this was the only way to find him so what's stopping me?

Because if nothing happens, what then?

One way to find out.

I lift the coal above my head and smack it against the display.

CHAPTER TWENTY SEVEN:
"…we could…"

Nothing. No bright lights or swirls in time, just Andy looking at me aghast.

"What are you doing?"

It seems pretty obvious to me.

"You can't do that," he adds which means he clearly did know what I was doing, or attempting to do, because the coal appears to have remained intact apart from some black powdery residue.

"You might break it."

Ok so maybe he doesn't know.

Andy picks up the lump of coal.

"What's the point of me going to the trouble of getting this back if you're just going to destroy it?"

That *is* the point.

He wraps his hands protectively around it, looking at me scornfully.

I hadn't anticipated his attachment to my coal. Maybe it has magical powers that compel him to protect it. Well if so they don't extend to me. I'm tired of pussyfooting around and anyway it doesn't belong to him. So I grab it back and smash it once more against the exhibition case.

"Stop!"

But I smash it again.

And again.

And again.

Eventually the shards of coal splinter enough to reveal the metal within.

"Why?"

Andy appears to have accepted the fate of the little lump of coal.

"I need to break it," I explain.

"I can see that, but why? It might have been worth a fortune!"

Didn't think of that.

"Too late now," I say. I brush the remaining bits of coal dust from the metal and look to see what I'm left with.

"What is it?"

I hold it up for him to look at.

"Oh, that's interesting."

I wait for him to add something else… something useful.

"What is it?" he repeats.

To me it looks just like the end of the memory stick that Andy stole from Barton.

"It's from a memory stick, isn't it?"

Andy takes it from me for a more detailed examination.

"I suppose it's a bit like one, but look here, where it could plug into something, there's a jagged edge, more like a key design."

I wrestle in my pocket for Andy's stick and take a close look at it.

It looks the same to me.

"There at the end."

Andy points at the lattice of metal at the bottom of the stick. I can barely see any difference.

"See how it has a different configuration? I don't know what this is supposed to be connected to."

"Maybe it only fits into prehistoric computers."

"Possibly, but it doesn't matter, the information is still useless if we don't own a machine that's able to read it." He says. "Unless you know of such a computer?"

"I might."

One or two, but getting to them is another matter.

How do I get to the right time zone or whatever it is that changes the interior of the rooms?

So far I've always managed to get back to Andy or him back to me. But it's been more luck than management.

"So how do you get yourself to this computer then?"

I look around the room for inspiration and see that tucked up behind one of the spotlights is a camera; presumably the same one that was pointing at the safe. I wonder if anyone is watching me at this moment.

Suddenly the lights go out.

I stand very still and close my eyes. The glare of the spotlights remains stained onto the inside of my eyelids.

For a second I think I can hear giggling.

I open my eyes. More fog.

"Did you switch off the lights?" I ask Andy.

"No," he replies.

Sometimes things feel different in the dark, like something has disappeared or been added, but when I switch them back on nothing obvious had changed at all.

There has to be some easy way.

I feel in my pocket for my door key. I can tell straight away that it's not there but I still frantically rustle my hand around the various pieces of paper just in case.

"Have you seen my door key?"

"I don't think so. Where did you have it last?"

Usually that would be a very irritating question but in this case it's just pointless. Where I last had it is not necessarily where it still is.

"Have you tried the door? That's where it was last time. What do you want it for?"

"I think I might need it to find out what is on this memory stick. Wait here I'll go and check."

I leave him with no choice as I step carefully down the stairs, keeping out a hopeful eye out for a glint of metal.

I head for the front door. What key did I need for the computers? It had to be the vivid yellow balloon which conveniently was the one most recently attached to the house key.

There's nothing in the lock.

Maybe it's still on the outside of the door, I don't remember taking it out when I followed Andy into the cottage. With little expectation I open the door and look but it's not there. I step outside and look around although I realise how absurd it would be to find the key just hanging around outside.

I'm about to go inside and start searching irrationally under sofas and inside fridges when I notice that the name plaque, covered in daisies, to the right of the door.

Last time I looked at this plaque I was almost tempted to leave the door key behind it – had I been tempted to do that before? At home I always kept a spare key behind a picture frame outside the flat door as I was always prone to losing my key, so nothing new. Could I have ever left a key here?

I almost don't want to look – it is only possible to cope with so many disappointments before you want to give up.

Blimey!

Several keys are bunched up together on a row of hooks.

Am I responsible for putting all these here?

I don't know whether to laugh or cry. If I put these here it would suggest that I have been here for a very long time. And look where it's got me, stupidly running around looking for keys to what?

Information that is either pointless or forgotten. Any second now I could have another black out and be at square one again. And yet I feel I'm really close to finding Frankie; I just need the right source of information at the right time.

At the front of the row is the ammonite key, did George put it there when he came to visit? Or Peter? Is he still around, watching, giggling at my idiotic floundering? I just hope the one I'm looking for somehow miraculously found its way here.

I scoop about half a dozen key rings including a tiny tennis ball and a toy bus and am tempted to slip them all in my pocket but I think that at several points I must have decided to leave them all here realising that I would rediscover them. And also, eventually, I would have time to find out where they all lead to – but for now I need to find out why, or if, this information from the coal is so important. I sort through them but none of them are the key I'm looking for. Disappointed, I shove the keys back on the hooks. As I swing the plaque back something falls to the floor. I move my foot and there lying on the ground is the estate agent's key with Brightstone and Nephews' name still floating in their yellow balloon. Was it hanging from a hook after all? How could it not have been?

Time to see if it works.

I pick it up, pull the door to and twist the key back and forth in the lock.

I wait a few seconds as though postponing my grand entry might have any positive bearing on the extraordinary result I was hoping for.

And then I go for it.

It's dim inside. I avoid the urge to switch on the light and wait for my eyes to adjust to the gloom. The floor is reassuringly bare and if I move the edge of my foot along the floor I can accumulate a sizeable amount of dust.

I'm about to take a step forward when I hear a car approaching. I quickly push the door to and crouch below the letter box. Of course the car might be passing by or visiting a different building, although so far there has been no sign of anyone in any of the other cottages on Field View.

The car slows down and I stay still as I hear someone getting out and heading towards me.

There's a sudden hard knocking. And then a familiar voice:

"Miss Norton, are you here yet?"

John-James.

I can't go through all that again.

I sit nervously hoping that he won't try the door.

0f course he will.

I impulsively thrust up my hand and push hard against the handle and immediately feel it straining to push down.

He lets go and I'm hoping that the unlikelihood of me sitting behind the door will work in my favour and it won't occur to him to try pushing harder.

Luckily I hear him walking back to the car – perhaps to get a key – and I take my chance and run for the stairs. I race up the staircase and stumble into the attic.

'Welcome Sarah.'

I haven't even switched on the light and yet around me several screens have burst into life and are emanating an eerie glow across the room.

I can feel my wrist pulsating slightly as though a splinter is being tugged out with a needle.

"Shh."

Relief that I have managed to locate the computers is dampened by my anxiety at having had to keep John-James at bay. I wonder if he remembers our last meeting – maybe he hasn't yet experienced visiting this room or being scared off by that strange woman. Why else would he be here if not to show me around again? And that woman's familiarity is still niggling away at me.

I suspect it won't matter to John-James if he thinks we've met or not – he'll still blabber on, which means I ought to get a move on.

I get out the device that Andy took from Barton Hall. I look at the initials F.N. taped to the front – it could mean anything – but at the moment, while there's still uncertainty, there's hope. Maybe it would be better if I didn't discover what's on it, just for a while longer.

I might get my wish.

It doesn't look like it could fit into the complicated opening but as I look more closely I think the USB port might have been designed to accommodate a variety of devices. I push it in.

"Sarah Norton – do you require to open the file?" the computer bellows.

"Shh."

"Sarah Norton – do you require a reduction in volume?"

"Yes!"

So far there has been no evidence that John-James has attempted to re-enter the cottage but nevertheless the last thing I need is any attention being drawn to myself.

"Sarah Norton – do you require to open the file?" the computer repeats quietly.

I'm not entirely sure.

"Yes."

One of the large screens fills with light and I am almost blinded by the brightness.

I close my eyes for a second and then reopen them, not daring to believe what I thought I had glimpsed.

It looks like Andy's lucky guess has proved correct.

For there, in front of me on the screen is a picture of Frankie.

It is wonderful to see his face again, even if it is only as a photograph.

I recognise the picture. Frankie would have been around three years old. He's sitting in his blue-and-yellow buggy, smiling up at the camera with a face covered with ice cream.

We'd just been on a trip to a kid's museum and he was about to fall asleep in his push chair as we headed back for the train when we came across a little kiosk selling ice cream. I think it was the first time he had ever attempted to eat ice cream from a cone before and it went nearly everywhere but his mouth –especially over the purple jumper that his gran had just finished knitting for him.

Why is this picture here?

There is some writing underneath. It confirms that it is Frankie Norton aged three years, four months and eight days.

Below is a longer paragraph which virtually reads word for word what I had just remembered about the circumstances of the photo; even down to the bit about him spreading most of the ice cream over his face.

Could the computer be reading my thoughts and transcribing them onto the screen?

I need to see what else is on the file.

"Scroll down," I instruct the computer and I am rewarded with another image of Frankie.

Again I recognise the photo. It was taken in one of those children's play areas attached to a Sea Life Centre. There are pictures of dolphins on the wall behind him and Frankie has his face painted as a pirate complete with facial stubble and an eye patch.

Underneath, once again there is information, giving Frankie's age as just turned four and a few details about the trip to the play area. I remember it was just after his father had taken him to the hairdressers and I had hated the fact that he had lost his lovely long hair. He wasn't trusted again.

The screen keeps moving and more pictures appear – all ones that I vividly remember taking – and all in ascending order of age with about a gap of a year in between each.

So it doesn't take long to reach the year that means the most to me. The year he went missing.

I scroll past a picture of Frankie proudly kneeling alongside a small group of boys – all arms tightly folded except the boy in the middle of the top row who is holding onto a rather small trophy. It was very cold that afternoon. I would have been more tolerant of the weather had I known it was to be his last sporting competition.

And there it is.

The last photo I remember taking of Frankie.

It was recorded on my 'reasonably priced' mobile phone and you can barely make him out but he's definitely there, squashed up together, at the back of the school hall, with the rest of his class. He's resentfully wearing a floppy red Christmas hat and has his mouth opened very slightly – fulfilling the barest minimum requirement for the compulsory singing of carols. I wonder if he would have made more of an effort if he knew it was the last time he would ever perform for his mum.

Undoubtedly not.

I can hardly dare to continue. What if there are no more photos or what if it is worse and the girls were right and there's a photo of him lying mangled on a mortuary table.

The computer obediently scrolls down.

And scrolls down.

Every now and then there are dates written at the side of the screen. But then empty space again.

I am on the verge of giving up when I see the top of a head.

Frankie.

Sitting in a push chair covered in ice cream.

Are the pictures on a loop?

I let the computer continue but they're just the same old photographs.

"Stop!"

The screen freezes on the photo that was taken at the Sea Life Centre.

There is Frankie, smiling as usual against a backdrop of dolphins but instead of a stubbly pirate looking at me he is now sporting some kind of fish face. What's that all about?

I don't remember him having his face decorated as a shark.

I suppose he might have gone with his grandma but it is uncanny how he is standing in exactly the same place with the same tilt of his head.

And then there's the information underneath. 'Just turned four – and a late birthday treat.' It is identical to the remarks written below my pirate-faced Frankie.

"Scroll down." I instruct the computer and a series of photos whizz by until I see the one I want.

Frankie in his push chair.

I look closely as though it is some puzzle from a spot the difference competition. And there it is. The jumper, it's no longer purple but a dark navy blue.

"Scroll down…"

And once again I stop at a picture of my son smiling up at me from his pushchair – his face barely recognisable behind a beard of brown ice cream. What kind of mother would give a young child chocolate ice cream?

I keep scrolling. The series of slightly differing pictures remind me of Simon's news clippings – but I know that at least some of these have to be genuine.

Finally the screen stalls; Frankie is glaring unhappily amongst a host of classmates, resentfully wearing a pair of antlers and a red nose. The last photo.

Except it isn't.

After a few moments the screen continues to scroll. And a completely new photo appears – one I don't recognise.

When Frankie disappeared he was only ten. Now, five years on he would obviously be older, but the photo in front of me is surely not of anyone younger than their late teens.

And yet surely it's the same eyes, nose, mouth.

I look closely to see if it might be a photo-fit. The papers may have run pictures from time to time suggesting what Frankie might have looked like in the years after he went missing. And for the first time I wonder if anyone has noticed my own disappearance.

But the photo doesn't look like one of those bleak missing posters. It looks like it's been taken on a sunny day.

The boy who could be Frankie is squinting into the camera and holding up a pint glass. He's sitting next to someone but all I can make out is part of a dress, a colourful red shift and purple tights.

Could this be Frankie from the future?

I've been bobbing back and forth in this cottage – could I possibly go forward in time to find him? Maybe one of the keys behind the daisy plaque could take me to him?

There is some writing underneath similar to the comments below the younger versions. It unhelpfully notes the picture as being an afternoon out with friends.

I scroll down some more, perhaps hoping for something more concrete – maybe a wedding photo or a picture of an old man who looks to have had a contented life – but there is nothing more, no more dates, nothing.

So what do I make of all this?

Did Andy really just happen to come across this lying about an office in Barton Hall?

And if he didn't, why is it important for me to see this?

It's time to find out what my piece of coal has to tell me.

CHAPTER TWENTY EIGHT:
"…have the..."

I remove the USB from Barton and replace it with the device from the coal. It falls out again. I bend down and look at the complicated arrangement of the USB port and then at the complicated arrangement of my stick.

Surely it must fit. Why else would this bank of computers be here? Wasn't I supposed to come here and do this? What was the point of pushing the idea of breaking the coal if I can't find out what's on it? Why make everything so complicated?

I twiddle with a combination of positions but it won't fit and I'm wary of breaking the memory stick. I finally slump down on the floor and stare at the camera.

"What am I supposed to do?"

Why put me through all of this and then just leave me sitting here without a clue? If someone wanted me to find out what was on the stick why didn't they just tell me to break the coal and pop upstairs straight away?

Except this wasn't *my* upstairs.

My first memory in five years wasn't even in the cottage. I was waiting at a bus stop a couple of miles down the road when suddenly Andy appeared and supposedly saved me and brought me back here. So maybe none of this is to do with me, I just happen to have stumbled over a silly bit of coal and irrationally attached some great significance to it.

For all I know I've never even been here before – there's no sign of anyone being here – not living here at least. There's no sign of normal debris like old clothes or toiletries or even much in the way of food. There are the photos that George showed me which were apparently taken outside the cottage and the film of me and Simon that I saw on the computer screen, but no real evidence like a brush with my hair on.

I look towards the screens. Might they provide proof of my life, perhaps me brushing my teeth or sitting reading a book? Or anything? Anyone?

I look back up to the camera but there has been no movement nor is there any sign of a light that might suggest it is being operated.

My wrist is itching. I look to where the light emanated when I was in Barton. Maybe I'm still DNA activated. I'm wary about speaking to the computer but I don't want to waste an opportunity to find out something useful. Maybe the file of Frankie's photos was just a hint. Could Frankie have been here? Simon was.

"Computer screens on!" I command hopefully.

The room is suddenly illuminated with a sinister yellow glow. I think it worked. Now what?

"Show Frankie."

Nothing. Maybe I need to be more specific.

"Show Frankie Norton."

Still nothing. Maybe it's not working.

"Show Sarah Norton."

The screens fill with identical images of me staring at a bank of computers. Okay so the camera *is* working. I glance up at the camera and see my selves turning towards it.

I'm not over keen on staring at myself at the best of times but seeing a multitude of my ungroomed faces is just too much. When exactly did I last look in a mirror or brush my hair?

Embarrassed by my unkempt appearance I try and restore some order to my wayward hair by struggling to comb my hands through it. Why hadn't any one said anything? I suppose the look fits with George's assessment of me. I look quite frightful.

I can feel and, more alarmingly, see my cheeks redden.

"Stop showing…"

I don't get to finish my sentence. Perhaps my connection with the computer is so strong it can read my thoughts for the ghastly kaleidoscope of me disappears, only to be replaced by further images of myself.

I give a tentative wave but clearly this image is not live – or if it is, it's not the same me sitting here.

The Sarah Norton I am looking at is standing in the kitchen downstairs. Why, given all the money spent on this technology, couldn't any of it have been spent on a modest update of that grubby little kitchen, obviously starting with a well-stocked wine rack? The me downstairs is eating a sandwich – probably strawberry jam – and studying a piece of paper – probably another note from myself. I wonder if I can zoom in and see what it says but before I get a chance to give a command I have put the paper down and picked up a small object. Could it be my coal?

"Zoom!" I call, before this too, disappears.

The camera obediently zooms in and I'm suddenly presented with an oversized image of my face. Again.

"Zoom lower." I'm not sure if this is a proper command but I am immediately rewarded by an undesirable close up of my chin.

"Lower," I call before I discover how five years of neglectful inattention to my beauty regime has affected the quality of my pores.

The camera dutifully pans down. I'm wearing the same jacket that I have on now – shame there isn't an X ray function so I could browse the pockets. I wonder if they contain the same odd assortment of notes that are in mine.

I'm also, I see, wearing the same patterned shirt I have on and judging by the colour I'm pretty sure those are the tops of the same durable trousers. So the chance of finding the key that leads me to an attic filled with a wondrous wardrobe of beautiful clothes is looking unlikely.

However, an attic with an assortment of soaps and cleaning facilities would be useful. I give my sleeve a sniff. It doesn't smell too bad – perhaps when this strange adventure is over I should negotiate a deal with the manufacturers of this superior stain and odour resistant clothing and endorse their product with five years' proof of its enduring effectiveness. I just hope the body inside has a similar immunity against dirt.

"Stop!" The camera has descended too low now and I can't see my hand.

"Zoom out."

The camera slowly reveals more of my torso – not a complimentary angle. Surely if I'd really been in a coma I should be skinny now – you can't have an extra glass of wine or two when you're unconscious.

The camera finally reveals a clear picture of my hand which is holding one of John-James' napkins, when the screen goes black.

So much for advanced technology – even my old laptop could last five minutes before conking out. I'm just about to give the monitor a tried and tested shaking when the screen brightens again.

There I am. Still. Only although I'm still wearing the suit, I'm not in the kitchen anymore. If I ever start writing notes again I must remember to include something useful such as suggesting I buy a new outfit because that doesn't tell me anything about when this tape was made except that it isn't now.

It takes me a couple of seconds to realise I'm looking at myself in the attic, but not in front of the screens. I'm back with the small safe. The camera is pointing directly down towards it just as I remember and I'm kneeling in front of it.

I don't really want to watch myself idiotically trying to figure out what numbers I need to put into the combination lock, or staring vacantly at the top half of the safe which will remain tauntingly shut. I look back to the screen to see if I can make out the shape of the lock but the top half of the safe is no longer visible. I urge myself to move out of the way but when I finally do I realise it is too late. The key hole is no longer there. The door is open.

"Rewind!"

How on earth did I manage that? Have I had the key all along?

I reach for the necklace that I had been so excited about. Did I manage to get it out of the amber without me noticing? I'm pretty sure I haven't had any memory lapses since the last time I looked at it.

I'm right.

The strangely shaped metal still glows through the orange amber. I hold it up to the light in case there is a subtle little opening that might provide me with access to the bit of metal. If there is, it's too subtle to see but as I continue to look I realise if it is a little larger and attached to a bit of plastic it would look very similar to the memory stick from my coal.

Did I open the safe with the contents of my coal? I don't remember doing that either and I was definitely present when I cracked it open a little while ago. So unless I'm looking at a future version of myself I didn't use either the contents of the coal or the amber.

I wish I would budge out of the way before the pictures disappear again.

On the screen, I look like I might have dropped something because I suddenly slump down now.

"Zoom!" I shout before I pop back up again.

The camera zooms down to my feet.

Idiot computer. I need to see what's in the safe.

I'm on the verge of panning up when I get a glimpse of what I'm picking up.

It's still not easy to see but I can make out a solid shiny shape that looks a bit like a toy gun. It's the taser thingy, the Alternator!

It looks like the same one Andy said he found downstairs under the sofa.

I take it out. Maybe I squirreled a few of them back from work one day and secreted them around the place.

Would I have hidden one behind the sofa?

My torso rises and obscures the safe once more.

Idiot.

I wonder if I can rewind.

I need to see what's in the top of the safe.

"Rewind!"

The pictures scramble backwards and I see myself move unnaturally quickly.

I think I should have been more specific with my instructions because I watch myself disappear in a blur that seems to be whizzing back and forth towards the attic door.

"Stop!"

It's a bit difficult to tell if I have succeeded as I am now just staring at a stationary object.

But then the attic door opens.

And finally! I must have got round to writing that memo after all because the horrid, yet sustainable suit that I have been parading is finally gone.

And I've lost weight.

And it isn't me.

To be fair I am looking at her from behind.

All I can tell so far is that she is skinny. She doesn't appear to be wearing retro tights and shifts so that probably rules out the mad sisters. So if I have come across whoever it is in the last few hours it leaves Ms Malone and the woman who looks vaguely familiar who told me off earlier.

And then they suddenly look directly up at the camera.

Do they know I'm watching?

But I was just there myself a few moments ago, I think, or maybe I haven't yet arrived. Either way, no one could suspect that I was at the other end of the camera.

Surely.

It's the woman from downstairs, the one who told me to switch on the fridge, the one who looks vaguely familiar.

She turns her back on me but she has moved slightly so I can also now see the safe.

She turns her head and grins as though she's in the opening credits of some cheesy sitcom and glances up at me.

I would swear she knows I'm watching her. I instinctively feel like ducking out of the way but she couldn't possibly be seeing me.

She turns back and I get the feeling she wants me to see what she is doing. Her body shifts unnaturally more to the side as though to give me a better view.

I can see now that she is holding something – a novelty napkin exactly like the one John-James used to hold his sandwiches. In fact it must be *exactly* the same one because it also contains a helping of soot.

So that's how that got there. Was she trying to hide it or was it put there for me to find?

And if she put the napkin in the combination safe then it seems likely that she also put it in the notes.

Ha. I knew it couldn't have been me who wrote all that rubbish to myself. All that stuff about 'this is not a game it's deadly serious!' and 'getting back on track'. It must have been this woman all the time. But why would she be telling me to break the coal if she knew it was already broken?

My head's hurting. None of it makes any sense. I'm sure I'm missing something and it looks like this woman is trying to tell me it.

I watch very closely trying to work out what is going on when she dips her hand in her pocket and takes out a small plastic bag.

It looks like it contains metallic sherbet and as I am thinking this she actually licks her finger and puts it in the bag. I expect to see her put the grains to her mouth but instead she rubs her finger very gently over the soot so whatever was on her finger falls down on to it. She then carefully covers the grains with some of the coal dust and places the napkin in the safe.

If that was her way of an explanation then she is seriously over-estimating my abilities of deduction because I remain clueless and more confused than ever.

When I took the soot out of the safe it never occurred to me to delve around in it, and if that was what I was supposed to do why didn't the note just tell me to poke around in the dust instead of having a go at me for not doing my duty.

I certainly wouldn't have abandoned it in the fridge if I'd known there was something valuable in it.

The woman closes the door to the safe and once again looks directly up at the camera.

Why can't she just spit it out and get to the point?

And then she smiles and looks as though she's about to speak.

I nearly fall off my chair with embarrassment. She really does know I'm watching! But if she's going to tell me to break the coal or switch on the fridge I think I'll scream.

"Hello Sarah. Perhaps this time you can actually get the job done. You don't want to be ruining your reputation, especially as getting to see Frankie again depends upon it."

Thanks. That helps a lot.

Why can't someone just tell me what on earth it is that I'm supposed to be doing?

And who is this woman and what does she know about Frankie?

"Nothing to say Sarah?"

She can hear me?

"You were always one of the quieter ones, but I could always tell there was a lot going on in your head."

What is she talking about?

"It's one of the rather annoying side effects that we have to go through this ritual every time we meet. And yet I leave you enough hints around the place."

What is she talking about?

"Still not placed me Sarah? I suppose it was quite a long time ago. To you at least. I thought the logo might have given you a clue."

She twists her back away from the camera for a second and then turns and holds something up towards the camera. It's the Alternator.

She's pointing at the logo, the coiled symbol representing Spiral Industrials.

"You must remember this at least, the ammonite? You were so enthusiastic about them."

And finally the penny drops.

The woman holding up the Alternator is my old teacher, Miss Clyde.

CHAPTER TWENTY NINE:
"…opportunity…"

Miss Clyde taught me over twenty years ago. I know she was only a student teacher but this woman staring up at me doesn't look a day over thirty. Either she's taken extraordinary care of herself or this can't be Ms Clyde, but it is.

Yesterday this woman popped into my mind after finding the odd collection of fossils in the attic, surely that was just a coincidence? But then there was the sign above the door at Barton and the logo on the Alternator. Even so, what has Ms Clyde got to do with all of this?

"Do you know where Frankie is?" I shout at the screen.

"Not exactly."

I turn around and there she is, standing behind me.

I quickly look back at the screen. I am surrounded by Ms Clydes.

"But he's alive?" I ask.

"I believe that he is."

What's that supposed to mean?

"So you know where he is?" I repeat.

I try not to sound too desperate, but I've been disappointed before.

"Not precisely."

"What does that mean?"

"It means that I can help you, give you the opportunity to find him, but you have some work to do for me first."

"*You're* my client?"

"We employ you yes. Spiral Industrials. And usually you are, as you claim to be very reliable, but this time, for some reason, you didn't follow orders."

"What do you mean?"

"For a start you didn't use the correct access key to the cottage, meaning you failed to acquire your instructions."

I think back to when I think I first entered the cottage. It was with Andy, but he told me that when he was driving his bus he'd dropped me off near the cottage earlier in the day. Had I already been inside the cottage that morning?

"What instructions?"

I wish I could remember what happened. It hardly seems fair to berate me for something I don't have any memory of doing. And there have been so many keys, how was I supposed to guess which one I should use? How was I even supposed to know that it made a difference? And I'm pretty sure I didn't have any useful instructions apart from the cryptic bits of advice I apparently deemed fit to impart to myself.

"To break the coal? Is that it?"

Ms Clyde sighs as though I'm a particularly dense student.

"Absolutely, but I'll come back to the coal."

"Look," I begin, trying my hardest not to sound as if I'm inventing excuses for the absence of some homework. "Perhaps if the instructions had been clearer I would have been able to follow them. And I don't know if you realise this, but I've been having trouble with my memory lately. In fact I don't remember anything about you or any job offer."

Ms Clyde smiles.

"But you do remember me, don't you Sarah?"

Is she referring to her teaching practise? It's true that she did make an impression on me but I think it's very vain of her to suppose that I'd recall a student teacher from over twenty five years ago, even though I do.

"Maybe," I reply.

She thrusts out a thin arm "Eleanour Burrows, although you knew me by my maiden name, Eleanour Clyde – or Ms Clyde to you; I was very modern."

I take her hand loosely in my own before thankfully she pulls it away.

"I appreciate that there are certain side effects to what you are doing. But I can assure you that you did agree to all my terms and were happy to accept any inconveniences along the way."

Really?

"I have it in writing," she adds.

She perches herself carefully on the edge of one of the tables and sweeps at her lap as though brushing away crumbs.

"I'd hoped to make a good impression on you Sarah, I must say I quite enjoyed teaching you. And I'd hoped that the name of the company might have stirred a memory or two and you would appreciate the little museum."

"You put that together? How did you find all those fossils with the objects in them? They must be millions of years old."

"Really," she begins in that condescending tone and I'm beginning to wonder how I could ever have liked this woman.

"I would have thought you would have realised that those things couldn't be from the past," she says.

"So how were they were fossilized?"

Ms Clyde examines me as though deciding whether it's worth the trouble of providing an explanation.

"We have been through all this before of course, but I suppose I can explain it simply."

How rude. If she thought me stupid – why would she employ me? And it's hardly my fault if I can't remember all her riveting lectures.

"Actually let's go to the museum – it's a far more interesting attic than this – don't you think?"

"Do you need a key?"

"Of course not, once you have experienced an existence then it's really quite simple to move around."

"The light switch!"

Am I still trying to impress this woman? It was hardly the deduction of a master detective.

"Not really necessary actually, but it does help your brain to have some explanation of why a room spontaneously changes." She walks over to the light switch and the attic goes dark. "Many things, as even *you* probably realise, are not always as they seem."

Suddenly the room is once more illuminated by a series of spotlights and there in front of me is the museum.

She pauses and looks at me.

Can she read my thoughts? I can feel a nervous titter coming on but her icy glare keeps me quiet. This sounds serious.

She frowns.

"And many things can be manipulated to appear as you would like them to seem," she says. I haven't a clue what she is on about but I'm not going to give her the satisfaction of confirming my ignorance. "Simply put, I made them."

"Of course they had to be fakes"

"Obviously they're not from millions of years in the past but they're clearly real. You can touch them after all."

I wonder if she's noticed that one her exhibits is missing but she seems to be too pleased with herself at the moment to notice anything.

"It's very easy really, especially as they are mainly made from simple elements like carbon."

I'm still not going to ask.

"I just programme the information in and the objects are created."

She pauses again.

"It's a bit like 3D printing of course, but you just use a combination of proteins and amino acids."

I hope she never went on to teach properly, she would drive students mad.

"So is the printer in here?"

"Can't you remember where you found the coal?"

"It was in the fridge."

"Exactly."

"Exactly," I echo, hoping to emphasise how ridiculous she sounds, but it's me who just sounds childish. She's making me feel thirteen again and it isn't a feeling I particularly want to remember. As I walk around the museum again I recall that I wasn't exactly popular in school and realise now that I didn't help myself by doing stuff like openly displaying an enthusiasm for fossils, or showing a liking for teachers. Suddenly other little memories begin to flood my mind of sneering, gangly girls passively tormenting me with equal measures of taunt and indifference. I realise that Ms Clyde is staring at me again as though waiting for my brain to catch up and return to the now.

"You mean the printer is in the fridge?" I ask?

She tuts. Clearly she feels she's waited in vain.

"The fridge *is* the printer. Normally that model is used just for creating perishables."

"You mean you can programme it to make food?"

I have a picture of Jean Luc Picard ordering hot Earl Grey tea in his ready room on the Star ship Enterprise. I just knew that would become a reality – no more cooking!

"I do."

"So why wasn't it full of food?"

"It's a machine. You wouldn't expect a computer to print out an essay before you even touched it would you? And anyway the socket..."

"That's why you told me to switch on the fridge. But I didn't programme anything."

"It's hardly very difficult, but no you didn't. All you had to do was put the bits of coal in there."

"To make the coal whole?"

"Well it wasn't to make your tea."

I wish I'd known. I would have been able to have that delicious jalapeno-strewn vegetarian pizza after all.

"Though George, I believe, did make you some wine," she adds.

Maybe he's not so bad after all.

"You know George?"

"Of course and what happened to him? It was very unfortunate Andrew used the Alternator. Having to re set it wasted a lot of time."

How does she know about Andy?

"So George definitely wasn't hit by a taser?"

"No. And its unfortunate resemblance to that instrument prevented it from keeping its proper title – my time and space realigner – otherwise known as a TASR"

I hold down a snigger. She doesn't come across as the cheesy sort – maybe she just watched too many episodes of *Doctor Who* as a kid.

"So what does an Alternator do?"I ask, ignoring her nerdy acronym."

She glares at me.

"It enables people to experience different times without destroying themselves," she says matter-of-factly.

Of course.

"You can time travel?"

"Sort of, how else do you explain what has been happening to you?"

Ms Clyde has clearly reserved her best disdainful glare for this moment.

"Yes. How could I have been so stupid," I reply with as much sarcasm as I can muster. "I just assumed I was going mad."

"Indeed. It can appear that way I suppose."

"Even more so if you're told that you're mad," I add.

Why am I being so defensive?

"You mean Peter? I must have a word with the boy. He's not always that blunt, but to be fair you're not likely to remember his comments. In fact I don't know why *I'm* bothering."

"So the Alternator allows you to travel back in time?"

Could this be how I get Frankie back? I could stop him from leaving for school that day and never let him out of my sight ever again.

"I believe I just told you that."

"How?"

"How's the easy bit. Most people know that it's theoretically possible to go back in time,

"It is?"

"You can see the past every time you gaze at the stars and if you could look back at earth from one of them, through a telescope, you would be seeing images of dinosaurs wouldn't you?" I would? "So if you got to earth faster than the light or took a short cut through a fold in space then you would be going back in time. In theory."

"Theory? I thought you just said it was possible! I thought you said you'd done it?" I thought that was how I was going to find Frankie!

"Not exactly. It's very easy to back in time but unfortunately it's not easy to survive."

"What do you mean?" Although she was intensely annoying, Miss Clyde was most definitely alive.

"Well if you went back in time to see some dinosaurs you would be dead before you were born and that doesn't make sense does it?"

It's not the only thing not making sense.

"So you can't travel *back* again?"

"Not if you died before you set off."

"But you'd still be alive, wouldn't you, while you were there at least."

"Of course, unless you got eaten by a tyrannosaurus," she laughs and deep crimson lipstick spills into cracks formed by the stretching of her thin lips. I'm reminded of hours spent on the beach helping Frankie dig long trenches down towards the sea only for them to be filled up in seconds by the incoming tide.

"So?"

"So how can you be in a position to be able to go back to see the dinosaurs if you already died millions of years ago?"

The amusement in her face has gone.

"I'm not sure what you mean," I say, "but anyway I only need to go back five years. I haven't died since then I don't think."

I attempt a chortle of my own but she doesn't smile.

"No, but just because you didn't already die doesn't mean you won't and then of course you wouldn't be able to go back in the first place. Haven't you heard of the grandfather paradox?"

I think she is deliberately trying to make me feel stupid.

"So how *do* you do it then?"

Her dark grey eyes suddenly brighten.

"Let me explain."

CHAPTER THIRTY:
"…to regain…"

Miss Clyde throws out her arms and interlocks her long fingers before making a solitary clap. It would appear this is one explanation that she never tires of making.

"Okay, so I asked you if you had ever heard of the grandfather paradox?"

I have. But I never expected it to be a particular problem for me.

"Something about travelling back in time and killing your granddad isn't it? Apparently if you kill your granddad then you can't have been alive in the first place to go back and kill him. Oh." I think I finally see what she's on about with the dinosaur. "Though why anyone would go to the trouble of travelling back in time and then be stupid enough to kill their own granddad, I've no idea."

"Yes," she nods. "That's not quite the point, the point is that the possibility is real. Science, you see, is all about the possibilities, which is where the Alternator comes in. Quite simply it solves the problem by removing that particular probability." She sighs and brushes more imaginary crumbs from her lap. "Of course you've had this explained to you before."

"Sorry."

"It's quite simple really." I wish she'd stop saying that. "It's just a matter of quantum physics," she adds unhelpfully. "Let's see if I can make it really easy this time."

She crosses her legs and looks to the corner of the ceiling as if searching for inspiration. I hope she's recalling the Ladybird version, otherwise we're both in trouble. After a moment she smiles.

"Okay, so I know you have a basic knowledge about particles behaving strangely at a quantum level. Remember all those popular science programmes you loved to watch?"

"Well only some Christmas lectures," I say. "I vaguely remember some lights or maybe ping pong balls that apparently proved something like quantum particles being able to be in different places at once."

"Indeed, but more importantly, they can also be in different times at once. So all the particles begin like this, and they only change into normal behaving particles when one of two things has happened. Firstly, when the particle is measured or 'observed' it ceases to act strangely."

"A bit like a security camera encouraging improved behaviour?" I suggest, making glancing up to the corner of the ceiling.

"No."

"But the act of observation alters behaviour, like an omnipotent god stopping its people from sinning?"

"No, not unless particles contain consciences."

"What am I thinking about then, something about God being the original observer of the first singularity and that's why the universe acts predictably?"

"I have no idea what you are thinking about, but if there were no laws about time and space then it makes just as much sense that the first observer could have come from our future, or at least from one our futures."

Why didn't I just keep my mouth shut?

"Ok, what do you mean by one of our futures?"

"Yes, the alternative, what you know as the Many Worlds theory, suggests that, instead of the weird particle following just one predictable function, it actually exists in all of them. So when you observe the particle and it begins to act more acceptably well, the other particles in the other places don't just cease to be. Instead they have their own existence with a different version of us observing it. Basically, instead of there just being one possibility, all possibilities happen. All futures happen.

"I thought that was just something made up by science fiction writers."

"I know you do."

"What?"

"Never mind."

"But what has this all got to do with your Alternator and the grandfather paradox?"

"You haven't realised?"

"Give me a minute."

Or a year or two.

"The Alternator allows you to return to a very slightly different time, one in which you will not kill your grandfather."

I think this explanation must be a little too over simplified.

"But you said it was just a theory."

She tuts and carries on.

"I think even *you* realise that's not the case anymore. Just think what has happened to you in the last few days. So you see, with endless permutations at your disposal, if you travel back in time there will always be at least one version of yourself that fails to kill your grandfather."

"So?"

"So it's the loophole that ensures that we can change the past."

"Okay, great but what's it got to do with me?"

"It's why I employed you Sarah – it's your job –to exploit that loophole."

Has she got the right person? Even in five years I doubt I would have applied for and completed a course in time travel. I doubt there's even any such course.

"The last job I remember having was working on insurance fraud," I tell her, not confident that this will put an end to the matter.

"Yes, I had expected better from you," she says.

"Like being a director of an international company?"

Almost another smile.

"Who told you that?"

Of course saying it out loud just exposes how stupid it sounds. I can't believe now that I was so vain as to have believed John-James' flattery.

"I can't remember."

She narrows her eyes and I suspect she already knows.

"So can you remember *which* International company you are a director of?" she adds facetiously.

I wish I hadn't opened my mouth. This is a bone she's not going to stop gnawing.

I look at the Alternator in her hand with the ammonite logo, the one she professes to have created.

"You work for Spiral Industrials?" I ask her.

Maybe we're on the board together.

"You're a director of Spiral Industrials? What a coincidence."

She's mocking me.

"You said you employed me. Is that the job you gave me? I must have really impressed you back in high school."

"If you like," she answers dryly. "But it was what happened to you afterwards that caught our interest."

I do a fast mental run through my activities after I left school and, apart from having Frankie, which I remember impressed no one but myself, I just held a series of lame jobs. Even my insurance fraud work sounds more impressive on my business cards than in real life. So I'm at a loss as to how I ever came to anyone's notice, least of all an incredibly successful international company.

"So what was it?"

"Your work, ironically, is connected to a very specialised branch of the company"

"Ironically?"

"Or maybe more serendipitously if you like."

"Another coincidence?"

If she notices my mocking tone, she doesn't show it. I should practise that.

"Actually our meeting wasn't a coincidence at all."

"But we met at my school. You were my teacher, you taught me about ammonites."

I wave my hand around the room as though the existence of this exhibition of fossils somehow proves that our first meeting was a harmless fluke.

"I would have thought by now you'd have got used to the fact that there is no real sense of *when*."

"You mean you went back in time to be a student teacher? I could think of a lot better things to see and do if I had the power of time travel."

"It was part of the interview process. We had to check that you were suitable. Compliant."

"Compliant? You went all the way back to one of the most miserable times in my life just to see if I would bend to your will? I think most students tend to follow rules in school."

"Perhaps most do, but not always with a student teacher and one teaching a particularly unpopular subject. Yet you were a model pupil; very eager and engaged."

"Great. So I passed the sycophantic test. Maybe you could have avoided providing extra ammunition to my bullies who were oh so delighted to hear about my new found passion for fossils."

"Ah backbone, a little fortitude never does anyone any harm."

Only someone who has never been bullied would say that.

"And it turned out I enjoyed myself. I loved teaching, it was so easy to bend impressionable minds and it was a wonderful break from the office."

"So you were never really a teacher?"

"I know. You'd never have known. Maybe I missed my true vocation, I think I did a pretty good job. Do you still remember about Ammon? I believe you were very interested."

I'm not going to admit to that.

"So this museum exhibition is just here because of our love of fossils?" I say.

"Not especially, but I thought it was rather amusing and might prompt a few memories between your blackouts."

"Very thoughtful, but I don't think it worked."

"You're wrong. If anything, it worked a little too well. Instead of following orders you've been scampering all over the place needlessly looking for clues."

"I've been looking for Frankie."

"And how's that going?"

I glare at her.

"Perhaps if you didn't waste time stealing things you might be doing a better job of finding him."

How dare she? She strides over to the end of the room where a light shines down onto the empty display.

So she had noticed.

She holds out her hand and I slip the necklace over my head.

"Sorry." I feel myself redden but I'm not sorry, I'm angry. "I didn't realise it was yours. I can't remember. In fact I can't remember anything. All I've done the last two days is try to find out what is happening to me and try to remain sane and yet all I've got in return are even more ridiculous questions and insinuations that I am indeed losing, or possibly already have lost my mind. So I think I've had enough. As you rightly point out I'm no nearer to finding Frankie, so I think it's best if I just leave. Here, take the necklace and you can keep your job as well, whatever that is."

I stride towards the attic door.

"Sarah."

I turn.

"These artefacts aren't just a little hobby of mine. I made them but they all mean something. I thought the little anachronisms were aptly amusing but they do actually embody all the significant alterations."

Significant alterations?

"What do you remember about the last time you saw Frankie?" she asks me.

"He left for school and never came back."

Ms Clyde looks intently at me as though giving herself a moment to come to some decision.

"Perhaps yes, but not always. Not the first time."

Ms Clyde holds up the amber necklace.

"I wonder what made you choose to take this one. Maybe you need some answers after all."

"Close your eyes," she orders. "I think it's time I showed you what really happened to Frankie.

CHAPTER THIRTY ONE:
"…to maybe..."

"Hello mum!"

The attic has changed and now, standing in front of the safe, is Peter.

"What are you doing here?" I snarl.

"That's a fine way to talk to your son."

"You're not my son."

"Yeah yeah, but in answer to your question, I would like to be getting a move on. We've already missed the train because of you."

"To Peterborough?"

This prompts a burst of giggles.

"Enough Peter," Ms Clyde snaps.

"What've you brought her here for anyway, don't she know?"

"Doesn't Peter, not don't," she corrects him.

Blimey. Maybe that teaching lark was second nature after all.

"Pardon mother."

"You're Peter's mum?"

"Not much of one," Peter answers for her. "I'm sure you'd make a much better one Sarah, if it wasn't for all the strange men you keep bringing home!"

"I don't."

"Anyway we'd be done by now if that latest one hadn't picked up the Alternator and shot Uncle George."

"Yes," adds Miss Clyde narrowing her eyes at Peter, "I can't think how he managed to come across it."

"I tried to get it back," he says.

"Not before it was used. It's all very well you complaining about wasting time Peter, when I've had to sort out a brand new realignment cartridge."

"But it didn't do much mum, it was only a slight alteration."

"You what?"

"Haven't you been listening to anything?" Peter says. "The Alternator creates new versions of reality – it alters what can happen to you."

"Is that why George didn't remember us meeting him at the cottage?"

"It would appear as though he's had some memory loss, but actually seeing you at the cottage never happened to him. Well, not that version of him."

"But he said he treated me at Barton Hall. He remembered me from then."

"Yeah, of course he did."

"But you just said that he was a different version."

"Yes, the new version only began around the time he was Alternated and because he wasn't the intended target it would more than likely only cause a slight difference."

So *who* was the target?

"Of course it's not guaranteed. I wouldn't want to risk it but most people wouldn't even notice if there was an alteration. It might be as insignificant as getting your face painted as a pirate instead of a fish. George probably had more wax in his ears or wore a different coloured tie or something."

So they do know about Frankie. But the face painting happened *before* he disappeared.

"It will just appear like he's a bit forgetful and people do that all the time, do things or go places and have no memory of them."

Like me?

"I doubt that anyone else would have even noticed this time," Ms Clyde says, having been unusually quiet.

"This time? Is that what you meant about Frankie when you said the first time? Did he not always go missing?"

"As I said, there are side effects – or perks – to your employment. Realignments are made."

"But what happened to Frankie?"

Please don't let what Amelia said be true.

"Was he in a car accident?"

Instead of answering she hands the amber necklace to Peter.

"Be a dear and put this in the fridge for a moment."

Before I can ask any more questions Peter grabs it and takes it out.

Ms Clyde walks over to the safe.

"I thought you were going to work it out."

"Strangely enough it never occurred to me to use a fridge."

"And yet you put the coal in there."

"But…"

"But what?"

I have no idea.

"We keep most of the documentation at Barton, in fact I believe you had a little peek at some of the information that Andrew stole."

I expect her to be angry about this but instead she smiles rather creepily.

"His initiative and cunning is impressive. He could be quite an asset."

"An asset for what?"

Before she can answer, the attic door opens and Peter reappears holding the bits of necklace.

"Thank you Peter," Ms Clyde says. "As I was saying, most information is kept at Barton and I believe you have met several of our team there, but the Significants and Originals are kept separately."

"The what?"

"Originals are what we describe as what originally happened to people. The tragic beginnings," she adds with inappropriate theatricality. "Significants are what they get changed to."

"Huh?"

"Would you like to open it? Any of the museum keys will open the safe, but here, use mine."

She puts her hand to her neck and pulls out a necklace of her own – a small ammonite attached to thin chain. She manipulates it slightly so that a small piece of metal comes loose. She passes it to me and I insert it into the safe.

I'm not sure what I was expecting, perhaps an old frayed ledger or a pile of computer discs, but then again why should I be surprised by what's in there? It makes as much sense as anything else. A bucket of coal.

"A bucket of coal?" Peter exclaims from behind my back. I expect an accompaniment of giggles but he seems genuinely surprised.

"I like coal," says Ms Clyde, "it's interesting. It takes millions of years to make and yet is easily destroyed."

I glance at her but it seems as though this is the full extent of her explanation.

"Of course it would help if you had some gloves."

"Now what?" I ask.

"Break the coal of course."

"Which piece?"

"See what falls into your hands."

I pull out the glove, grab one of the pieces of coal and smash it against the side of the safe.

I don't recall Peter turning off the light switch but as soon as the coal breaks, the light in the room flickers and we are once again standing in front of the banks of computers.

On the floor in front of me is a small computer stick, just like the one Andrew stole from Barton Hall.

I wonder why there are so many computers.

"Does it matter which one I use?"

"You choose," Ms Clyde says.

I pick up the stick, dust off some soot and insert it into the side of the nearest computer.

The screen bursts into life with disturbing images.

There are flashes of unimaginable horror; buildings collapsing, trains exploding, boats sinking and all with an accompaniment of screams. Kids with eyes as wide as saucers, bawling in terror as they reach out their arms into empty space. Parents white with panic as they dig their bloodied arms into mounds of shattered rubble.

"What is this?"

"Just wait," Ms Clyde says. "The image will focus."

Then the horrors quieten and, as Ms Clyde suggested, the images appear to zoom in. But this doesn't look horrific. I look towards Ms Clyde, to see if this is what she was expecting. The monitor is showing a TV show – rather too low brow I would have thought for Ms Clyde – but she seems engrossed so I return my attention to the screen. Then I realise what, or rather who, I am looking at. This must be the show Andy was telling me about. Was it all true? Unmistakably, on a colossal stage mottled with streams of light, is Simon Greaves. He is caressing a guitar and beaming confidently into an audience of squealing fans. I presume he is doing rather well considering the volume of appreciation. The camera focuses on what must be the judges table – four overdressed and overenthusiastic adults, their faces straining with glee. But their expressions suddenly transform from joy to horror accompanied by a roar of metal and screaming. The camera returns to the stage in time to see a section of the stage plunging onto Simon.

"That's enough," says Ms Clyde and she pulls out the memory stick.

"So Andy was right!"

"Right about what?"

"He said Simon was dead."

For once Ms Clyde looks a bit worried.

"He is just brimming over with surprises. Did he break any coal?"

"I don't think so."

"It must be the cottage. Did he just 'suddenly' develop a recollection of what happened to Simon Greaves?"

"He saw his name on a bit of paper, but then the paper turned blank."

"Did you notice anything unusual about the paper?"

"Apart from mysteriously losing its content?"

"Yes apart from that?"

"Are you referring to the yellow smudge?"

"I see. Did you use different keys while he was in the house, or did the lights go off unexpectedly?"

"Both."

"Looks like we have no choice then."

"No choice about what?"

"The cottage seems to be leaking information."

"It has? But why wouldn't Andy remember Simon's story? He said he was famous – millions of people saw him die on a live talent show."

"People forget stuff all the time," Peter sneers. "You don't remember it, do you?"

"I never saw it in the first place."

"But how can you be sure? Like I said, people seem to forget stuff all the time."

"Like George?"

"Exactly."

"But you can't fire your Alternator at millions of people."

Peter splutters.

"You don't need to."

I gesture to the screen where I had seen myself shoot the Alternator at Simon, as though it would help to unravel my confusion.

"What did I do to him?" I recall with panic what Simon had told me. "Did I cause him any harm?"

"Not intentionally," Ms Clyde says.

"It could have been worse," Peter adds.

"Like dying a terrible public death you mean?"

Peter explodes with more giggles.

"Shush Peter," Ms Clyde admonishes. "Sarah, don't look so horrified. You can't choose what will happen."

"It's a bit like shutting someone in with Schrodinger's cat," Peter says, "the Alternator creates the box and the recipient gets shut in. You can't know what will have happened until after."

"So he could still die?"

"Simon will be fine as long as he keeps a low profile," says Ms Clyde.

"You mean, like discouraging him from entering any talent competition?"

Peter giggles again.

"Something like that," Miss Clyde concedes.

"Although it's a bit presumptuous to assume he'd make the final every time he goes in for one of those silly contests," Peter adds. "Show business is very fickle you know and the chances of him being hit again by a stage prop are decreasing all the time."

"So I saved his life? I'm glad, but why him? Lots of people have accidents."

"Not all so expensively. Though of course you both made a lot of money out of that one, but obviously it cost them a fraction to pay you and mother here."

"Them?"

I feel like a goldfish just about to realise that there's more to life than a bowl full of water as it finally dawns on me why Ms Clyde said this was connected to my job.

"Insurance?"

"Ding!" shouts Peter gleefully.

"When we alter reality we save insurance companies from paying out a few thousand pounds?"

"Not thousands Sarah, not even millions, but billions of pounds. But you're not the kind of person to be just motivated by money. There are more important reasons why we do this."

Peter claps his hands and reaches for the bucket of coal.

"Pick another!" he squeals as though this is just some twisted parlour game.

Ms Clyde glares at him as she takes the bucket and offers it towards me.

"Which one?"

I look closely but they all look the same. I close my eyes and delve in. I pull out a piece and before I can change my mind I smash it against the wall.

I feel a little smarting on my wrist as Ms Clyde kicks away the broken pieces of coal and inserts the piece of metal into a different computer.

Once again there are flashes of terror and then once again the horrors quieten and zoom in on just the one terrifying scene.

There is a grass verge strewn with wreckage, maybe at the side of a motorway. A wheel is spinning aimlessly above what might have been the red chassis of a pushchair, but the red isn't paint. It's blood and there are bodies, lots of bodies. How did I not see them? Now I see a train coach being pulled across a railway track and I see several of the bodies are small and so young, children's bodies.

Another monitor bursts with light. Peter is standing in front of it mesmerised by the screen.

I turn my attention to the new computer and watch as a blur of rescue workers and ambulances frantically scour a beach. The images seem to slow and focus on young a woman – her face grey and bloated, screaming the name Mary over and over as she watches a body being repeatedly pummelled in the chest.

"Enough."

The screens go blank.

"What was that? How can I see…?"

Ms Clyde is still looking very calm.

"Memories projected onto the screen. You'd be surprised by the amount of detail retained in a moment of crisis."

Her lack of empathy is astonishing.

"That young woman, was that Amelia? And was that her sister? She looked to be in a very bad way."

"You know her?"

"We met at her home."

"So you know Mary's fine then."

"Yes, though Amelia was quite concerned about her and seemed to think I'd caused her to disappear. Amelia was very scared when she saw the Alternator. Now I realise why. Apparently she works at Barton Hall too."

"Small world!" Peter exclaims.

"Has all this got anything to do with the list of names from Barton?"

"Oh, she's catching on now," he squeals.

"Does George feature on one of these pieces of coal too?"

"If it wasn't for George, Peter wouldn't be here," Ms Clyde says.

"Peter's name was next to George's alongside a swirly symbol. Amelia and Mary too. Is the symbol important?"

"You have been busy. Yes the ammonite represents success, they got what they wanted."

"They've all been realigned? They got their loved ones back? George was involved in one of these tragedies? Amelia lost Mary but got her back, no wonder she was terrified of losing her again, and George got Peter?"

"Yes, speaking of whom, Peter, I think it's time you left – time you grew up."

Peter giggles and shrugs and leaves the room.

"But what about me? Why haven't I got a swirly symbol, why haven't I got Frankie back? What happened to with *my* past?"

Miss Clyde holds out a third stick, the one I'd been carrying around with me in the amber necklace.

Another sharp pain, and then I remember. I remember the day. We were all going on a fun day out, a museum for kids. I remember his dad deciding that we should go by train to make it more exciting. I remember the train was early – it wasn't the one we were planning on taking but it was heading for the same place and of course we boarded it. But the train was full – there were lively children taking up several rows of seats at the back of the carriage. I remember being irritated by their noise and wondering why they were on the train, forcing several people to stand in the aisle. I held Frankie's hand – he was only three –not even at school. There was one free seat right at the front just opposite the toilet and I had to put Frankie on my lap. His dad had to stand with the buggy outside the toilets. I remember looking around the crowded train and looking at a particular passenger who was standing in the aisle a little further up; he was very tall and had an unusually large forehead. I remember looking at it a little later and thinking how different that same face looked streaked in blood. I remember Frankie squirming restlessly on my lap trying to get up and join his dad. I remember his dad glaring at me; a silent order to prevent me from adding to his discomfort in the clammy congestion of the passageway. I remember him gesturing to Frankie to stay put. I remember that forever after he wished he hadn't. It was at that very moment that the train stopped. Everything, just for a moment, was quiet and still and then there was an explosion of noise and glass as a length of metal crashed through the window opposite us and smashed into Frankie's head.

Of course it was much later I heard that a farmer had lost control of a hired JCB and it had tumbled into the path of our train. The force of the impact had caused the arm of the JCB to fling round and smash through the window. As soon as it hit Frankie the arm had sprung back – it was as if a giant robot had punched quickly through the window and left.

I escaped with two black eyes and his dad had a few cuts, but of course we escaped nothing.

CHAPTER THIRTY TWO:
"…start…."

Miss Clyde looks at me with what can only be described as pity.

I collapse back onto one of the tables ready to feel the sickness rise inside me as I await memories of Frankie and my overwhelming loss but just as when Amelia told me of the car crash, there's something not quite right.

"This doesn't have to be what happened does it?" I ask Ms Clyde. "You can Alternate me or whatever it is that you do and change it."

Ms Clyde slowly shakes her head.

"Why not? Isn't it worth enough money, is that it? No big pay out for the insurance company just for the death of one little boy?"

"Sarah, I'm sorry."

"What for?"

"For you, Sarah."

No.

"I'm sorry, but you already were affected by the Alternator. You already changed the outcome."

"Then where is he?"

"Sarah…"

"Where is he?"

"I'm sorry…"

"But you said these were the originals, that they could be changed."

"Sarah the information in the amber wasn't the original event it was what we call the Significant, it was what you changed it to."

"Why would I cause my own son's death?"

"In the original train crash there were barely any survivors. It was worth the risk."

"You mean it was worth a lot of money."

"There would have been a very large pay out, yes."

"But I would never have taken a penny if it meant even a slight chance of harming my son."

"No, but you *would* take a chance on saving him. And all the others, including all those children."

"You mean what you showed me before, the bodies on the track, that was what originally happened? That was my train crash?"

"I'm sorry, yes. But you knew the risk. You knew there were no guarantees when you agreed to join us."

"Us?"

"Spiral Industrials."

"And Amelia, she's a part of this?"

"She was the one who used the Alternator on you. She was the one who caused the alteration."

"Like stopping a train from crashing? But it didn't work, it still crashed. How was there any change?"

"It has to be subtle. We look to find someone seemingly unimportant and they do something just a little bit differently, like collecting boarding passes just a little more efficiently so that a ship or bus or ferry or whatever gets to set out just a little earlier."

"Or you could arrange for a train to run a little later?"

"When you arrived at the train station you didn't catch the train you were supposed to catch?"

"No. There was another train running late, heading for the same destination so we ran towards it. I had to collapse Frankie's buggy quickly because the guard was ready to wave the train off."

"Delaying the train by a couple more seconds."

"You know, I always thought that if Frankie had got off my knee and gone to his dad, then he would have survived."

"Maybe, maybe not."

"I always blamed him you know, and now I find out it wasn't anything to do with him, it was me. All me."

"You tried to save him."

"What about everyone else?"

"They all survived.

I should be pleased I suppose, but it just all feels incredibly unfair.

"But this all happened years ago."

"I would have thought you'd have learnt by now that time isn't relevant here."

"So I haven't been wearing the same outfit for the last five years?"

"No, but you really ought to use the shower."

I knew there'd be one. It's probably next to the wine cellar.

"But if Frankie was three when he died, how come I remember him as older? I saw him play football and sing in the school play."

"Everything before the accident is unchangeable but after being Alternated there are countless possible versions."

"Like Simon? But the newspaper clippings showed several tragedies."

"The chances of finding him in good health aren't precise."

"And Frankie? But you said I could find him."

"Yes. You can't change what happened on the train, not again, but every alteration is different. You're looking for the one which leads to him being safe."

"So how *do* I get him back?"

"You can't. But someone else could."

"Who, how?"

"Has Andy ever mentioned the Manchester bus killings?"

"Yes, but what has all this got to do with Andy?

"Did he tell you about his involvement?"

"He was there? He didn't say he was there. Was he driving the bus?"

Please let him not have been the one who did the stabbing.

"He was one of a few survivors."

I remember him talking about some people on the bus – hadn't he thought the letter to Martha or Mary had been from one of them – Jakob – another inmate of Barton?

"Like many other survivors – yourself included – he came to Barton. All the people that you met there – all the people that you saw on the screen were once all involved in tragedies; all of them survived."

"And were all of their tragedies 'quietly reimagined'?"

"Not all."

"Just the costly ones I suppose."

"So the killings on the buses haven't been changed?"

"No, in his timeline, it's still happened."

"But there was never a cult?"

"No, but the story of the cult being responsible for the bus killings seemed to have worked up until sometime around now. This now."

"You mean nobody was suing the bus company?"

"Not yet. But if they did it would be more catastrophic than just a bus company going out of business. But something changed and a new investigation was opened."

"Leading to catastrophic financial ruin?" I say, intending sarcasm.

"Exactly."

"That's why we have been keeping an eye on the individuals involved."

"To stop them suing?"

"We can't stop them, but we can take away their reason to. And if that doesn't work, well, we have an alternative method."

"Such as getting Andy to alter the original events?"

"Actually we had originally decided to use Jakob, if it was necessary. You spent some time assessing him in Barton."

"I thought I was a patient there."

"You also thought I was a teacher."

Student teacher.

"So something's going to happen to Jakob?"

"Not anymore. It would have done but he didn't really take to you, he thought you were crazy."

How rude. How typical.

"But that doesn't matter now, we have a much better candidate. Amelia has been keeping an eye on Andrew. Who knew he would be so gallant?"

"So she did know who he was!"

"Yes, Amelia was happy to put her car at his disposal when his bus broke down and he has been so accommodating."

"Compliant, like me?"

"Yes. I mean these are very useful qualities – very useful. That is why we allowed you to keep bumbling around, to see how biddable he could be." Now she's making out it was all a cunning plan. "Of course there was a bit of a problem when Andrew used the Alternator on George but we were able to give you a few nudges and a few self-penned notes so it's all worked out well."

"I'm glad you think so."

"Thank you."

"So now what?"

"We finally get down to business, you finally get to complete your job. To break the coal!"

"But it's already broken."

"It isn't meant literally Sarah, it just means to create a new reality, a new Significant and potentially the outcome you're hoping for."

"So what do I do then?"

"You need to slot the metal cartridge from your coal into the Alternator and find Andy. That will become the only evidence of the original incidents."

Ms Clyde hands me the Alternator and I feel about in my pocket for the contents of my piece of coal. What if I *hadn't* broken it? Too late now.

"The Alternator will be able to just remove that one incident?"

I think back to George and how he had no recollection of our meeting in the cottage.

"That's not how it works, I'm afraid."

"So if I zap Andy he isn't going to remember me."

"Probably not. Certainly he won't remember what has happened this last couple of days."

"So I lose my only friend, and possibly the only person in my life who has ever gone out of their way to help me like this. Do I want to give that all up?"

"This is why you shouldn't get involved," Ms Clyde adds.

"The longer you leave it the worse it will be."

"What if I refuse?"

But I think I know the answer to this and it won't be about losing a job and a friend.

"Then you will never see Frankie again."

She walks over to the light switch and before I can stop her the attic goes dark.

CHAPTER THIRTY THREE:
"...afresh..."

I wait a moment to see if my eyes adjust to the darkness but I can't see anything. I head towards the door and feel for the switch.

I was expecting to see the spotlights illuminating the strange museum but a rather harsh light reveals very little. No banks of computers or small safes, just a few neglected looking boxes and bits of old wood, a normal-looking attic.

I feel strangely nervous. I was supposed to find Andy but I have no clue about where, or rather when I am.

I go over to the boxes and have a look inside; just a few old Christmas decorations, nothing odd about them at all.

I head back towards the door and as I pull it towards me I hear my name being called.

Andy!

"Sarah, Sarah, is that you?"

"Yes."

"I thought I'd lost you for good."

Not just yet. I put my hand on the Alternator. Can I really go through with this? What will happen to Andy? Will he lose his memory too? Perhaps he will suddenly 'wake up' in the road not knowing what's going on. Maybe I should give him my train ticket.

I can see Andy at the bottom of the stairs holding the door open for me.

"How did you get in the attic? There's nothing up there. I should know, I checked often enough.

"Longish story," I say as I descend.

"Wait here you said, and then you just disappeared."

"Sorry."

I grin at Andy but something is different, he narrows his eyes and turns away from me.

"Except this time it wasn't just you that disappeared."

As I follow him into the lounge I see that the furnishings that were here when I left Andy have vanished.

There doesn't appear to be anything, not even the dust and debris that had garnished the cottage when I was last here. Now everything looks immaculate and very clean. Is this Andy's real timeline?

"What happened?"

"I was hoping you would be able to explain. When you didn't come back I went outside to get the wine and to look for you but when I tried to get back in, the door was locked again."

"You broke in?"

There don't appear to be any doors hanging off their hinges or shards of glass strewn over the perfectly polished floor.

Andy glares unreasonably at me.

"Actually, after a while I found your secret stash of keys – quite a colourful collection."

"Which did you use? Did it have a key ring attached to it?"

Andy cocks his head as though I've asked him something strange.

"Yeah, weird thing. I rifled through the bunch and then I spotted this one that had a gorilla on it and as a kid I used to collect them. My bedroom was literally plastered in them"

I stare at him open mouthed.

He's describing Frankie's room.

Please no. Or please?

"Do you have a mother?"

Now he really does look at me strangely. I look back closely. No way is this Frankie from the future.

"Of course."

"And do you see her often?

"Not really."

"When did you last see her?"

Surely if it had been when he was eleven he would have mentioned the remarkable coincidence when I told him about Frankie's disappearance. But I need to get that memory out of my head. Frankie was three when he last saw his mum.

"Why? I'm not sure, probably a couple of months ago. I know I should visit more often but it's not so easy when you're working and she doesn't exactly live around the corner."

"Of course, sorry. So you used that key?"

"No, I was reaching for it but when I saw this little bus swinging and well I couldn't resist."

"You were drawn to the bus?"

"Well yes, it seemed the obvious choice. Anyway the key worked, but when I got in, all the furniture was gone, the museum too. It was like they had never been here. The place smelt like it was brand new or freshly repainted. And then even stranger – I turned my phone back on and I got a signal."

"That's good," I offer encouragingly.

"I guess so. Well, while I decided what to do, I went on the internet to check a few things out."

"Like what?"

"Well Simon Greaves for a start. Turns out you weren't going mad, he did get ill in the early stages of a TV talent show, but he got better and by all accounts stayed that way.

"I checked out Barton Hall as well, and although it's owned by Spiral Industrials there isn't anything remarkable about it. It's been a recuperation and psychiatric hospital for a few years but without incident. You however," he pauses and looks at me dramatically for a moment, "are a bit of a surprise."

I'm all ears. Anything that happened to me since my trip on the motorway will come as a surprise.

"First of all I looked for Frankie. I thought I would look him up and see if there had been any developments or sightings."

"And?"

"Well, it wasn't easy."

So he knows something.

"Given what you said about Frankie and that his disappearance was in all the papers I assumed there would be a lot of information about him, but there was nothing."

So Ms Clyde was telling the truth, he didn't just disappear. But there has to be something – a train crash perhaps?

"You mean you think he doesn't exist? You know it's not always easy to find someone on the internet straight away. It was a while ago."

"Believe me I've had plenty of time to search. The only reference to a Frankie Norton is a small article about the tragic death of a young boy who died in a neighbour's pond."

Was that the result of the Alternatoring of Simon, or have I been trying to get back Frankie for longer than Ms Clyde suggested? All those keys. All those attempts. Could it all just have been a waste of time after all?

"Then I used the card that you gave me."

"My business card?"

"Yes, the Reliability is My Reputation one?"

"The very same, and it seems that this isn't the first time that we have met."

"You know who I am?"

"I didn't recognise you, I only saw you once briefly. I believed you when you said you knew nothing about the Manchester Killings."

"But I don't."

Andy holds up his phone for me and I take it from him; a picture of me shaking hands with someone I have never seen before.

I glance around the room. This is the first time I've been here when it's looked like this. Has the bus keyring taken Andy back to his original time line?

"You were not just a just a small-time fraud investigator," he says. "You were part of the team which discredited the victims of the Manchester Bus Killings. You helped the bus company get away without paying any compensation."

I did? Does this mean that I don't need to use the Alternator on Andy? If there is no payout then why would Andy need to forget about what happened?

"I don't remember."

"Sure you don't. No wonder you have plenty of money to buy your fill of cottages. And is that why you were keeping an eye on me – turning up every couple of months to make sure I wasn't going to do anything about it? Well too bad."

"What do you mean?"

"I shouldn't have given up in the first place. I should have had the guts to carry on and prove there was no cult and that the bus company should have taken more responsibility for what happened."

Andy is glaring at me. I barely recognise him. I was scared that by using the Alternator I would lose him but I realise I already have.

I feel in my pocket for the Alternator and find the train ticket. I and thrust it into his hand.

While he's distracted by the ticket I take out the Alternator and the bit of metal from my coal out of my pocket and instinctively slip the two pieces together. Of course this isn't the first time I have done this.

Andy looks up and sees the Alternator.

"Not so innocent are we?" he asks coldly. "I found your instructions in the kitchen. Break the coal? Use the Alternator? You had me fooled. Do you even know what that will do?"

Only what will happen if I don't.

The choice is now very easy.
"Sorry Andy," I say, and shoot.

*

The room goes black.

*

A moment later I'm standing next to a bright orange sofa.

There is no sign of Andy; the only trace that he was here is his phone that I am still holding.

I look at it hopefully – the screen, which moments ago showed a picture of me congratulating some official has now been replaced with the words no related item found. I scroll back to his previous search for Frankie and hold my breath. Nothing would be good – nothing could mean that he's just an anonymous kid living a normal, boring, tragedy-free existence. But as soon as I hit enter, the screen fills with links referencing a motorway pile up and dates for memorial services. I click on one and immediately I'm faced with a picture of Frankie. He's smiling and holding a football, there are shoulders and shins on either side of him, bits of other boys cropped from a group photo – bits of boys who I presume carried on growing. Frankie didn't survive.

Not today. Not this today.

"About time."

I turn around and standing in the gloomy light of the door stands Miss Clyde. Alongside her are George and the sisters.

"It didn't work. I gave up my friend for nothing."

"You'll see Andy again, probably sooner than you think," says Mary with a smile.

"If he's like you he'll want to find answers and a better ending," George adds.

"But he hasn't lost anyone."

"He might not have a child he needs to save, but he needs redemption. He will never forgive himself for allowing his passengers to die. He will be forever looking to make up for it."

"By saving his passengers?"

"Maybe, but I'm sure you will be seeing each other on some journey or another."

"Now what?" I ask.

Miss Clyde slips her hand into her pocket and pulls out a piece of paper and hands it to me. On it are a few details about Andy followed by the words 'Alteration Complete.' Under that is a reference to Frankie being killed as a result of a freak traffic accident. At the bottom is an instruction for me to place it in the folder.

"Take the completed cartridge and the key back to the train and try again. Use your ticket."

"I gave my ticket to Andy. I don't think I can do this. I've just seen the death of my son. Again. Who in their right mind would agree to do this? To see their child die over and over?"

"A mother."

"But I can't live with this."

"I know." Ms Clyde says. "We're not entirely heartless. You'll get Frankie back – you've seen the possibilities already – you saw the picture of him as a young lad and you've seen how Mary was returned to Amelia. And when you do there will be no more need for this",

She holds up an Alternator , a smaller version than the one I used on Andy and aims it at me.

"We'll give you hope. When you come round the paper will be blank and all you will remember about Frankie is that he is missing. The last thing you will recall is that you were on your way to a meeting."

"With you?"

"Yes, your first meeting. Here," she passes me another ticket, "try and follow the instructions this time."

I look at it. What's so special about Peterborough?

"Now close your eyes."

"Do you honestly think I'll get him back?"

"Of course."

I want to believe her but I know that until I see him alive again I will never stop searching. As many lives as it takes. As many lumps of coal it takes to get the right break.

*

I'm standing at a ticket booth, presumably waiting for a ticket.

EPILOGUE: "to break the coal."

I'm standing in a foyer holding a bright orange folder.

I thought I was going to be late for this meeting in Leeds but incredibly I came across the place almost as soon as I left the motorway.

The foyer is enormous, with high walls and marbled floors, more like a train station than the entrance to some offices. Even the reception area looks more like an elaborate ticket booth with its intricate frame topped with a beautiful clock, reassuring me that I am not late for my 3.15 appointment. I approach the receptionist who gives me a welcoming smile – not the usual indifference with which I am typically greeted at this type of office. This place seems different, not least the unusual corporation logo which dominates the foyer – a large ornate ammonite curling around the company's name. Spiral Industrials. I've never heard of them before but their email intriguingly implied terms I would find hard to refuse. And since Frankie's death I have taken on very few jobs. I need this assignment.

I realise I have been gazing vacantly up at the ceiling but when I look back at the receptionist she is still smiling patiently at me. She is quite young but has an old fashioned style that would not look out of place on a 60s movie set.

"Sarah Norton?"

I'm very impressed. Not only has she noticed me, she has also worked out who I am.

"Yes. I have an appointment."

"Yes, Ms Norton. They are expecting you. If you want to take a seat for just a second, I will just print out a visitors' pass for you."

She begins typing onto a laptop while I move towards an incongruous orange sofa to her right. The seat is already partially occupied by a youngish man with brown curly hair and a wide smile. I didn't realise there were going to be other candidates interviewing for the job.

However, before I can get acquainted, the young receptionist calls me back and hands me a card. It looks a little like a train ticket but it is slightly larger and more ornately decorated. The name of the man who I spoke to on the phone, Peter Burroughs, is written at the top, alongside the time and date of the meeting. Very efficient.

The girl points to the bottom of the ticket which informs me that the meeting is to be held in conference room 8.

"You'll need this to get through the safety systems – I'm afraid there's a high level of security in the building and I wouldn't like you to set off any alarms. But don't worry, someone will be here to escort you in a moment."

As if on cue, a door opens to my right and a small woman in an immaculate suit with short dark hair appears.

"Sarah Norton!"

She strides over to me as though she is welcoming a long lost friend. I don't usually get this kind of enthusiastic reception for the kind of jobs I take on.

"Sarah, I'm Eleanor. Please follow me. I'm afraid we're in the room right at the very end, I hope that's okay? As you'll soon discover, the position involves a lot of travel. And you'll have to excuse us but we're in the middle of refurbishing – not to my taste – but my son has a bit of a passion for trains. Anyway, we have all been anxiously awaiting you. We're only a small company but we're very confident we will be extremely successful, especially now you've agreed to help us."

"I have?"

The woman turns and for a moment I think I recognise her from somewhere.

"Absolutely!"

And before I can protest, she extends her slim hand towards my own.

"Welcome aboard Ms Norton – I hear you have a reputation for reliability."

LINDSAY WILSON

Lindsay Wilson was born and raised in Scarborough. She now works in Wakefield teaching Maths and English and lives there with her husband and two children.

25639232R00163

Printed in Poland
by Amazon Fulfillment
Poland Sp. z o.o., Wrocław